the TV PRESIDENT

also by Elise Valmorbida

MATILDE WALTZING

'There have been countless books on the migrant experience, but few recall this rite of passage with such wit and daring'
 —*Sunday Herald Sun* and *Sunday Telegraph*, Australia

'Valmorbida writes with energy and challenges the conventionality of what language can achieve . . . engaging, often funny, sometimes poignant'
 —*Canberra Times*

'Words in this text are quartz-like objects that contain miniature worlds folded within . . . This is a miraculous work: iconoclastic, compassionate and brilliantly witty'
 —Rosi Braidotti, author of *Nomadic Subjects*

THE BOOK OF HAPPY ENDINGS

'In *The Book of Happy Endings*, Elise Valmorbida achieves something rare and precious, and she writes like an angel'
 —John Madden, director of *Shakespeare in Love*

'Valmorbida brings her gift for elegant language to this collection of narratives about the search for love'
 —*Publishers Weekly*, USA

'Intelligent and life-affirming'
 —*Library Journal*, USA

the TV
PRESIDENT

★ ★ ★ ★ ★ ★ ★ ★ ★ ★ ★ ★ ★

elise valmorbida

for dear John
with warmest wishes
and how many years....?

X X X
elise

ⒷB *editions*

First published in 2008
by CB editions
146 Percy Road London W12 9QL
www.cbeditions.com

Printed in England by Primary Colours, London W3 8DH

ISBN 978–0–9557285–7–0

To the memory of Sam Patterson, writer and friend
(1926–2003)

'It's not what you are that counts, but what people think you are.'
—Joseph P. Kennedy's advice to his son John F. Kennedy

'Television is now the main personal link between the people and the White House.'
—JFK

With special thanks to Greg Loftin, Tara Wynne, Cleo and Jim Hamilton, Alison Flood, Suna 'Thelma' Setna, Annemarie Neary, Anne Aylor, Steve Mullins, Elizabeth Fairbairn, Mum and Charles.

Thanks also to Jeff Flood, Mark Spencer, Denise Atkins, Tom Price, Vivian Castleberry and James Harrison.

And thanks every week to The ZenAzzurri writers: Anne Aylor, Rob Carroll, Susan Clegg, Aimee Hansen, Richard Hughes, Margaret Laing, Roger Levy, Steve Mullins, Annemarie Neary, Sam Patterson, Sally Ratcliffe and Richard Simmons.

★ ★ ★ ★ ★ ★ ★ ★ ★ ★ ★ ★ ★ ★ ★ ★

DRAMATIC TV BATTLE

The first episode of *The TV President* will delve into the lives of not one but two of the nation's top JFK lookalikes. From regular gala events and Hollywood auditions to highly irregular 'conviction tests' set by the program makers, the new Kennedys will pitch themselves against each other in a bid for the No.1 position. Cherry Pickering, the show's producer, states: 'We have archival footage, historic re-enactments and over a hundred unblinking unsleeping unflinching cameras behind the scenes. *The TV President* promises to deliver the greatest election ever seen.'

★ ★ ★ ★ ★ ★ ★ ★ ★ ★ ★ ★ ★ ★ ★ ★

Jack and Jack

It was 5:30 p.m. and Fresno baked. John F. leaned on the steering wheel and read the signs as he drove. *Gaming Center. Trading Center. Divorce Center.* He peered up and down the deserted streets. Bail bonds buildings and empty lots. Just three old skyscrapers on a flat line. Closed doors and windows wherever he looked. This was his home. No place for a president to live.

John F. turned at last into Olive Avenue, the summer sun hitting his head from every direction. The sidewalks here were full of Bohemians. Well, nearly. The Tower district looked like LA. Well, nearly. John F. could feel his hair gel soften. A breeze tickled the shiny front of his forehead. He turned the radio on.

In pride's dazzling hall of mirrors demons dominate. They inject the deadly virus of vanity into our veins. We become their sick junkies, desperate for a fix. And, before we know it, life has no value, unless we can see our puny little selves glorified like false idols in the desert of other people's eyes—

John F. changed stations, twisting the knob until he found The Best of Music. He pulled up at the stop light and checked his hair in the mirror. The edges were still sharp. An old woman on the crosswalk stared at him, gasped, tripped over a hole in the road. John F. smiled his beneficent sun-relaxed campaign-winning smile. The lights changed. Simon & Garfunkel burst into song.

John F. would rather have been a hammer, but he knew all too well that he'd mostly been a nail. It didn't bother him anymore.

He had come lower than middle in his graduation class. *He* had lived in the gloom of his brother's shadow, inheriting the family ambition like an ill-fitting hand-me-down. He'd even been through The Last Rites four times before the actual day—and just as well.

A nail could surprise them all by becoming a hammer.

John F. drove slowly through a hazy shimmer of gazes. The faces of outer Fresno turned to follow him like wide-eyed sunflowers in a field. In this respect, today was a day like others—but today was also historic. It was his first day in the top job. He'd been elected. He'd won the State by a landslide. His photo would be all over *The Fresno Bugle*, *The Voice of the Valley*, *The Modesto Bee*. Possibly even *USA Today*.

In San Francisco the judges had declared one Kennedy flawless until he smiled. Another contender was cursed with a squint. The Death Valley candidate had, among his lesser faults, a stain on his tie. Surely anyone serious about his candidacy would have brought a spare. And the guy from LA wore too much makeup.

As for the others . . . Well, God was in the detail. It wasn't just about measurements. It went deeper than the deep-set eyes, higher than the upturned hair, wider than the broad cheeks. It was about love. Who else had adopted his name, converted to his faith, submitted to the surgeon's knife and taken personal-development classes in winning? These days, losing was the only thing he really got emotional about.

John F. pulled into his drive. The convertible coughed to a stop. His little white house positively shone in the Fresno sun. Bounding from the back yard, the K-9 Corps gathered and barked on the front porch: Clipper the German shepherd, Shannon the Irish spaniel, Charlie the Welsh terrier. Caught inside behind the screen door, the Russian pups whined. Jackie would be at the salon as usual. Messing about with other people's hair. Apart from the name, his wife never did play her part.

With sweaty fingers John F. took the TV producer's card out of his pocket.

Cherry Pickering

Producer, Reall Life

The TV company had chosen him. He turned the card over and read the handwritten message for the hundredth time.

Will you be The TV President?

John F. clutched his hot head, leaned back into the upholstery and grinned.

Elwyn Barter grinned. Most people fell apart when they smiled, dissolving into themselves, but his smiling parts were perfect and he knew it. From his podium he beamed down at the crowd.

'All living things in the whole wide world are divided into five Kingdoms. And mine, ladies and gentlemen, is the Fungal Kingdom.'

He had saved the slime talk until after the prize. It was his party piece, and this was his gala now. He had won. He looked more like *him* than anyone else in New York State, and as for his voice—

'You're a botanist?' The fan at his knees gazed up at him, eager.

'Mycologist,' Elwyn corrected her. 'President of the puffballs!' He lowered his voice, leaned forward and widened his eyes. 'I keep a colony of rare fungi under my bed. Ordinary looking jars with screw tops. There's something cloudy inside each one—'

Suddenly the reporters itched with questions. *And what do they live on? Is that like . . . er, candida? Where would we be without penicillin or porcini?*

'Our fungal cousins feed off dead organic matter. Although some don't wait for it to die. They prefer to eat from life—dal vivo!'

The banquet room went quiet. He had overdone it. Why did he always overdo it? He was not used to fame. He laughed.

'But, my friends, let's talk about why we're here—let's talk about winning! Victory has a hundred fathers, defeat is an orphan.' He replicated the presidential voice exactly.

He glanced at the judges. They looked relieved.

The fan was agog. She wore a diamanté brooch in the shape of a ring.

'*Ich bin ein Berliner!* —You know that's a kind of donut,' Elwyn said, his eye on the brooch. 'As far as I know, I've never been a donut but we are 50 per cent identical to a banana. And lettuce isn't far behind. Whatever we look like . . .' He paused. '*Whoever* we look like, we're all from the same ancient alma mater.'

He had digressed again, returned to himself, when all they really wanted was The President.

'What do you feed them?' The fan massaged the dewlap under her chin. Her lips glistened.

He couldn't resist. Every voter deserved an answer. 'Snake scales for some, the fussy eaters. Hair. Fingernail clippings. Flakes of skin—mind you, that's hard to catch!'

A sushi waitress touched his hem and asked for his autograph.

'Which one?' he grinned. He drew an old-fashioned fountain pen from his inner pocket. His nails were cut clean and short. He leaned over and signed his own name, resting on her shining upheld tray. His knuckles nudged a heap of ginger.

The waitress examined her stained chit.

Elwyn Barter

Disappointment clouded her face.

'Just kidding!' He winked and took out his special autograph book. He opened the cover with deliberation and scribbled, ripped the page out along its perforation, blew across the moist surface.

'Exactly the same as You Know Who.' He winked again and addressed the crowd. 'Just check the books. My Inauguration. The United Nations. The Test-Ban Treaty. You name it. I signed it. My fellow citizens of the world, ask not what America will do for you . . .' He put on the all-purpose statesman's look: an aura of intense concentration, a vision beyond.

Inimitable! someone called out. *Amazing!*

Photographers aimed, shot and fired their flashes.

'What's it like to open a superstore?' The eyes of the waitress were bright and wet. 'Can you have anything you want?'

Elwyn suddenly noticed the TV producer from Reall Life. She was standing coolly to one side, scrutinizing him from pristine top to toe.

'Yes,' he said, gazing at the waitress with a president's boundless love. 'You can have anything you like.'

She blushed.

He held the State of New York. Who else could do better? But the TV producer was stony-faced. Elwyn searched for his imperfections reflected in her hard little eyeballs. He thought he'd swung it—were there superior winners from other states? Who else had his gift for impersonation? Perhaps he'd been too provocative. Perhaps she could tell he was gay. His eyes were too symmetrical, he knew that. He'd said too much, he did that when he got carried away, he'd overdone the slime—

The TV producer made her way to the front of the crowd and

passed him something. He turned away to read her card. His hands trembled.

Cherry Pickering

Producer, Reall Life

On the back, she had written her personal message.

Will you be The TV President?

★ ★ ★ ★ ★ ★ ★ ★ ★ ★ ★ ★ ★ ★ ★ ★

CULT TV EMOTION

'More people voted with their handsets last night than turned out to vote in the last federal elections,' was the proud claim today by the Vice President of controversial TV production company Reall Life. 'And there are no dimpled chads to count, no lawsuits, no recounts either. No scope for human error or bias. The handset never lies.'

Viewers of *The TV President* know the set-up by now: Elwyn Barter, a fungal specialist from New York City, battles for the top job—and the jackpot—with John F., a rebaptized motel manager from Fresno, California.

The two breathtaking lookalikes have signed away 3 months to 'live' the series as it unfolds in real time, privately baring all for the cameras. The candidates are not permitted to meet in the flesh, but they have submitted to their first Conviction Tests: a screen-to-screen studio debate complete with in-seat live-audience voting, followed by a coconut carving contest recalling the young Kennedy's resourcefulness when stranded on a desert island in World War II.

Slick East Coaster Elwyn Barter was voted top man in both tests thanks to his uncannily accurate voice and a forger's gift for handwriting—even when pushed to the limits on coconut shell. Home viewers, however, have been swayed by the commitment shown in John F.'s private life—his unshakable devotion to th Roman Catholic faith, his camera-shy hair-stylist wife Jackie and his K-9 Corps dogs. Furious at losing the first round of tests, the motel manager delivered an apt quotation from the man himself: 'Forgive your enemy, but don't forget his name.'

The emotional stakes are high. The winner takes all and the size of the prize hangs on the show's commercial success. Cult viewing.

★ ★ ★ ★ ★ ★ ★ ★ ★ ★ ★ ★ ★ ★ ★ ★

Fresno Jackie

With the Russian pups curled up next to her on the bed, Jackie watched as her husband stepped out of a white limo, the bombshell lookalike at his side. They were arm in arm. John F. was pretending he was with a real date. The couple were instantly surrounded by photographers and flashes going off. The screen got so bright it made Jackie blink. She blinked as Mardie Scrutt laughed and threw her head back just like Marilyn Monroe. The camera went close in. Between the flashes, Jackie could see up Mardie's nostrils, down the back of her mouth. Jackie didn't know this woman, but she hated her. John F. was looking pleased with himself, more presidential than ever, like he'd won first prize at the fair. He didn't look so pleased this morning when he'd informed her of this particular Conviction Test. She'd wanted to scream and ask him questions, remind him of his marriage vows—but Reall Life was watching, listening, recording, waiting to broadcast her feelings for all the world to laugh at. So she'd kept her hurt inside. She was getting good at putting on a front. Churning on the inside, holding it all in.

John F. had flown away by lunchtime. Now a chauffeur was running to him and Mardie, opening up a huge LeizureScape umbrella to shield them from the media glare. If they were meant to be re-enacting some old secret affair, why was the media there anyway? Why was anybody looking?

Jackie was looking. If she was looking, everybody else was looking too. She imagined the girls at the salon, people all across America looking into their TVs, cellphones, computers—how could she keep herself from looking?

A little picture of herself flashed in the corner of the screen. *GET THE WIFE'S REACTIONS!*

There was acid in her throat. The taste of vomit. All anyone had to do was press the right button and they could watch her watching her own husband fooling around with another woman on national TV.

Now John F. was tripping through gold front doors with a look on his face that said he'd never seen a fancy hotel before. Eyes popping out of his head. Smirking. This was the Motel Manager from Highway 99 who knew the hospitality business inside and out—the decent man she'd married sixteen years ago. Mardie Scrutt was no better than a call-girl. She was wearing a low-slung satin dress, no bra. Her nipples stuck out. A strap slipped off her shoulder and the dress gaped open at the top of her bouncing breast. The camera zoomed in and froze on the picture. The Reall Life logo flew from its corner to the centre of the screen. A message appeared. *Sorry! Only premium-rate payers can enjoy this viewing privilege. Do you wish to upgrade?*

Jackie curled into a ball. The pups shifted in their sleep. She reached out and stroked Igor's downy-soft head. She'd seen enough. Her husband would be horsing around with Mardie in the hotel lobby, now. He would be telling rude jokes. It would go no further, Jackie could be sure of that. Maybe John F. and Mardie would be getting into the elevator. Acting like they were on a date, the way actors in films pretend they're in love when really they have bad breath and arguments. Maybe they were parading down some high-class corridor with gold chandeliers and rugs on the walls, maybe they were heading for their suite now. It would go no further. It would be against the law to go further, Jackie felt sure of that. It was all a show, a game of make-believe. John F. would never actually have an affair. And he never could be intimate with the lights on.

The Reall Life logo twinkled and the message turned over. *Upgrade now to resume play!*

Jackie swallowed the acid taste, gulped. She didn't want to upgrade. She knew the cameras were watching her, here in the privacy of her own home, listening to her, so she couldn't show her worry, couldn't say anything or do anything that would give her feelings away. She picked up her handset and started to press the buttons. She might have been turning the image brightness up. She paid two hundred dollars. She wanted to scream but she stayed very quiet. She upgraded.

Thank you for choosing to upgrade. Now sit back and enjoy the rest of the show!

The Reall Life logo flew back to its corner. The frozen image dissolved.

The cheating couple were in the suite already, Jackie could hear them laughing, but she couldn't see them. The camera was sliding all over the boudoir, showing big vases of roses, candelabras, bunched drapes with huge tassels. All Jackie wanted to see was John F. and Mardie, but Reall Life was prolonging the moment, zooming in on curly furniture legs and plumped-up cushions. Jackie heard the clink of glasses.

At last, they came into view: John F. and Mardie were standing by a shiny white grand piano, holding long-stemmed champagne flutes, toasting the election.

To HyperFriday! they said together and Mardie giggled.

The bubbles tickle my nose, she said. Her voice was cute and breathy. *It's a long time since I've had real champagne.*

You won't be saying that tomorrow night, Marilyn, John F. said, gazing into her face like a lapdog.

I promise not to get too jealous, he teased.

There was something funny about his eyes. They looked black and staring. He should have been talking about his own wife here at home watching him, getting jealous, but he was talking about the other presidential candidate.

When you meet up with him, it'll be ME you're thinking of, John F. said like he owned her.

Mardie seemed to find that hilarious. Her dress strap fell off her quivering shoulder and the top of her big round breast was on show again. Quick as a whip, John F.'s hand leaped out and grabbed the bare flesh, squeezed the nipple, slipped the strap back up. Then both of them burst out laughing, leaning their heads in to each other.

Jackie felt sick. She felt the floor open up into a huge hole ready to take her falling body. She was falling into hell.

A little picture of herself flashed in the corner of the screen. *GET THE WIFE'S REACTIONS!*

Jackie watched as her husband trailed a slow finger down the woman's satin front, over her stuck-out nipple, along the curve of her belly, all the way down to her private parts. The camera zoomed in on his wandering hand. It—he—stroked at the satin and Jackie could see the shape of Mardie through the fabric, and it looked like she was wearing no underwear.

But Jackie was wrong. The hand gathered up Mardie's skirt and lifted it, bit by bit, exposing an old-fashioned garter belt, white and virginal like the 1950s. John F.'s hand played along the trembling cellulite on Mardie's thigh, poking in and out of her nylons' lacy edges, tickling. How long was it since he had touched Jackie in that way?

Porno, she felt like screaming. But she kept her feelings pressed inside. She smoothed the frown from her eyebrows and set her face to neutral against the show. The camera sidled across from Mardie's crotch to his. Tight inside his pants, his hard-on seemed to fill the screen.

Jackie swallowed so hard she coughed.

The Reall Life logo left its corner again and twinkled. A new message appeared.

Your credit has run out. Do you wish to top up now?

Jackie felt herself choke. What could she do? She panicked. She looked at her pups. So innocent. They knew nothing, which made her feel worse. She tried to swallow but it made her cough. She could not show her feelings. It could not go any further. John F. would turn the lights off so the cameras could not see. John F. would not go any further. He'd said he would just pretend.

Jackie picked up her handset and paid some more.

The program took forever to resume. The Reall Life logo taunted her, twinkling and dancing, acting skittish.

The lights had been dimmed. John F. and Mardie were underneath the piano, kicking its shiny white legs. He was making little moaning noises. Jackie had never heard him moan like that before. The picture was grainy, hard to see. But Jackie could see enough. Everything was blurry through the tears in her eyes and the tears poured out of her eyes and kept pouring so fast she couldn't see.

A little picture of herself flashed in the corner of the screen. GET THE WIFE'S REACTIONS!

All she had to do was press a button to view her own reactions in real time. Instead, she picked up the handset and threw it at the television as hard as she could. The pups woke up and barked. Jackie screamed and screamed while John F. moaned and the dogs barked and Jackie screamed and John F. kicked and Jackie screamed and John F. barked and Jackie moaned.

★ ★ ★ ★ ★ ★ ★ ★ ★ ★ ★ ★ ★ ★ ★ ★

SEX-CELEBRITY DEATH SHOCK

Mardie Scrutt, more familiar to the nation's viewers as *The TV President*'s buxom blonde, was found dead at her home yesterday in 'suspicious circumstances', according to a senior detective investigating the case.

Detroit resident Ms Scrutt, 38, originally from Bird-in-Hand, Pennsylvania, was known to have been depressed in recent months following her new-found notoriety as the 'Ms Monroe' who had sexual relations on camera with two presidential impersonators at the famous Carlyle Hotel. Ms Scrutt was formerly best known for her roles in Hollywood's straight-to-video *Goodbye Norma* and the troubled cable series *Happy Birthday*.

At a special meeting with the press today, Reall Life producer Cherry Pickering stated: 'It's a tragedy, and our condolences go to Mardie's husband and children. We at Reall Life had no awareness of her personal situation, but everyone in the crew will testify that she was a consummate professional. We remain everlastingly thankful for her vital contribution to the success of *The TV President*.'

Reall Life's controversial hit series has attracted historic viewing figures, cult web communities, substantial Wall Street portfolios—and heated opposition. Interviews with outraged civic leaders have been incorporated into the program's evolving magazine format. There may be protesters' barricades outside the company's headquarters and numerous lawsuits in the offing, but the program-makers remain undeterred. The show, it seems, must go on.

★ ★ ★ ★ ★ ★ ★ ★ ★ ★ ★ ★ ★ ★ ★ ★

Jack and Jack

Half-asleep and full of dreams, Elwyn stretched—aware that his armpits were on full display. *How much hair?* he thought. *What growth formation? Moles, scars, distinguishing features?* It was too late anyway. It wouldn't be down to underarms. Not now. Not when there was so much else in the balance. He heard the titter of a thousand viewers gathered outside the hotel.

He had slept rigid as a corpse all night. He rubbed the sleep from his eyes, yawned, sat up and stared at the camera which was poised like an insect at the end of his vast bed.

'Friends . . . Americans . . .' Elwyn addressed his audience in the voice. These days he rarely spoke in any other way. It was his advantage over the motel man. 'We're eyeball to eyeball and I think the other fellow just blinked—as my Secretary of State might say!' He held the camera's gaze. How long had he been planning this moment? He had rehearsed every single Kennedy quotable in the book, finally rejecting them all as too obvious, too . . . *Fresno*. His mother had agreed. His mailbox was full of suggestions. As if there wasn't enough junk from every male who claimed to have been his ex. *Existence is so fickle, fate so fickle. Victory has a hundred fathers, defeat is an orphan. We stand on the edge of a new frontier.*

'Did the other fellow just blink? I hope so!' Elwyn's perfect laugh was deadened by the cushions and swags of his presidential suite. He heard applause.

'My fellow Americans, only you know the answer to this question. But I ask only for your support.' He fell back and stared at the hothead lens on the ceiling. His eyes were sore. He kept them open to tease out two deep and fearful tears, squeezing so that they trickled down his temples and onto the pillow satin.

'I ask only for your support,' Elwyn breathed. He was full of love for his unseen voters. He might have cried a little more, but he kept himself in check. Two tears showed how much he cared; any more would provoke questions. He closed his eyes. He had time.

He had given up so much of himself. Every inch of his soul. Every twitch of his body—even sex. Ever since he'd lost weight and found his JFK face, he'd been celibate. Then he recalled the Monroe affair and silently corrected himself: *virtually celibate*. Did an actress count? They had both warmed up with a dose of love Drugz off-camera. Poor Mardie Scrutt, clearly out of practice, had pulled and tugged him like an educational toy. But he had managed to overcome himself, and her. Some time after the event, she'd emailed him with the shocking secret of her pregnancy. So much for the 'special edition' LeizureScape condoms! Elwyn couldn't bear the thought of a child. The world was already overpopulated. His baby—he didn't doubt that it was his—would have been a media jackpot. A historic throwback with a whole life to live in the glare of cameras. It was too cruel. Elwyn had tried to bury his unease along with everything else. He had come this far. He remembered the cemetery at home under his bed: his rare specimens, neglected, reduced to dead liquid or dusty powder. He used to be a mycologist who happened to be a lookalike. Now he was a lookalike who happened to be a mycologist. He had flipped over, easy as a coin.

Elwyn kept his eyes closed. He had time. The pillow was softest satin, cool against his skin.

He had lost his fungi but he had not lost the race. Who could have predicted such a close contest? He thought of the money. A thousand dollars for every classified species of fungus. No, more. Green bills pinned to the tree of life. If he won. But it wasn't just about the money. The battle had gone beyond that. He dreamed of life after the show. Hollywood's bestselling face. The deals, the dolls, the endorsements. The king of the new aristocracy, the most desirable man in the United States . . .

Elwyn opened his eyes. The crowd cheered outside. He didn't know which lens to pick. He decided to ignore all the cameras, wrapped himself in his bedsheet and stumbled like some party-costume Caesar into the bathroom. On the way he caught a glimpse of Dallas through the window. The mob was at least fifteen deep along the sidewalk, dwarfed by giant screens. Were the people hailing him? Was he the Chosen One? *Defeat is an orphan.* Or had the Other One just waved from a balcony? These days, he was always having to second-guess. It poisoned his perfection.

Elwyn stepped behind protective glass and let the power shower blast his head. He wondered if the camera above would pick up his lurking bald patch through the steam. He tilted his face upwards. The hair and makeup team would sort him out. Wardrobe was next on the schedule, armed with the clothes that made the man—each item a Commission Exhibit replica—without blood, of course, or tell-tale clues.

Commission Exhibit 393: Kennedy jacket.

Commission Exhibit 394: Kennedy shirt.

Commission Exhibit 395: Kennedy necktie.

Then Jackie.

Then The Governor.

The Governor's Wife.

The Limousine.

From here on, Elwyn sensed it was all down to natural selection.

'Bless me father for I have sinned . . .' John F. mumbled at the priest kneeling in the corner of his presidential suite. There was no lack of cushions for the old man's knees.

John F. was thinking of his wife Jackie. He was feeling guilty. He was thinking of the Ten Commandments. The Catechism he'd learned by heart when he converted. The Holy Sacrament of Marriage. Thou shalt not divorce—but Jackie wanted one, ever since the Marilyn affair. *Just you wait until after the show,* she had whispered into his ear. Was this First Lady pillow talk? No wonder they'd chosen a lookalike for the motorcade. Apart from the name, his wife had never played her part.

Father Paine was a real priest. The casting people had discovered him at the airport. He didn't seem to mind the cameras. He smelled of stale tobacco and fresh cologne. Too much cologne. His eyebrows were bushy, like Moses in the films. He wore foundation makeup, and thick concealer on a glaring pimple.

John F. wished for a confessional box. He hankered for its intimacy.

He had rejected Reall Life's offer of some downtown Irish theater prop—it was open at the back, rude as a hospital gown.

John F. lowered his voice so that the microphones would not hear. 'It is one month since my last Confession and these are my sins—'

'What's that? Speak up!' Father Paine boomed.

Had they done this on purpose? John F. looked up at the ceiling. The camera moved on its pivot and met his gaze. No answer. There was nothing for it. Truth had no secrets. He pictured himself on the floor with Mardie, underneath the grand piano, feeling bold as a—he was ashamed.

'I committed the act of adultery.'

The crowd roared outside. Were they applauding him? Or had the Other One dazzled them with more of his fancy talk?

'Ah,' the priest said. 'Adultery.' His nose rested on the steeple of his fingers. 'But that's not all, my son.'

John F. sniffed. 'Those who look only to the past or present are certain to miss the future.'

'Another man's words? That's not good enough,' the priest said.

'I . . . I—' John F. broke down and wept. Big tears the size of Fresno grapes.

The crowd roared again.

Father Paine nearly smiled. 'You have to say the words out loud, my son, so God can hear you.'

John F. blubbered. 'I yearned for— I wanted— I wanted to be a hammer. I— I didn't—I didn't want to be a—a nail. I committed the sins of pride, and vanity, and greed, and lust, and . . . I—' John F. took deep breaths like a woman in labor. He couldn't speak.

The crowd was singing now. Slow and mournful. *Yes I would . . . If I could . . .*

John F. was gasping. They sang for him.

'You must be careful not to hyperventilate, my son,' the priest said. He checked his watch. 'Come on, then: for these and all my sins . . .'

'For these and all my sins I am— I am truly—'

The applause was unmistakable now. It was for him. John F. felt his breathing quieten. New tears, grateful ones, sprang out like tiny leaks from his eyes as Father Paine delivered absolution in Latin, loud and clear as an actor. The priest waved his blessing hand a little wildly, John F. couldn't help but notice.

And then he heard voices.

Hair and makeup! The words came from beyond the door.

Wardrobe!

The priest raised a single eyebrow. 'You don't want me to perform the Last Rites, do you?'

John F. winced. 'I've done that, Father. Four times already. Just like *him*.'

The door opened.

The priest got up to go. He hesitated. He seemed nervous.

'You filthy apes!' he muttered.

He grabbed the crucifix at his neck and held it up to the hothead above him. He yelled. 'Damnation! Damn you all to Hell!'

John F. crossed himself as the priest was dragged away.

'God will be the final Judge,' John F. said to himself. Then he looked the nearest camera in the eye. 'Mr Barter, you're no John F. Kennedy!'

And the crowd cheered.

The two limousines were waiting side by side. Parallel. A perfect match, detail for detail. No one could say that one was positioned ahead of the other. Someone had probably measured. 'Jackie' sat in the back seat. Another 'Jackie' sat in the other back seat. Reall Life had done their best to conceal any differences.

As Elwyn stepped into his car, he glanced across and saw the Other One at close range for the first time. His rival was more handsome than he'd expected. Here in the flesh, the modest motel man looked smarter, sharper, harder. He even looked bigger. Fit for conquest.

Hot and breathless, Elwyn held back his sudden desire to stare. He felt alive and powerful, but he also felt distracted. There was an unprofessional tremble in his knees. A flutter in his endocrine system. A precursor to erectile function. Lust. For a moment he forgot about everything else. Then he remembered to grin: the sun-warmed well-hung most-loved grin.

His fans applauded. Smiling children waved little flapping banners.

Elwyn sank into the padded seat and patted 'Jackie' on the hand. He liked her matching pink hat and suit. It was reassuring. He needed to project the statesman's aura now, the grand vision from within. (He tried not to picture the Other One sprawled across an out-of-town motel bed, oiled and wanting.) Elwyn adjusted his trousers, Commission Exhibit replica—he couldn't remember which number.

'Are you nervous?' he asked.

'Jackie' shook her head. She was stiff with fear.

'Cat got your tongue?'

'I been briefed not to ad lib.' Her voice was high and squeaky.

She'd said enough to be classified. It helped him concentrate. Rural department store beautician. Degree in Cosmetic Science. A groomer. A breeder. Not even an actress.

The Governor and his Wife waved from the jumpseat in front. Was that accurate? Was that a microphone in the driver's collar? Was that a lens in the ashtray?

The limousines pulled off, side by side. A team of cheerleaders broke into a pom-pom frenzy. The people roared. Their voices vibrated like war drums deep down in Elwyn's belly. He caught a glimpse of the Other One in the wing mirror and looked away. (He was on top of the President now, taking him from behind, making the motel walls shudder.) He reminded himself to focus, to take control of his rowdy hormones.

'You know the word *crisis* in Chinese is written with two characters . . .' He patted his companion's perfectly manicured hand again. 'One character means danger. The other represents opportunity.'

He saw himself on a giant screen, mouthing the words in sync. His voice was amplified to fill the silence of the Other One. The people applauded. Elwyn knew to focus on the stranger at his side, the woman he loved, the woman he had betrayed. She smiled uncertainly. He knew to emanate imperial calm. (He was ramming the kneeling President into a peach-colored motel bed.)

The crowds cheered.

An epileptic collapsed in a fit by the roadside. People in uniforms rushed to his side.

'Just a diversion,' the Governor said. 'Routine.'

Elwyn remembered that detail. Part of a conspiracy theory. He guessed a second Epileptic was convulsing in twin motion on the other side, by the other limousine, for the Other One—he kept his gaze pouring outward, loving his people, securing their votes. He checked the wing mirror, but the angles were all wrong: no sight of the pin-up in the parallel car.

The motorcade turned off Main into Houston. Motorbikes in neat lines. Police in smart uniforms at the edges—were they actors in costume or law enforcement officers? A blonde woman waved a home-made sign. *Hooray for JFK.* Her eyes were brimming with emotion, but it was hard to tell which president she adored. Elwyn figured his chances were one in three. At least one of his rivals was dead. He willed the blonde to love him and only him. Every vote counted. He gazed into her eyes. But he couldn't help himself from glancing upwards. The sixth floor corner window of the Texas School Book Depository was half open. Of course these days it was just a museum.

The Governor's Wife turned to speak.

'Mr President, you certainly can't say that Dallas doesn't love you.'

She delivered her line with utter conviction—at least she was a professional.

'That's obvious,' said Elwyn.

Was the other Governor's Wife this good? Would the talent of the extras skew the people's vote? His 'Jackie' was more like a Patsy.

The crowds repeated the words, thunderous and ponderous. *You can't say Dallas doesn't love you. You can't say Dallas doesn't love you.* And then they fell silent, as if on cue.

'Coming up to Elm,' the driver said to himself.

This was where the limousine would slow to 10 miles an hour to make the hairpin turn. Elwyn looked for live oaks, picket fences, grassy knolls.

Someone on the street jerked open a black umbrella. Elwyn flinched. Did the Other President flinch?

'Retail is detail,' the driver said, without turning his head.

The Governor was more reassuring. 'No cause for alarm, Mr President, the real troublemakers have been kept out.'

That meant the fundamentalists. The radicals. The phobes. The religious opponents of Reall Life.

'Jackie' kept smiling and waved.

Thousands of bodies braced, breathed in as one, froze into abrupt silence. It was like driving through a picture.

John F. didn't know what had hit him. He felt a bare-knuckled punch in his forehead, an almighty slap across the ear, a flash of light. A firework exploded at his throat. A rock struck his face. And another. He was the adulteress and they were stoning him. Jesus did not stop them. They were without sin. John F. jolted and jerked in his fairground car. When would the ride be over? He was going to be sick. He could not see. He craned to see. Bent double. But all he could see was the light: dazzling, almost blinding, the flare shrinking to a pinpoint at the end of the tunnel. He was nearing the tunnel. The picture was crackling and burning and hissing and full of flying things and interference and buzzing and pain and static.

They had chosen him. He had won.

Fresno Jackie

Jackie curled up on the living room sofa with Shannon, Clipper and Charlie at her feet and Igor on her lap. The dogs were her only family now. There was a police cordon around the house, a crowd of press men and women beyond the picket fence, helicopters overhead, a line of vehicles as far as the corner. She felt like a zombie. John F. had stolen a march on her, left her behind. She'd wanted a divorce, but he went ahead and died. Not just any old death, like normal people. That was never going to be enough for him. He'd forgotten how to be the motel manager from Highway 99, proud of the hospitality and hygiene certificates on his lobby wall, the honest man with no time for guns or drugs or call-girls, the simple handsome boy who had asked her father for her hand, big wet shadows of sweat on his shirt and red raw shaving nicks on his jaw. And Daddy had worried that this son-in-law wouldn't go places, that he didn't have enough metal in him. Well, Daddy was wrong on both counts. John F. had gone all the way to Dallas, and he was full of lead.

Jackie stroked the head of the pup asleep on her lap. Keeping her eye on the screen, she reached for her box of Snax and fished out a handful. She fed them into her mouth, one at a time, like dimes in a slot. Then she inspected her fingers. Through the salty powder she could still see the stain of henna.

You shouldn't be fooling around in people's hair, he'd said.

To please him, before Reall Life, before she'd finally given up on him, she'd colored and straightened her own orange friz to give it The Look—the cut, the height, the side parting, the hairspray—nothing too hard about that kind of brunette, but there was more to a woman than her hairdo, she of all people knew that much, and there wasn't a thing she could do about her freckle-white face or the rest of her. Besides, she just wanted to be Fresno Jackie, not the other one. She was named after her Irish grandmother, nothing to do with a Frenchified First Lady with brains all over her suit.

'Just you wait until after the show,' she'd said into her husband's ear the next night after the Marilyn affair. The cameras were watching in the dark but she'd learned to get around them, and the dogs always whined in their sleep which helped to mask the audio, and she was so soft in her whispering that some preachers later took to sermonizing about the loyal wife who stood by her man despite his affairs—no, *because* of his affairs—who found it within herself to kiss her straying husband and pour sweet nothings into his ear in order to win him back. But they were wrong. John F. had done it with another woman on national TV.

'Try laying such a thing aside as idle talk,' she'd breathed at him. (Thank God Daddy was dead.) 'Try un-saying that at the salon.'

You shouldn't be working in a salon, he'd said under the sheets, as if that was the right kind of answer. *You should be a society hostess, a mother, a model or something.*

'And you should go to Confession,' she'd said back. Meaning in a quiet church somewhere. Not national TV.

National TV. Before, after, and everything in between, including his moans. It was the final straw and she couldn't even show it. But wasn't that what you were meant to be doing these days? Letting it all out? Saying how you feel? She couldn't let her feelings show. The cameras had been all over her, like those dirty men on public transportation who can't keep their hands to themselves. She'd had to grit her teeth and play her part—whatever that was. It wasn't so easy for her. She didn't look like anyone, except her Mom, and she had Aunt Geraldine's clever hands, short and stubby, pale and orange-freckled, with small splayed nails. Where was Aunt Geraldine now? Where was anybody? What was Fresno Jackie going to do now?

The helicopters were so loud she thought they'd take the roof off. She could hardly hear the television. They were showing people all over the country, crowded together in all kinds of places, with tears streaming down their cheeks, piling up bouquets of flowers, or standing in lines to write messages in official books, or watching the giant replay screens without saying a word, or telling interviewers how they felt, or whooping like wild Indians when the latest poll announcements tipped in one or the other's favor . . .

It was so hard to think of him dead. Impossible. The idea went in and out of focus, like something she had to remember and kept forgetting.

Shannon was having a nightmare. He woke up with a bark, shook his fuzzy soft ears, yawned and fell back to sleep at her slippers. Charlie whined, sneezed and turned over.

She couldn't remember the last time she and John F. had had sex. Unless it was that time they went to Yosemite and stayed in a lodge with bears all around going through the trash and slashing people. That was years ago. Something tiny had seeped in and kept on seeping until, before she knew it, the tiny something had seeped into every inch of her, and when she looked at him all she could see was his faults, the fat on his face, the noises he made when he was thinking, his smell in the bathroom, his airs and graces, the way he held his knife and fork 'presidential style', the way he raised his voice in quiet places, the way he searched for his reflection in shiny surfaces just to check his hair or his smile or the way his head moved, and the way he went on and on about this date or that fact or what he ate for dinner or which guy in the CIA hated him or what size shoe he took.

She should have known it when he changed his name officially. Or when he started having things done: all that plastic surgery, his teeth, the car, even the dogs. Or when he converted—she ought to have known it was the beginning of the end, long before Reall Life got hold of him. He'd never converted for her. She ought to have seen the end coming. It was impossible to think he might be dead.

Jackie caught a glimpse of herself on the screen. In the picture she looked white and sad and lonesome after all the crowds. She was sitting on the sofa holding a big box of Snax and watching TV. The lamp was on, the shades were down, Shannon and Charlie were asleep at her feet, and one of the pups was curled up on her lap. It was probably Igor, it was always Igor, the clingy one, her favorite Russian baby, even though she never admitted to preferential treatment. John F. was out of sight.

For a while she thought it was a replay.

She'd got in the pawn-men from KashKwik to remove the cameras and microphones, every last Reall Life lens and bracket. They'd filled her trashcan to overflowing. They'd left marks in the furniture, blind holes in the ceilings, torn paint where the tape was. She didn't have to be on show anymore. Her part of the contract expired with John F.'s death, that much she knew for certain, she'd queried it with the lawyers and they didn't say different at the Divorce Center. It wasn't her fault if Reall Life didn't get to her trash before everybody else did.

Jackie felt her belly lock as she watched her spaniel Shannon on TV, waking up with a bark, shaking his fuzzy soft ears, yawning and falling back to sleep at her slippers. She waited for it: Charlie whined, sneezed and turned over.

Those damned pawn-men had missed the TV.

Jackie jumped. The dogs jumped. The Snax box fell.

The Reall Life spy-camera was stuck on the side, hooked in the TV's armpit so long she'd stopped seeing it. She yanked at its root until it tore. She plucked it out, the last eyeball. She threw it to the floor and half expected it to squirm.

'Asshole,' she said, now that she knew no one was listening or taping. The victims never said that on *My Little Eye* or *Say Cheez* or *Expozé*. People always turned sheepish when they realized they were caught in the act, hiding something, or being dumb, or cheating. They were always embarrassed. Everyone safe at home laughed at them, the way bullies laugh, but the shamed ones never got angry and broke a camera. It was like they were grateful for the attention. And they were on a contract. Jackie knew all about that now. There were so many things John F. could not do. So many things he had to do.

Igor jumped off the sofa to sniff at the uprooted dead thing, and looked up at Jackie as if she had an answer. She did. She put an XMart catalog on top of the camera and jumped, again and again, with all her weight. Charlie and Shannon got out of her way. Jackie heard plastic and glass crack but she kept on jumping. She jumped for every month she'd been on show. She jumped for every one of John F.'s moaning thrusts. She jumped for every hundred thousand dollars she'd inherit if he won the election. She jumped until she twisted her ankle and hobbled back to the sofa, only now aware that the entire K-9 Corps had lined up to watch her jumping. Her children. Her family. Dogs. Just dogs. Named after someone else's dogs. She was a widow with no family and her ankle throbbed. She fell onto the sofa and buried her face in the cushions. She felt her crying mouth pull wide as a grin, so wide it almost hurt, and deep noises came from her throat and her insides, and she jerked, and her mouth pulled wider as she sobbed and she thought of skulls that look like they're really happy but actually they're dead. They have nothing to be grinning about. They don't even have a skin anymore.

Slippery Jack

Elwyn's eyes popped open. The lighting was low. They had moved him from the trauma room to a private one. He remembered ambulance carts and corridors. Wheels that needed grease. The percussive racket of the press pressing behind barriers and doors. The press. The press. His neck was sore. His right arm hurt. A plastic intravenous plug was wedged into his left hand. Blood like a big black bug sat on the pale sheet. In the pale sheet.

Back and to the left, he thought. *Back and to the left*. But he had lunged forward and to the right. His small-town pseudo-Jackie had screamed and thrown her bouquet into the air like a demented bride. The noise of her was still in his head. The sight of her. On the car floor clutching at his knees. Rough little bundle of shaky pink wool. What of the simulations? Had the audio started? *Back and to the left—* he had steeled himself for his last ever Conviction Test, rehearsed it silently off-camera days beforehand, sitting on the toilet in the dark. He had waved, smiled, adjusted his hair, lifted his hands to his throat, grimaced, jerked back and to the left. He knew his role. It was a sequence. Like a dance. Not meant to hurt.

No cause for alarm, Mr President, the real troublemakers have been kept out. Was that part of the script? Was that real? Was that some kind of signal?

They had removed his back-brace. He was wearing a hospital gown. He was wrung out, but he was himself again. Full of penicillin, no doubt. Fungus imperfectus. Was his brain damaged? He tested himself. *Zygomycota. Basidiomycota. Ascomycota.* He could remember that much. He could say the syllables in his head. A man had jerked open a great black gilled umbrella charged with hypothetical toxic spores. *Agaricus. Amanita. Boletus. Calvatia. Cantharellus—Phallus—* ah, *phallus.* He checked and it was still there. Invertebrate. Intact. Pain-free. A low soft sound like a rising wind swelled to a roar in the distance, or perhaps it was as near as a hospital TV. Was it possible? Could they see him? He looked for the camera in the gloom. He searched for the infra-red lens, the receptive mesh of a microphone. *Tree Ears. Trumpet of Death. Caesar's Mushroom.* He had always loved the common names.

Slippery Jack, he thought to himself. A bullet had caught his bicep. Another had flown past his jugular and deep into the upholstery. *Slippery Jack. You've survived your own assassination . . .*

And fell asleep.

The Big Dealey—Today's Bets

'THE MISSIONARY POSITION' 3-WAY BET
Suspect: Father Paine
Firing Line: St Thomas of the Wounds
Holy Apostolic Church & Ministry (steeple)
No. of bullets: 1 or 2 or 3
Motive: Religious Belief
Odds at 12:30 p.m. CST: 40/1
Total no. of bets placed on all suspects: 12,666
Bets close HyperFriday—only 5 more days!

Father Paine hunches over the Visitors' Book. He takes another pen from his pocket and writes in big swirly curls.

God created Adam and Eve, not Adam and Steve. God giveth and he taketh away. Next time Our Loving Father will smite the defiant son down. He has had his warning. God is merciful. Hallelujah.

Father Paine pauses before signing the entry.

Mahogany King, Louisiana.

'A good black name,' he says with satisfaction.

He is alone in his earthly realm, the Interfaith Chapel at Dallas Fort Worth Airport, Secure Side. He had wished for a cathedral, a basilica, an abbey, a Vatican—but God has His ways.

He takes another pen from his pocket. A blue ballpoint. He writes in a long thin spidery hand, leaning to the left a little.

God is peace and love. That guy pretending to be JFK that was bad karma a real bad vibe and God knows God SEES ABSALUTELY EVERYTHING!!!!!!!!!! it cudnt last he had it coming!!! Dallas is the GRATEST god bless America!!!?

Father Paine sighs. It is pure genius, especially the punctuation. He feels like a cigarette. He signs the entry.

L.B.J.

He flicks back the pages of the book. There are Americans from every state, Mexicans, Puerto Ricans, Australians, Africans, Indians,

Russians. He takes another pen from his pocket. A fountain pen. The Bishop's. He borrowed it at their last meeting. He puts on a high-class accent inside his head.

This has been my first voyage to the United States of America. Your country is most charming. However, I was disappointed that a strong Christian nation such as yours should find degenerate sexual acts to be suitable matter for widespread home entertainment at all hours of the day. Not to mention the graphic depiction of violence. Such amoral behavior has ended in tragedy and now is the time to repent and mend our ways. Yours in appreciation of this calm and quiet spot within a populous airport/ world.

Father Paine has calculated that his English gentleman should sign himself in the manner of the Queen of England.

E.R. London, Buckingham.

There's a district near Garland called Buckingham. He doesn't want it to be confused. He thinks awhile before adding clarification.

E.R. London, Buckingham Shire.

Some of the chapel visitors cannot spell. Some of them are bordering on the illiterate. Most of them are Christian. They are angry, alcoholic, divorced, blessed, saved, grateful, afraid of flying. Many of them are real. He hasn't written words for everyone. He takes another pen from his pocket. A red nylon tip.

When I saw that priest on the TV I nearly died an went to heaven. That was the best. Man, he was strong as 9 acres a garlic. The rest a that stuff was boring as a warm bucket a spit. That priest should a been president. Then we know which way our countrys gone. Father Paine for President. We got G-O-D on our side. The Only One. None a that other un-patriotic stuff. Father Paine for President. The Way and the Truth. Father Paine for President. Amen.

A. Governor, TX.

The door suddenly opens and a tall dark stranger in overalls enters the chapel.

'Excuse me,' the man says. He peels the mini Persian rug off its rack and places it carefully on the oatmeal carpeting, angled toward the back corner wall.

Father Paine checks the time. It's 3:55 p.m. He's taken longer than he thought. He hasn't had a cigarette in ages. The red pen is still in his hand and the Muslim is looking at him. He feels himself blush.

'Their spelling,' he shrugs, motioning pen to page. 'What's happening to the Crusade against ignorance and darkness? In my day, if you had yourself an education you could do anything. Anything. That's how we got a man on the moon.' He has said enough. His chapel is more lonesome than the moon. 'Where are you from?'

'Terminal B,' the Muslim answers with a sly smile. 'Excuse me.'

The Muslim turns and stands and closes his eyes and clasps his hands and starts saying things. Then he kneels down on his mat and does the bobbing action, like a cat. Up and down and regular. His name is probably Adman or Emad or Mohamed if their wall-notice is any indication. Father Paine knows that laminated photocopy wall-notice by heart. He has said Mass here God knows how many times and stared at it. He has yet to find out what kind of thing an iftar is. One day he'll try and call those phone numbers just to ask. Anonymous. And where, he wonders, do their womenfolk get to praying? He has never seen them on his floor with their rumps in the air.

'Well I've got an appointment with the Bishop,' he says importantly, and heads for the door. But the Muslim doesn't seem to be listening.

Father Paine catches the little red train to the parking lot. This is the third busiest airport in the world—or second busiest, depending on which brochure he reads—and his chapel is smaller than a trailer! No wonder the turnout is so mean. It's an insult. It's not even his chapel. He has to share it with the likes of Mohamed and any other Joe that walks in off a foreign plane.

Father Paine gets to his car and squats a little to scan his face in the two-way window glass. There's still a scab on his temple. The pimple blew its top the very next morning after the Big Day. He used to hope for better skin in old age, but God has His ways. He unlocks the car doors and falls inside. Why is he full of aches and pains? He needs a cigarette. There's nowhere you can smoke these days, not even in tough old Texas. He looks around, surveying the parking lot. There is no one. He pulls a pack from the false bottom under the dash and lights up. The first breath of smoke feels like heaven.

'Oh breathe on me, oh breath of God,' he sighs. He wonders if

31

that might be blasphemy. He feels the nicotine steal into his heart and rattle his old brain. He is too advanced in years to give up this routine. It's a vaccine against Alzheimer's. He read that somewhere. But why the Crusade against tobacco when there is so much else that is pernicious in the world? There are no more certainties. People need certainties. An eye for an eye. They need black distinct from white. There are too many grays.

Father Paine sucks on his cigarette and licks its stained filter tip, already wrinkled and soggy with his teething and his spittle. He has been working up quite a lather. Some ash falls onto his pants.

'Dust to dust,' he says aloud. The car is full of smoke. His eyes are stinging. There are too many grays. He can feel a sermon coming on.

'In our society we tolerate everything but intolerance,' he says. It's always good to start by catching them off guard. There's nothing like a paradox to make the little lambs curious. That way they feel a lack, a thing they need to know. Then their shepherd can be relied on to deliver the answers. It clinches their trust. It's like selling insurance.

'We tolerate anything and everything but intolerance. That's why there is so much confusion in our world. Drugs. And divorce. Genetics. Homosexuality. Suicide.' He doesn't add the word homicide. He has a fleeting vision of himself pressed against a rifle, his head popping out of a hole in the steeple like a worm out of a carrot. He feels a pain in his shoulder.

'Why should we *tolerate* the drug addict? Why should we *tolerate* abortion? Why should we *tolerate* homosexuality? Because the so-called *Tolerant Ones* would accuse us of intolerance if we didn't. As if our intolerance was the sin! Ladies and gentlemen, here is the sleight of hand. Here is the illusion. Intolerance is not the sin. What is the sin? Tolerance is the sin.' Father Paine waves his hands through the thickening smoke and it billows around his fingers like a special effect. It adds a certain emphasis. Another clump of ash falls onto his pants.

'Say no to tolerance! Tolerance is the lazy lily-livered luke-warm lug-worm of complacency. It was tolerance that allowed the Jews to use the temple as a marketplace. It was tolerance that allowed Jesus to be crucified while another man sat by and washed his hands. It was tolerance that . . .' He is stuck for a third example. There must always be three. Every decent orator knows it. Every senator, pope and general. Three is enough to sound like many, rich and various—but not enough to lose your audience. Three has a beginning, a middle and an end.

His cigarette is a stump burning at the crook of his fingers. He lights another one direct from its end. He butts out the first. His ashtray is overflowing. He is inspired. God is speaking to him, through him. He feels like Moses. Or Paul. He is surrounded by Jews. Or Ephesians. A huge crowd of them fills the car, the parking lot, the whole of Dallas Fort Worth Airport. His voice is on the general speakers, everywhere, booming through the restrooms, the check-in areas, the moving sidewalks, the departure lounges, the runways where airplanes wait hushed and listening, the back rooms where customs officers pause awhile before resuming, wistful and wiser, their gloved inspections of baggage and bowels.

Father Paine sucks hard on the new cigarette to get it going.

'We don't have to tolerate the Tolerant Ones! We need rules and codes and certainties. We need a map. We need a path. We need a . . .' He is stuck again.

It has to be three things. Like the Trinity. Like the Holy Family. Like the three Wise Men. Or four can work, sometimes, like the four rivers in Eden, the four evangelists, the four horses of the Apocalypse. Five is occasionally useful, depending on the situation. Seven is better. The seven deadly sins. The seven dwarves. And on the seventh day. Twelve is the kabala itself. To die for. Forty has its uses, too, as in forty days and forty nights, Ali Baba's forty thieves.

But never a two. Two is an argument, a contest for winners and losers. Two always ends in tears. Like Cain and Abel. Adam and Eve. Lambs and goats. More than any other number, Paine hates two.

Two presidents are two thieves hanging on two unholy crosses and deserving to die. Did the thieves of yore both look the same? Did God know which one to smite and which one to save?

Father Paine feels a prickling of guilt and coughs. He can barely see his hand for the smoke. His eyesight isn't too good at the best of times. He stubs out his second cigarette and starts the car. The air conditioning comes on with a blast and his remorse thins.

'I wish I had a witness!' he says, just like a fat black presider in Testimonial Valley.

33

In his mind's eye he can see huge spotlights, glittering vestments, a distant stage with a choir of forty arranged like heavenly seraphim, a host of twelve Salomé-style dancing girls, and three movie screens suspended from above. He likes the numbers. Forty. Twelve. Three. Those big operators could fit his chapel in one of their surplice pockets! In the pot they piss in for Lent!

Father Paine has never been *big*, not even at his zenith before the unfortunate Charismatic Incident in Hebron. Now he is the fisherman with the tiny boat, the empty net, coveting his neighbor's catch. He would be grateful for a house of worship in a Grand Prairie mall—his own retail space—sandwiched between a donut-stop and a frozen-meat outlet.

'Heaven and Hell on earth, Amen!' He slaps the dashboard.

No, in truth, he hankers for more than that.

A crowd of thousands. A vision mixer and a director. Hymn words on a LeizureScape teleprompter, bold and glowing on a big screen. Contribution envelopes collected by ministry officiants with white gloves. Microphones everywhere, clipped to official collars and hanging like spiders from the ceiling. Live transmission on the world-wide web. A global presence.

'I wish I had a witness, Amen!' he says, louder, raising his hands as if to bless the steering wheel.

He had a calling from Reall Life. God gave him an opportunity. It made him feel like Moses, on the Planet of the Apes. He wanted to make a good impression, but he had a pimple on his temple. Television can do harsh things to a face. They dragged him away but that was dramatic, like a martyr. Memorable.

Father Paine strokes his scab. He thinks about having another cigarette. He feels small and white and plain.

Events didn't work out the way he'd figured on the Big Day. It was a circus. So confusing. Like *The Pattie 'n' Cathie Show*. Identical cousins. They walk alike, they talk alike . . . And his eyes are not what they used to be.

He hears the sound of planes landing and taking off. There is no one in the parking lot. Just cars.

'I wish I had a witness!'

Fresno Jackie

Jackie figured that her dead husband in the morgue would win. All the pollsters were saying so. But it was going to be close. The wounded double who lay in Parkland Hospital was sneaking up on John F. without so much as lifting a finger. He was reckoned to be a strong finisher, just because he was alive.

There was no second prize.

Jackie was sitting with the dogs in the living room again. These days she couldn't seem to move herself away from the main TV. It wasn't special, like setting time aside to watch a favorite show. It wasn't avid like a hobby. It was like sleeping with the help of Drugz. She could feel the pack of eyes outside, the fingers waiting to open her up, break her barrier. She had stuck brown paper on all the windows and door glass. She had her K-9 Corps, but she ached for John F.'s warm body.

That Elwyn Barter guy was doing well in the opinion polls on account of his heroism. They were showing him unconscious in his hospital bed. He was all wired up to machines. He was under observation. Medical equipment and cameras. His pain was good, the reporters were saying. He was a survivor. Everyone loved a loser who pulled through at the last minute. By living beyond his assassination day, he was America's best chance of acting out the great unfinished drama.

That was his Unique Selling Point, a marketing man was saying. There was TV in him yet.

He stood for Hope, a psychiatrist was saying. Enough to wipe all that guilt and grief clean away. Heaps of it. Decades of it.

And yet her husband John F. was the martyr who had given his life for the people—his life!—not once now, but twice! What greater sacrifice could a man offer his country? He was the ultimate double, the perfect remake. He was authentic beyond belief.

They showed his dying face again and again. The starry look in his eyes as the first shot found him. As if he had wanted it all along—as if he wasn't even surprised. The moment of impact. Close up. His face filled the screen. He was so handsome. Radiant. Shining almost. A flickering look at her, as if to say *Jackie, I'll see you in heaven.* And then the blood. Exploding like tropical flowers on his hair. Then pouring. They showed it all.

Jackie, I'll see you in heaven.

Jackie, I've won.

Jackie, you're a millionaire.

That's what she saw in his eyes before he gave up the ghost.

I love you.

How long since she had said that to him? *I love you.* Had she been too hard on him? She remembered the tender way he used to look at her sometimes, cozy as a big kid, or the pride on his face when he drove her down Olive Avenue in the convertible. Had she been too hard on him? The way he gave in to Reall Life, the affair, the shooting—was it all her fault somehow? Had she been a bad wife? Would he forgive her in heaven?

A wind whipped up outside and rattled the shades. Either that or someone had got past security. Jackie felt her heart turn over. Adrenaline pumped into her head. The dogs pricked up their ears, raced out of the room and barked, barked, barked, kept on barking. Igor jumped off her lap and wet the carpet in zigzags all the way to the front door. Someone was on the porch. Jackie could sense their weight. The shades rattled again and something outside fell and broke. She flinched. Her arms were goose flesh. Her heart thundered. She could hear the house boards creaking, insects, the electricity pouring through wires.

It's your delivery, called a voice through fibers of wood. *Groceries and mail. Officer 1122 at your service, ma'am.*

It had been organized. He was her only contact with the outside world. Or was he an impostor?

The other President was on TV again, getting silently shot in 1963. It looked blurred and distant, almost fake.

Jackie heaved herself off the sofa and tiptoed towards the front door. She peeled back the brown paper from one corner. There was a head behind the rippled glass. Flashes were firing from the sidewalk, or perhaps she imagined that. The dogs were still barking. Their noise did not block the sound of blood streaming inside her arteries. Carefully she patted the paper corner back in position.

'What's the security code?' she squeaked at the thin dark space between the door and the frame. She felt a tiny current of air there. It made her shiver. The dogs stopped barking just for a moment.

'What's the security code?' she repeated. Her voice was almost nothing.

Hairport, answered the outside voice—although he couldn't have actually heard her. He was prepared.

'What's the key to everything?' she said at the crack, this time louder.

Hair Today.

He knew what to say. It was safe. She could open the door.

Slippery Jack

Elwyn was sure of it now: cameras were trained on him even here in his hospital bed. He had tested the evidence. All he had to do was move or groan, and there was a response: an instant, distant roar. Whether the sound came live from some parking lot outside, or whether it was transmitted from a monitor in a room nearby, he could not be certain. He was afraid to open his eyes. He was afraid to fall asleep or ask for Drugz, even though he needed both. He imagined his nurses and doctors watching themselves on their screens, ministering to him in their brand new personalized hospital drama. Turning him over for his injections. Changing his bed pan. Taking his temperature, his pulse, his pressure. He wondered if any of them had refused to sign a model-release form, if anyone had resisted the temptation of celebrity. Probably not. They had all become actors. Perhaps they had started dressing up specially for their new roles. Ironing their work-clothes with extra care. Having makeovers and manicures before coming in to do their shifts. One in particular seemed to be in costume rather than staff uniform, like a Sexy Nurse. Her name badge made it worse. *Head Nurse Mitzy Muchmore*. He half expected her to reappear with a Naughty Schoolgirl or a French Housemaid by her side.

But this was not his fantasy.

He wanted a President. A motel manager with a handsome broad grin. A man who must have greeted, registered and turned a blind eye to all kinds of late-night Naughty Nurses in his time—did they have call-girls in Fresno? *In his time*. How much time did the Other One have? The Other One had been hurt, Elwyn could assume that much. But no one would say what state the Other One was in. It was against the rules. Reall Life had kept him and John F. apart—no statistics, no sightings—until the Big Day.

Elwyn did not open his eyes. Head Nurse Mitzy had returned, alone. He could smell her. She had doused herself in perfume. He recognized it. As if the cameras could detect a fragrance! He wanted to sneeze. He pretended to be asleep. He peered at her through the distorting filter of his eyelashes. She took the file off the end of his bed and studied his records. She pivoted, for no apparent reason, and held a still pose. She made a balletic gesture with her hand. She dropped her pen and bent over to pick it up, hinging at the waist. She was performing for her unseen audience. She knew where to look. Through the blur of his lashes Elwyn located the cameras: one in the top corner, and one (he guessed) behind his head. There may have been others. He was in pain. Mitzy Muchmore took hold of his wrist and felt his pulse. There were logos printed on her pockets: *Fuelz. Drugz. Armz.*

Elwyn slipped, like sand, in grains, into sleep.

Fresno Jackie

'What are you dressed up like that for?' Jackie had asked.

'Biological isolation,' Officer 1122 had replied.

Hidden inside a facemask and baggy anti-chemical overalls, he had taken away her garbage and furnished her with groceries. The wrong breakfast cereal. Hygienic products. Dog food. Snax. Drinx. Drugz. Her mail. The usual stack of catalogs. A sack of letters. All the envelopes had already been opened. Security had checked for poisonous powders. They had sorted the public from the private correspondence—how did they know who was her personal friend? All kinds of strangers were her friends now.

I know just how you feel.

I've had exactly the same experience.

Some of her new friends thought she was Jacqueline Bouvier Kennedy. Others thought she had been in the car. Many of them wanted her money. Most of them poured out their hearts to her, told her their deepest secret secrets, commiserated, mourned, wept with her—even though she wasn't weeping. Should she have been crying some more? John F. would have told her. He always used to know about things like whether to cry or worry or get mad or which shirt to wear. Until he won his first serious contest. Before he fell in with Reall Life.

I cried more than when my wife died.

He treated you real bad. They're all like that.

I too am a hairdresser.

You drove him to it. You forgot your place.

My son also was shot in the war. He died for his country.

I am praying and baking for you.

Don't you go rebounding on some Greek typhoon now.

Jackie ripped apart one envelope after another. She couldn't stop herself. It was like a compulsion. She scanned each page. Beige, white, patterned, thin, thick, scented, crisp, fragile. Soft paper. Hard paper. Black-edged. Deckle-edged. She threw it all onto the floor. She kicked at it like fall-dry leaves. The pups sniffed and played around in it. They chewed it like homework.

Same as you, I want to kill myself. I am so lonesome.

She might have written that one herself. It broke her heart. She crunched it into a ball.

Her regular mail amounted to just four envelopes. The officials had bound them in rubber bands. Two bills. A black-bordered letter of condolence from the salon—they were in no hurry to have her back—had she seen them on TV? An official notice from Dallas. She was required by law to attend the morgue and identify her husband's body.

Slippery Jack

When he was conscious, Elwyn attempted to move unseen. In fractions of an inch, slowly, slowly, his good hand crept all over his skull. The President's head was the likely target. The head of the head of government. Slowly, slowly, he checked for injury. He dreaded what he might find. A ridge, a bandage, a contraption, a crater. How would he know if he had suffered brain damage? Could he trust his fingers? He examined himself until he could be certain that his head was intact. His neck was collared for the whiplash. His pillow was raised. His bad arm throbbed. His condition had improved, but he was no good at pain. He was squeamish just thinking about it. At college he had envied the dissectors' sang froid, the vivisectors' ability not to imagine. He could never have studied zoology or medicine. Smuts didn't squeak. Mushrooms didn't feel a thing, and molds did not need to be bound or sedated.

He noticed a logo on his blanket. *AutoCorp*. He wondered when it had appeared.

Elwyn dreamed. He was riding in the car with John F. and they were holding hands like infatuated schoolboys. The wind was blowing in their hair. They gazed at each other and laughed as they each began to say something, speaking at the same time, and stopped. Idly they picked lint off each other's jackets. They straightened each other's ties. It was preening, just like birds or baboons. They picked and preened but then the lint became sticky and got under their fingernails and it was gray and greasy like blubber. They had lost their heads. Both of them. They were covered in gore. Elwyn gasped and wailed. His voice was strangled.

He roared himself awake. 'Don't leave me!'

His eyes were open now. It was dark, with little winking lights, red, and green and white. A great rush of rain welled up in the darkness. When it subsided, he knew it was applause.

Could cameras see in the dark? Of course they could. His eyes would be video-green and startled-looking, flashing like cats' eyes at night. He had seen that on TV. The haunted look. He closed his eyes.

Applause.

For the first time, the sound of it made him feel bad and small. With clapping came gunfire. Hiding inside the rain there were bullets. Unseen eyes were trained on him. Hundreds, no, thousands of unseen eyes were feeding on him. Every single person in the land knew exactly who he was, where he was, could pore over his pores. His heart was beating too fast. Anonymity was the prize! The assassin was in the crowd. The killer's eyes were trained on him. The madman was out there, looking. Lurking. Or maybe he was inside the hospital already, just waiting for the right moment to shoot. Which one would he shoot first? Maybe he was dressed up as a doctor, an actor, preparing a lethal injection, flicking the loaded syringe with his expert fingers. It was the death penalty. So easy, so obvious.

Everything sounded loud now. The hum of the cameras, the clicking of machines. Elwyn thought he had escaped, but he was going to die again, this time for real. They would inject him and he would die on camera, while the world watched and clapped. By the time they realized, it would be too late. His arm throbbed. His agony was real. Those bullets had been real. He wanted to cry out. The Drugz were wearing off. There were shooting pains up and down his right side and in his neck. He wanted his mother. He wanted to hide. He was a sitting duck. Wired up and pinned down by the cameras. He wanted to disappear, but he couldn't even twitch without them noticing. Reall Life was waiting for another assassination stunt. Would they stop the gunman? Would they intervene? Maybe they wouldn't. It was great TV. They had been caught by surprise once already. Reall Life would—

Elwyn felt sick and cold and wet with sweat all over.

Had Reall Life hired the assassin? The idea was appalling. It was murder, live. He was trapped, wounded, unable to squeak. A lame sitting duck. He had to get out. He had to get away. He had to run away from Reall Life. He struggled to sit upright in his bed, pains tearing through his body, his eyes wide open and staring. It was dark.

The little lights, red, and green, and white, kept winking. He could hear everything so clearly now. Machines, applause, beats of blood in his own head. He felt faint. The crowd was going wild. He was wild. He had nothing to lose, everything to lose. The gunman was in the crowd. He tore at the plug in his hand, and threw the tubes away. He groaned, clutched at his gown and jumped off the bed, ready to run, but his knees were soft as cloth. In slow motion he staggered into the drip unit and fell to the floor with a crash of hard and soft. Then the alarm and the cheers. Then oblivion.

Jack in the Box

'It's for security,' Jackie announced to the press crowd outside her home, before stepping into the limousine. 'There are lots of freaks out there.' She knew her words were muffled by the layer of encapsulated activated carbon over her mouth. Plenty of scope for misunderstanding.

Biologically isolated all the way from Fresno to Dallas, she cut a fine figure in every reflection she saw. Heads turned. Officials took her aside. Press men shouted questions at her from behind barriers. *Why don't you have a Reall Life bodyguard? Who killed your husband? What are you going to do now you're all alone?* She perspired on the inside but, from her white hood and facemask to her white overboots, she was invisible to the world outside. She felt safe. She didn't have to speak unless she wanted to. No camera could steal her soul. And no one could know that her hair was a mess, or that her eyes were sore after nights of missed sleep and crying.

She picked her way along the concrete path that led to the morgue entrance. Her overboots made it hard to walk with any elegance. A crowd of reporters and photographers pressed from behind, held back by police guards. Their flashes snapped. Their voices called out more yearning questions. Everywhere she looked there were flowers. Heaps of them, bouquets, bunches, wreaths. And teddy bears carrying personal messages, condolence cards filled to the edges with sorrow, hand-scrawled mourning balloons that bobbed in the breeze. *Jack and Jackie. We love you.* Her sea shone with cellophane waves that caught the light and danced as she walked.

To mask her face and mark her grieving, Jackie had considered wearing a big black hat with a full-length lace veil. Officer 1122 would have delivered it along with her mail and groceries. But Jacqueline Bouvier Kennedy had done something like that, and Fresno Jackie was not about to start playing historic First Lady. Especially when her own husband was dead—

Was he really dead? Could Reall Life be working on some kind of

Say Cheez trick? Was John F. waiting for her here in this building, playing dead on a medical table with a phony tag on his toe, shaking with laughter and ready to start the celebrity life all over? The doubt made it hard for her to feel any one thing. She felt a rush of grief and then, in the middle, or underneath the hurt, another feeling. Mistrust. The feelings curdled in her stomach, made her sick, made her focus: self-defense.

Instead of a huge black hat with a full-face lace veil, Jackie had considered a beekeeper's outfit or an astronaut's spacesuit. In the end, she had settled on her own personal Biological Isolation Garment. She had browsed through the different colors and styles online. She had chosen white. It was more discreet than camouflage or orange. The fabric was comfortable, air permeable and fire resistant. These were facts she could be sure about. Guaranteed.

The morgue elevator was like a hotel elevator. The walls were apricot-colored acrylic glass and the ceiling was mottled bronze-effect. The advertisements were sponsored by LeizureScape. Jackie had expected someplace more industrial. Dripping and murky. The police officers felt warm next to her, or perhaps she was imagining it. She craved for warmth, to lean against a warm body. She'd hardly registered their faces, but she'd noticed logos on their badges. A tiny lens peered down at them from the ceiling corner and she wondered if Reall Life had anything to do with it. She had filled enough screens since the morning, private plane and all. Dallas Love Field was bristling with cameras and ID-readers. She guessed every airport was the same, especially these days with all the Terror Wars.

A friendly recorded voice announced the floors as the elevator descended. They were going down. Very, very slowly, it seemed. She remembered some story where the stairs kept going down, too far, and in the end it was hell.

Apart from the black purse, her baggy white reflection looked like it must be someone else, somebody off the news. The elevator doors opened. Her nose itched.

Was he really dead? Was he lying there now, chatting with some concealed cameraman, telling a rude joke? Would she have to be shamed and grateful, smiling and bashful, like all those mugs on TV before her? Would Reall Life let her keep her mask on? She felt sick. Scared and angry and full of sorrow all at once. Sicker than—

'Mrs Kennedy, this way please,' one of the police officers said. The voice was far too serious. It was melodramatic. He had to be an impersonator.

Jackie checked for cameras, but for once she couldn't spot any.

She was led along a corridor to a room like a fridge and a sterile table with a pale cloth cover over an uneven human-sized form. Big words on the cloth said something about DISTRICT.

This moment would be the surprise ending, the scene of all her shame and mockery. It was more than she could bear. Her breaths rushed loud as the sea, her skin crawled with itches. But she was grateful for her overalls. Nobody could see her face.

As the cover sheet was turned back, Jackie prepared herself for John F. to spring up like a jack-in-the-box, for an announcer to step out from behind a drape, for a TV camera to roll across the tiled floor towards her, zooming in on the blush beneath her mask.

But he did not spring. The body before her was still. His head was a mess. There was nothing left of his face or his smile. Just a great gaping bag of tattered flesh and hair. Even his ears were little red rags. The cloth cover was drawn back carefully to reveal his whole body. His legs were rigid as a showroom dummy—but there were moles, freckles, hairs. Tiny feathered crimson veins. Deeper blue veins. His hands seemed to be swollen. She looked for his wedding ring. It was not there. Through the overglove fabric, she felt her own fingers. But she knew she had taken her wedding ring off, just as he had done. She started breathing again. She shocked herself with the sudden noise of it. She did not cry. This poor unfortunate man was a stranger. Unrecognizable.

'This is not my husband,' she said. She clutched at her purse as if it held her life.

'Excuse me?' The officers spoke as one. Their expressions were anxious, Jackie registered that much, but she could not piece their faces together to make them whole. A moist nostril. Signs of dandruff. A pierced ear.

Jackie unzipped her mask and peeled back her hood. The odor of the room hit her. It was clean and cold. She could smell rubber and science, disinfectant and sweat—her own nervous perspiration.

'I said, this is not my husband.' Her voice was clear. 'This is not John F., the person I married. What have you done with him? I do not recognize this man.'

The Big Dealey—Today's Bets

'THE CUBAN MISSILE' 2-WAY BET
Suspect: Artime Cubela
Firing Line: The Texas Live Oak by the Grassy Knoll
No. of bullets: 1 or 2
Motive: Industrial Sabotage
Odds at 12:30 p.m. CST: 19/61
Total no. of bets placed on all suspects: 824,085
Don't forget: just 4 days to go before bets close!

Artime watches the news with his lights off and the curtains drawn. His room is a mess. His things have been thrown everywhere by the authorities. How many weeks have passed since their visit? He stares at the screen as the Anglo hairdresser in the big white anti-chemical suit walks up a path to the local morgue. Reporters and onlookers hang behind her like exhaust. She doesn't have to work. All she has to do is exist. All she has to be is the false president's wife. She is worth as much as a politician or even a sports star, rich enough to buy a villa anywhere she wants in Miramar or Miami.

Still lying down, Artime flexes his strong arms. He punches his bare stomach. It is hard enough to hit hard because he works out. But he's a man with ideas too. He is the entrepreneur behind the JFK Ultimate Ride Experience, otherwise known as JURE. —Who is this redhead who calls herself Jackie, comes from nowhere and does nothing to earn her status?

Artime can't believe how many flowers she gets. He tries to calculate the number. The cost. He wonders if someone paid for them to make an impression. He tries to add up the total weight. The length—if he laid each carnation end to end, each rose, each lily—what distance would they make on a long, straight, smooth, American road? He is used to thinking like that. His clients like to hear how long things are, how heavy, how old. It's like giving his mind a work-out.

Anyway, he has nothing better to do with himself now. He has no car. The authorities have taken his beautiful real American car, his customized 1961 Lincoln Continental convertible. They have claimed it as their own. Robbed a negro in broad daylight. They have even taken away his disks. He is like a store back home, an ice cream parlor with menu boards and staff in uniforms, but no ice cream. An empty chewing gum dispenser six feet high, covered in juicy American names and flavors and dust.

Artime can't take his eyes off the screen. The authorities have cracked the surface but the picture still works. He opens a can of Drinx. He spills some on his front. It fizzes down to his navel. Tickles his white-scar tattoo. He flicks through a hundred, two hundred, channels. So much shopping! So many channels! It still amazes him. His poor family back home have no choice. Just one channel with sad Russian films which gave way, like cars, to Chinese ones—or the Minister of Water, Milk and Bread mumbling for hours with the Minister for Electricity. There is no danger of good drama in Cuba. If you open the window for fresh air, the bugs come in.

The Americans are talking about Artime on the news. Aerial footage of the Big Day motorcade shows a disturbance in a tree by the Grassy Knoll. Any man with an eye for detail could see the shadow of a big dark body in the upper branches of the Texas Live Oak: the Founder, Sole Proprietor, Driver and Chief Executive of JURE—the JFK Ultimate Ride Experience! But after everything he has done, Artime feels like a sideshow, a bit part. A *Big Dealey* bet. They don't bother to arrest him.

'Nothing more than a bet!' he spits at the screen.

They have taken away his real American car.

Real American car! Real American! Artime used to say, away from the police, the ubiquitous police, close into tourists' ears on the cobbled streets of downtown Havana. *Real American car! Real American!* It wasn't too hard to pick the real tourists. The government plants dressed well enough, looked white enough, clutched at their maps and acted dazed just like turistas. But Artime was no fool. He had an eye for detail—gestures, fashion—and he knew how to avoid getting caught.

For his regular job in Cuba, the legal one, he used to be head of recreation at the Hotel Presidente. He was the black habanero who taught the sunburned girls to salsa. He called their bingo numbers in four different tongues. It was not enough. The Great Castrator took away his tips and taxes and paid him peanuts.

For his irregular job in Cuba, the illegal one, Artime patched in the damaged body of his dead father's Dodge. He used plaster and house-paint. By the end it looked like blue ice cream. The trims were missing. The glass was cracked. The inside stank of fuel, and the engine coughed black smoke, but the tourists never used to mind. They'd pay him more in a night for one round trip than a doctor earned in a month—only better, because they put American dollars in his pocket. Cash money. No rewards for The Great Castrator. Enough in the end. Enough for the dinghy without a motor, a pleasure craft for tourists with two silly paddles. Just thin rubber and air between him and the ocean floor.

After four days at sea with Yuri the lifesaver from Alamar, their air escaped. (Ah, Yuri! Named in the Russian style by a Party-loving father.) The dinghy deflated, filled with water, fed their food to the sea. They took turns to blow it up by mouth. *The kiss of life*, Yuri joked. Just human breath between them and the ocean floor.

When his gut was full of raw fish and salt, Artime lusted for America more than ever. He dreamed of ice cream and chewing gum. A real real American car. He had his own slogan to match any party slogan. *Better to die at sea than live in Cuba.* But he didn't die. And his friend didn't die. Yuri went all the way to Las Vegas and Artime discovered Dallas—first the vintage TV show, then the city—all those years ago, before the twentieth century closed.

Before Artime switches off the news he sees a cop talking above a big red viewers' hotline number, asking for information about the assassination.

Call: 2–4–1–KRIMETIME

Detective Pascillo is on every channel, it's a national alert. He looks like an actor. He is hunting for assassins.

'What kind of man are you? Are you a man to make some bets?' Artime says out loud. He's standing up to the cop. Man to man.

'Did I shoot a man, or did I shoot a car? You don't know which way to bet!'

51

Artime laughs without smiling. Perhaps he should call the TV cop and tell him what he thinks, that a special car is worth more than an ordinary man, that no other man can just steal her like that and get away with it.

'The car is mine. I can do with her what I want.' He punches his hard stomach. 'Is that a crime?'

He hits his stomach again. 'I shot the car. I hit the car.'

He stares at the ceiling. He's stuck photos all over the cracks—himself standing in full uniform next to the limo, girls wearing his chauffeur's hat, Japanese businessmen posing next to him in a line—and postcards sent from places as far away as Iceland and Australia. *We were moved by your tour. We will never forget it.* A photo of Yuri, now a wedding photographer in Las Vegas—he took his own shots kissing his bride. Artime gazes into his friend's triumphant eyes and tries to count the dollars. What's Yuri worth? He feels the spilt Drinx sticky on his stomach. Normally he would wipe it clean. Normally he would not be drinking on his back like some lousy cockroach. He closes his eyes and listens to the drone of the Ewing Freeway. Car after car after car. Everyone has a car in America except Artime.

A tree is rooted to the spot, before and after the Big Day. What better perch could there be for a man without an automobile? A tree remembers the paths of bullets. Artime knows about symbols. Dead live oak makes the best timber for boat-building. The authorities have taken away his beautiful real American car.

Why don't you try walking? Silvia suggested after the raid. His girlfriend is so Mexican, so forgiving. Sometimes he has to knock some sense into her.

There are too many walking guides in town. They speak fluent American. They know every detail, who said what and where. For them, the conspiracy is so deep and perfect it is like a religion, and nobody can mess with the details. They know dates. Hours. Minutes. Running times, driving times. They know tourist card numbers and firearm numbers and serial numbers and address numbers. They find links between names, until every name joins up with another name and makes big whispering circles. They are members of the Assassination Community, they belong, and they are all white.

No one cares if the walking guides have licenses. They are not entrepreneurs like Artime. They are fundamentalists. They are worse than politicians or priests repeating numbers and words. Assassinologists are no threat to Reall Life.

Only Artime Cubela has the car.

He corrects himself in his head: *had* the car.

He corrects himself again: AutoCorp have two cars just like his.

He corrects himself again: their two cars are damaged, wounded, full of bullets.

And Artime's car—have they crushed her now? The authorities took his car to protect the business of Reall Life. They have given the roads to the big brands. Since when do the authorities here behave like The Great Castrator?

Intellectual property, they have written, as if it is a sentence. He has stuck their letter on his ceiling, next to a postcard that says Liberty.

Unauthorized duplication and broadcasting of protected copyright audio source material. Unauthorized use of 'John F. Kennedy' and 'JFK' which are Registered Trademarks and Service Marks of LeizureScape Enterprises Inc. Unauthorized use of 'AutoCorp' which is a Registered Trademark and Service Mark. Unlicensed public re-enactments constituting gross infringement of Reall Life's exclusive license to use the aforementioned brands.

In plain English, their letter says, *the Use of these Brands in this Context.*

They banned him.

And a matter of historical accuracy: there were no black men (or women) in the presidential motorcade.

But Artime defied them. He'd put the black man in the motorcade and he was going to keep him there. For the first time in his life, in freedom, in Dallas, in America, he was thinking the old party slogan.

Better to die on your feet than live on your knees.

'But in America the customer is king!' Artime says to his own face in the cracked screen.

His customers want to be JFK, to see the streets as he did, from Dallas Love Field to Dealey Plaza. They want to be taken back to 1963, when the crowds wore hats and obeyed policemen. Before

AIDS and civil riots and the Terror Wars and women in the army. When beauty was truth and the Kennedys were beautiful.

Artime's car was—is—beautiful. It's a perfect replica of the original X-100. He has shown respect for history. If only the authorities could appreciate that! He did not make do with any old car. He waited for the right model to show up in the auctions. He spent money. All his money. Real American dollars. He cut open her steel body. Split her down the middle. Stretched her. Sprayed her midnight blue all over. Gave her jumpseats and a hydraulic back seat. He did not neglect her Secret Service parts: retractable steps, hand-holds on the trunk, radio antennae and platforms built into the rear bumper. Some tourists want to stand there like special agents on guard, but he must move them inside the vehicle for motoring safety. Some passengers sit low where the Connally couple sat. He guesses that the superstitious ones like to be wounded, not killed, in their imaginations. But he knows that the customers' first choice, and the most expensive one, is the back seat. It is always raised up as it was on That Day, to make sure that the presidential passenger is seen by everybody.

Artime's in-car soundtrack is—was—full of cheers and clapping. He recorded the President making speeches, Jackie giggling on the White House telephone, the voices of reporters, the Beatles and Marilyn Monroe. He downloaded the national anthem. The Pearl Harbor bugler mimed by Montgomery Clift for Frank Sinatra. The dreams of Martin Luther King. He added human heart beats.

Only Artime Cubela can bring to life the President's fateful journey, block by block, towards certain death.

Love Field.

Mockingbird.

Lemmon.

Turtle Creek.

Cedar Springs.

Harwood.

Main.

It's so easy for him to remember. It's a picture catalog of objects. (Then comes the compromise: Houston Street is one-way now, so his route turns into Market to get onto Elm.)

And when his customers see the looming Texas School Book Depository building they shudder. And when they hear the re-enacted speech of the Governor's wife, they feel the stab of dramatic irony. *Mr President, you certainly can't say that Dallas doesn't love you.*

And then they feel the horror. *Oh no, no, no.* The sound effects of gunfire and the wounded Governor's words which usually coincide more or less (Artime does his best to time it) with the white cross marked on the road: *My God. They're going to kill us all!*

And then the silence is tragic as he accelerates (unless there are traffic backups) to drive past the Dallas Trade Mart site and on towards Parkland Hospital, before returning to Love Field. The soundtrack is silent until they come to a stop with the historic announcement of the dead man's death.

After his tour, Artime's customers always hug him or shake his hand. They look into his eyes like parting brothers and sisters. And when they are gone, he counts up the undeclared cash earnings that fill his pockets, as generous as their sorrow. He polishes all the chrome fittings, and oils the leather upholstery, to prevent damage from the sweat of their hands or the salt from their tears.

—What would happen if he calls Pascillo now, tells him who he is, what he has done? How long will it be before the authorities come to get him for his crime? He is a suspect—what are they waiting for? But he cannot call the TV cop. He is not man enough to do it. He does not want to be humiliated by the authorities.

'We Cubans don't have any guts!' he says to his reflection. In his mind he can see vultures circling just like they do back home.

Jack and Jill

It was too late: Elwyn's eyes popped open before he remembered to keep them shut. He waited for the rain of dreaded applause, but it didn't come. There was something breathless about the quietness, like those long moments before thunder. He was alive. The light was bright and made him squint. He remembered crashing into the drip unit. They must have picked him up, put him back in full view, wired him up and pinned him down again. He was the target. But he was still alive. His blanket was printed all over with logos. He was the target.

There was a woman sitting at a distance from his bedside, staring at him.

Was this the assassin? Had Reall Life sent her? He was trapped. His bullet-wound pulsed with pain. Could the killer come dressed as a woman? Not a phony doctor, not a hit man, no Lee Harvey Oswald lookalike. She was between him and the door. He felt a rush of panic. He struggled to breathe. A female killer? He hadn't thought of that. This would be the last trick of Reall Life.

A huge cellophane-wrapped fruit basket filled her lap. Purple and green grapes bulged against giant plums and apples, monster mangoes. Was there a gun in there, or a grenade? This was the perfect way to hide a weapon, better than flowers.

The woman had orange hair and a black suit. She narrowed her eyes. She looked like she'd won a prize, but it hadn't made her very happy. Maybe she was having second thoughts. Assassins did that sometimes. She lifted the gift. Shaking. Towards him. Slowly.

He braced himself.

Then she put it down on her lap again. She inched her chair forward.

What was she playing at? They were torturing him.

She had no name badge, no logo. She was not dressed up as hospital staff. She didn't look like anyone. Impossible to classify. For no reason at all, a list of common mushroom names filed into his head, one after another. *Apricot Jelly. The Blusher. Hen of the Woods.* This moment mattered. He was about to die. Again. *Poison Pie*. Whatever he said or did, he knew it mattered. So he did nothing. He said nothing. He stopped breathing. *Swamp Beacon.*

The woman inched forward some more, still staring at him. The cellophane crackled. She was close enough for him to know that she was holding her breath too. There was no one else in the room—but Reall Life was watching, Elwyn felt sure of that. They were making him suffer.

Don't do it! he pleaded with his eyes.

The woman's pale freckled nostrils quivered and grew pink. She bit her lip. She was clutching a purse, pressed against the basket. Her fingers were white with clutching. Her blue-gray eyes filled with moisture and a tear spilled out. She was still holding her breath. He was still holding his breath, holding every muscle. Her shoulders tensed. Another tear spilled down her face. Was it remorse? He lifted his good hand, the hand with the intravenous plug wedged into the skin. He lifted his hand in her general direction. He was not used to moving. He felt so weak. He was not sure why he was moving.

Please . . .

Pain shot through his shoulders, seized his neck. His hand swayed and pulled on its tubing. It looked like a puppet's hand shaking on string. His fingers straggled. His arm dropped again. He let out a breath. She stayed perfectly still. And then suddenly her shoulders dropped and she let out a gasp.

'John F.' she cried. 'John! John!' The tears streamed down her pale pink cheeks. The cries came out of her like coughs. Her eyes screwed tight and her mouth pulled into an unhappy grin. Her teeth were small and tidy, like a doll's. She was inching forward on her chair, gripping her purse, pressing the fruit. She was calling him John.

At last, Elwyn breathed out. Relief. He understood. She was no assassin. She was the Other One's wife. The Lady of Fresno. The competition.

'No,' he tried to say, but his voice was hoarse, out of practice.

'John!' she cried out. 'Let me take you home!'

He tried to shake his head very gently so as not to stir up the pain in his neck. Then he changed his mind. He didn't know why.

'Yes,' he croaked. 'Yes, yes. Home.' He was President John F. of Fresno and this was his wife.

There was a protracted silence, so deep it pressed in upon his ears, heavy and airless like clay. It was as if the entire hospital had ceased to function. As if wheels had stopped turning and meters had stopped pulsing. As if even the air conditioning was holding its breath.

And then a crowd roared in the distance.

The sound filled him with horror.

'You're alive!' Fresno Jackie spoke loudly. She glanced up at the camera and then at Elwyn. She moved her chair alongside the hospital bed. Her face was really close now. Her expression was concerned, like a mother. Too concerned.

'I just knew it wasn't you in the morgue! They shot him. In the head, worse than before. Honey, they tried to tell me you were—' She opened her purse and took out a white handkerchief. She blew her nose vigorously, leaning over the fruit.

She was calling him honey. Was she mad with grief? Was she playing to the invisible audience? He didn't know what to say. His voice came out in a hoarse whisper.

'So the Other One's dead?'

'Dead.'

Elwyn gulped and his neck-brace felt painfully tight. He choked on the emotion of it, the narrow grinning crack between him and eternal death.

'Does that mean—' He whispered quietly so that the microphones could not hear. 'Has he won?'

Jackie leaned towards him. 'He hasn't won, not yet. The polls say different things. You know, it helps his case to be dead. But you're going to get votes because—well, people want you because you're alive.' She cleared her throat and raised her voice. 'And you converted—you were always more sincere. Everyone knows a genuine all-the-way-through-honest man when they see one. Are you getting enough food? Are they looking after you right? Can I make you more comfortable?' With her free hand, she plumped his pillow. The violence of the action sent pains shooting into his neck.

When she stopped, Elwyn whispered at her. 'The cameras are on me, 24 hours a day. I can't even—' He wondered how John F. would say it. 'Go to the—without people looking.'

'I know.'

Was she pretending with him? Elwyn imagined stepping into John F.'s shower, using his soap, sleeping in his bed, wearing his clothes . . . the prospect was irresistible. But more than this, more than anything, he wanted out. No more limelight. No more killers after him. He wanted to take the prize money and run. He didn't know where.

'Jackie, can you save me? Can we go back—to the way we were— before?'

'Before TV?' Jackie's face was twisted with anguish.

'Yes, no eyes. Just eyes for each other.' He knew it sounded like a line from a soap opera. She was going to save him. Where was Head Nurse Mitzy? Where was anyone? The phrase crossed his mind: quiet as a morgue. Jackie was going to save him.

Her face brightened. 'I brought something for you. Some fruit.'

Jackie lifted the basket by the handle and looked up at the camera. She positioned her offering by his chest. There was not enough space on the bed. She grasped his good arm and wrapped it around the basket, tubing and all.

'There,' she said, too loudly. 'Do you like it?'

Elwyn nodded. It hurt. The gift blocked his view of the camera. A big gold tag said *Foodz*. Was there a microphone inside all that fruit?

Fresno Jackie murmured softly into his ear, all the while crackling the cellophane with her fingers.

'I want to find out who killed him.'

He thought her tone had changed. He decided to risk the truth. He whispered back. 'You want to know who killed—your husband?'

She nodded and nuzzled above his collar, still playing the cellophane with her fingers. 'After everything, you know, I loved him.'

'I loved him too,' Elwyn breathed into her neck. The words fell out of his mouth, despite himself. Perhaps he had sustained head injuries after all.

'And I hate him,' she said after a while, still whispering, still nuzzling, still cellophaning.

'Me too.'

'We've got a lot in common.'

'Get me out of here,' he pleaded. 'Help me, Jackie. I can't do it alone. They're watching me.'

'If you help me find out who killed him. I can't do it alone. Can you be him for me? He always knew what to do. I've never felt so alone in all my—'

'I know,' he said. 'Me too.'

She drew back. Her lips were pressed tight, like her purse. Her white synthetic shirt was grayed and worn. Why hadn't she bothered dressing up for the viewers? Before the motorcade, he would have looked down his nose at this hairdresser from the suburbs. But Fresno Jackie was suddenly as beautiful and sharp and poignant as an apparition. She was setting him a task and he was the hero. There were insurmountable obstacles to be surmounted. He beckoned her back towards him. The fruit basket wobbled. Jackie leaned in to listen.

'It's a deal,' he whispered.

Without warning, the door opened and there was Head Nurse Mitzy Muchmore. She was pushing a small stainless steel medical cart.

'Here.' She strode across the room. 'Let me open that up for you.'

Mitzy reached past Fresno Jackie, lifted the gift and placed it onto her cart, where she cut through the wrapping with suture scissors. Her movements were abrupt and efficient. Elwyn thought of a homesteader skinning a rabbit. A theme tune played in his head. *Daniel Boone was a man . . .* That's what John F. Kennedy was. A real man. Fresno Jackie wanted her real man back. Elwyn didn't care. Fresno Jackie was going to save him.

'There,' said Mitzy. She was positioning the golden Foodz tag carefully in the middle of the grapes. 'Now you can really smell the goodness of the fruit!' She turned the whole basket this way and that until she was satisfied with the arrangement. Then she pushed the cart in by Elwyn's bed. Fresno Jackie had to edge her chair back a little.

'Thank you,' Elwyn croaked.

'Thank you,' Jackie smiled serenely.

'But that's not all,' said Mitzy. 'You've got lots of fans, Mr President. Naturally you do. Are you feeling up to some visitors?' She did not wait for him to respond. She beamed and turned towards the door.

'Let there be love!' she called.

The door opened and a shiny new medical cart appeared, heaped with bouquets of flowers and cuddly toys. Elwyn could not see who was moving the cart. It had to be a dwarf, he thought. Or someone with a remote control.

He and Jackie watched as the next cart came through, gingerly, then another, and another in procession, each piled high with cards and candy and flowers.

'They're sick!' Jackie groaned.

Elwyn stared as each child came into view.

They were wearing hospital gowns stamped all over with cartoon versions of the Drugz logo. A doll-faced African-American boy pushed his cart and pulled a drip unit on wheels behind him. A brave Hispanic girl used her crutches to move her cart along in jerks. Two cheeky Indian twins grinned and pushed their way to the front. Their four arms were in plaster casts. There was jostling and rustling and whispering and giggling as they took their positions and changed their minds. Elwyn wondered why the cute Korean boy had bandages on his head. Perhaps he'd had an operation. A pretty white girl with black-shadowed eyes and bluish lips smiled wanly and Elwyn was reminded of a kid at his junior school who had a hole in the heart.

All the Sick Children stopped with their carts in semi-circular formation as if they were the stars of a school concert. The room felt crowded. Swaying slightly, they began to sing the national anthem, their voices rising painfully at the end.

Get well soon, Mr President, the Sick Children chanted as one. *We want to be like you when we grow up. We love you.*

A sudden wail reminded Elwyn that Mitzy was still about, although he couldn't see her now without straining his neck.

Jackie turned toward the noise.

'That's so beautiful,' Mitzy cried out. 'It breaks my heart. So . . . beautiful!'

When the tears started pouring down the Sick Children's faces, even Jackie wept.

Elwyn looked up at the only camera he could actually see. He stared and stared at it, until he felt sure the lens itself was moist and crying. There was not a dry eye in the house but his own.

'Thank you,' he said meekly, softly. And then he remembered a line from somewhere. He knew it was religious, just the kind of thing John F. would say. 'Suffer the little children. Suffer the little children.'

And then he fell asleep.

When Elwyn woke, Jackie was at his bedside. She was close-up again. Her eyes were dry. The room was full of carts and gifts, but the Sick Children were gone and Mitzy was nowhere to be seen. Elwyn figured that there were extra cameras and mikes in among the flowers. His head felt clear and refreshed. He knew to whisper.

'How long have I been asleep?' he asked.

'Just a bit. Are you all right?'

'Overwhelmed. How are you going to get me out of here?' he asked.

'I'll think of something, honey.'

He would have cosmetic surgery. Eat himself back to obesity. He would dye his hair, rub his skin with boot polish all over, pretend to be an outsized Mexican with an accent and a moustache, like Charlton Heston in *Touch of Evil*. No one would know. He would escape with this simple woman from Fresno in her XMart bargain suit. He would turn a blind eye to the suit. He would do anything.

★ ★ ★ ★ ★ ★ ★ ★ ★ ★ ★ ★ ★ ★ ★ ★

TV PRESIDENT IN PERIL?

Viewers watched nationwide as the wounded presidential motorcade survivor was wheeled out of his Parkland Hospital observation unit in the early hours of this morning for an emergency operational procedure. The incident occurred just after 4:00 a.m. Central Standard Time when home audience figures and hospital staff numbers are low. The senior medic responsible for the move is yet to be identified.

'Our patient was showing signs of cardiac distress,' Media Liaison Officer Head Nurse Mitzy Muchmore said to the press corps assembled at Parkland Hospital, just minutes after the transfer to the operating room. Muchmore stated: 'Patients have been known to show post-dramatic symptoms long after the actual trauma is over. This could be a life and death situation for the President.'

The statements were delivered from the dais in a crowded nurses' classroom believed to be the same location where acting White House press secretary Malcolm Kilduff made his historic announcement of JFK's death in 1963.

Muchmore was guarded by a hospital administrator and a senior Dallas Police Department spokesman, both of whom endorsed her report.

But sources close to Reall Life suggest that not all has proceeded according to plan.

One production assistant, who wished to remain anonymous, said: 'We've run a check on all the operating rooms. It's like he just vanished.'

★ ★ ★ ★ ★ ★ ★ ★ ★ ★ ★ ★ ★ ★ ★ ★

★ ★ ★ ★ ★ ★ ★ ★ ★ ★ ★ ★ ★ ★ ★ ★

HEX OR HOAX?

It's a mystery. Presidential candidate John F. Kennedy of Fresno was last seen headed for emergency surgery at Parkland Hospital, Dallas, Texas, 4:04 a.m. Central Standard Time today, but his whereabouts following the transfer are not known and the senior medic responsible for the move remains unidentified. The location of John F.'s Californian hairdresser wife 'Fresno Jackie' is also unknown.

'Investigators still are trying to piece together what happened Friday in Dealey Plaza,' stated Sgt. John Kilgallen, a missing persons unit supervisor. 'This Mr. Kennedy was present at the shooting. He was an eye witness. We would ask him to make himself known to his nearest police department for interview by detectives.'

Kilgallen was unable to comment on any aspects of Kennedy's contract with headline-grabbing TV company Reall Life.

'It's a conspiracy,' commented Carlos Trafficante, 43, a contract worker at the now-legendary Parkland Hospital. Trafficante claimed to have seen a suspicious woman laughing with two Mexican janitors by a back exit. 'I saw the puff of smoke,' he said. 'I think it was from the cigarette. She got in the car with one of the men. It had unfamiliar plates from outer state.'

Commentators are suggesting that the presidential candidate was kidnapped in a high-ransom 'hit' linked with organized crime, although no figure has as yet been demanded.

Others suggest that this twist in the tale was orchestrated by Reall Life in order to boost ratings and the forthcoming TV election known as HyperFriday. No one from the organization has been available for comment and, since the press announcement in the early hours of this morning, all staff at Parkland Hospital have been placed under media curfew.

Bewildered voters and health officials were already grappling with a case of mistaken identity following Monday's amazing revelations by Fresno Jackie. Protected against potential terrorist attacks in chemical-biological isolation garments, Mrs. Kennedy denied that the deceased contender was her own husband of 16 years.

Last seen wearing a black suit with matching purse, the 36-year-old hairdresser was visibly moved as she embraced her survivor husband at Parkland Hospital, Monday. Within hours of this momentous reunion, sales of program-related games and memorabilia surged, and national polls started to see-saw.

The mother of the deceased has yet to be located for a second identification procedure which is expected to put the lid on speculation and rumor. Several women have come forward, and men also, claiming to have been intimate with the deceased. But their applications for access have been turned down.

'This happens every time there's a crime in the papers,' said a source close to the Dallas Morgue. 'Some folk want all the attention. Specially if it's what you call a high profile case. They'll say just about anything just to get theirselves on the TV.'

'We must query the assumption that any one of these people is dead,' said Conover Dillard, Professor of Media Studies at the University of Oxford. 'We need to put a question mark on everything. We must not be afraid to publish our most searching questions.'

With only two more days to go before the real voting begins, polls are looking closer than ever. Analysts agree that this election will be won in the swing states, as many as 17 of them. The Florida, Iowa and Ohio results will be key to the election outcome. Meanwhile, back in Big D, the search for Truth—and the man himself—continues.

★　★　★　★　★　★　★　★　★　★　★　★　★　★　★　★

Black Jack

'You've got to read the rules,' said Amanita. 'Anyone stays in my place's gotta read the rules.' She was sitting on a sofa as big as a car. She wore men's pajamas and thick glasses. Her eyeballs were milky as marbles. Early-morning sun sifted in from windows on all sides, lighting up her cigarette smoke.

Amanita's Inn was some kind of converted warehouse next to a huge parking lot with roads on either side, and a religious soup kitchen at the other end. Elwyn had met Fresno Jackie at the appointed place: inside a gold-colored SUV parked by the entrance. The rest of the lot was empty, apart from a homeless man asleep in an XMart shopping cart. He looked genuine enough. There was no one to recognize them.

Elwyn had been walking. In darkness. Three big blocks from the bus stop. Only poor people walked in Dallas. Only poor people caught the bus. It was Jackie's idea. He'd caught the same bus as the hospital janitors. He'd stumbled over great hot-air-belching vents. He'd dodged wires and hydrants and broken concrete and signs in the middle of the sidewalk. Dallas was not a place for walking. Dallas was a place for shooting. He was exhausted. *Dallas doesn't love you.* He hated Dallas.

He and Jackie scanned Amanita's rules, item by item. His hands were sweaty. His moustache itched.

'Nope, that's not good enough,' said Amanita after a while. She drew hard on her cigarette and blew high into the air, making a cloud above her head. Her wispy gray hair was another cloud.

'I might be half blind, but I ain't half deaf and I can't hear you reading the rules.'

Elwyn and Jackie glanced at one another.

Jackie shrugged and started to read at top volume. 'My home is your home.'

'Together!' Amanita barked.

Jackie was acting uncomfortable. Elwyn was acting Mexican. The boot polish from his fingers was beginning to stain the paper. The couple read obediently, together.

'I will treat Amanita's Inn as my home. I will not show bigotry or hatred or discrimination of any kind in my home. I will cut hatred out of my heart every night before I sleep and every day before breakfast which is at whatever time I prefer before 10:00 a.m. as long as I make a reservation and stick to it. I will not exercise my right to bear arms in the bedroom or any other part of my home. I will flush the toilet repeatedly during use to take account of the low pressure which the Water Board in their wisdom has inflicted upon tax-paying residents in the Dallas area. I will not make disturbances at night after 9:00 p.m., and that includes the volume of my in-room TV. And I promise to return the keys when I leave, or risk forfeit of my deposit.'

'Good, good,' said Amanita when they had finished reading. 'Mi casa es tu casa—now I say that in Spanish 'cos I may not be from here, not from Dallas, not from Texas, but I'm about as Mexican as you are, Mister . . . Mister . . .?'

'Black,' Jackie said, grasping Elwyn's hand. 'Mr and Mrs Black-Gonzalez.'

Amanita shook her head. She stared, so bare-faced it was almost rude. She held her cigarette to her mouth and inhaled as if it might be her one source of truth.

Elwyn could tell his accent had not fooled her. He and Jackie had arrived too early. They didn't have enough luggage. No one came to Dallas just for a vacation.

'Now I know you two are up to something, but as long as you play by the house rules, I don't mind what kind of private business you get up to.'

'Thank you,' Elwyn said meekly. He seemed to be saying little else these days. 'Thank you.' He used his own voice. It was unfamiliar. He was not JFK anymore. He was not John F. of Fresno. He was not a hospital janitor, not even a faux-Mexican. His arm was throbbing. His neck-brace chafed. He hoped Jackie had brought plenty of Drugz.

'Amanita's a beautiful name,' he said. He didn't want to give himself away but he couldn't resist unpicking the coincidence. 'Does it mean something?'

'Matter of fact, it's a kind of mushroom,' she smiled slyly.

Elwyn felt a quiver of professional pride. It was short-lived.

67

'Born with the cord around my neck made me a funny color.'
Amanita winked one cloudy eye and grinned. 'I was Mama's whippin'
child. She said I was so ugly she had to tie a pork chop round my neck
just to get the dogs to play with me. I think that's just a figure of speech,
but I do believe I was coyote-ugly, which is also a figure of speech.
Which has got something to do with the fact that I'm a free thinker
and I'm not whippin' anybody. Except the war-mongering politicians.
Now I don't mind if you're married or not married, gay or straight, or
both or neither. —What happened to your neck? Mama's cord get you
too?' She laughed, inhaled, blew smoke rings and coughed.

Elwyn touched his neck-brace. He wondered how much she could
actually see.

'Well, I've got your payment, thank you, so all's left is for me to show
you your room—I should say rooms. Mrs Black-hyphen-Sombrero
here's reserved all the rooms but you'll be sharing a bathroom. It's
interconnecting. You've got a singing cricket comes free, no extra
charge. There's only one, so you could call him a solo artiste. In dry
weather you can get fourteen in a toilet bowl. Open the door and a river
of 'em come in. But in damp weather the mildew gets to the eggs.'

Which mildew? thought Elwyn, as they went down the stairs. He
was beginning to feel like himself again, although he knew Jackie was
wanting someone else.

'I've got to wash all this off,' Elwyn said to Jackie at the door of his
room. The smell of melting boot polish was beginning to make him
feel ill. Worse still, his overalls reeked of someone else's body odor
and a week's worth of stains. They were authentic. Jackie had gone to
some trouble to achieve his anonymity.

'Let's meet in half an hour,' she said. 'Here's some underwear and
things. They're clean.' She pushed an XMart bag into his hands. He
had no idea what she had bought for him. Did she know his size? Of
course she did. He and John F. were a perfect match. For the first time,
this thought made him feel uncomfortable. He closed the door and
listened for the sound of her going to her room next-door. Then he
heard the cricket.

Their bathroom was dark with the light off. The cricket thrummed from inside, contentedly, as calm as purring, but extra loud. Elwyn could hear traffic from the street outside, its volume oddly amplified by some trick of the plumbing. He could also hear Jackie next door. She was opening and closing drawers, rustling plastic. Elwyn turned on the bathroom light and pulled back the nylon curtain around the shower. He watched as the brown legs scuttled down the plug hole. He turned the water on. The singing stopped and then started again. He wondered if there were two crickets.

Jackie appeared at the door on her side of the bathroom. She held out her hand. Another plastic bag. 'Drugz and bandages. For your wound. I can dress you if you want.'

Elwyn shook his head as best he could without aggravating the whiplash. He didn't know what he wanted. He wanted to scuttle down the plug hole and hide in the damp dark.

'That's where the cricket is.' He pointed.

'There's dead ones in the drawers,' Jackie said. 'John F. would die—I mean, you should have seen the motel, you know, everything was deodorized and kind of new—but Amanita's a low-risk kind of person.'

Elwyn took the bag from her and waited. Jackie looked him in the eye. Her face was expressionless. Pale pink as a seashell. He didn't know how to read her yet. She resisted classification. There was still a reasonable possibility that she was mentally disturbed, temporarily or otherwise. She turned and closed the door behind her. He locked it.

'John F. never locked,' she called out.

'Trust takes time,' he called back.

'There's not much of that.'

Trust or time? Elwyn thought. With his good hand, he took off his overalls and neck-brace. He ripped off his false moustache. In the shower he thought of all the soapy shoeshine water rushing past his clinging cricket like a great flood. He kept his bullet-holed arm dry. There was not a camera in sight. Not one single lens or microphone. He felt the first delicious surge of solitude. He thought how every animal died alone. He sang. And then he remembered Jackie.

Jackie and Jackie

Jackie threw herself onto her bed. It was small compared to a Fresno motel bed. The sheets were old-fashioned cotton, with real woolen blankets and crocheted cushions. There were handicrafts wherever she turned. It was like being in a historic homestead and she was a pioneer.

She felt proud of herself. She had escaped the eyes of the media. Against the odds, she had brought her husband back to life and managed his abduction without a hitch. For the time being they were safe in their hideaway. But they couldn't stay long. If that *KrimeTime* detective was going after all the assassination suspects, he'd be heading for Detroit in no time, homing in on the angry husband of dead Mardie. As far as Jackie was concerned, Bob Scrutt was Suspect No.1. She wanted to get to him before anyone else did.

What if Pascillo started searching for the missing president, not just the suspects? He had a special hotline, so the whole entire looming land of America was full of spies and witnesses waiting to call him up. Every stranger was a potential threat. Nowhere was going to be safe for long, even if she was smarter than a detective. And there was no telling what Reall Life would throw at her. She had changed their script. They didn't like that. She had outsmarted them. They didn't expect that, after all the humiliations they'd put her through. *Get the wife's reactions.* They'd got her screaming and screaming on national TV.

One week ago she was just a hair stylist from Mane Event. She had never left the state of California. She was somebody who looked like nobody, a side-order celebrity because of the man she had married and wanted to divorce. Now she was somebody in her own right and she had millions of dollars worth of credit to make herself invisible—all the money she needed to buy her way, all the way, to her husband's killer.

The road was long, Daddy used to say, but he wasn't talking about the road from Dallas to Detroit. The road was long. She took the roadmap out of her purse and spread it open on the bed. The only bumps in the land were from the crocheted cushions underneath the paper. There wasn't one single place along the route she'd ever heard of. Not even a real big city with a famous food. It was a road through nowhere and maybe nobody lived there, so she could fly like a bullet through the big wide open spaces, through nothing, straight to her husband's killer.

With her man by her side, she had her bases covered: it didn't matter now which way the elections went. On HyperFriday they would both be winners. She would have enough money for lawyers, bodyguards, hair salons, anything. And Elwyn had his part to play in Detroit. His acting days were not over yet. The assassin could try to assassinate the president all over again. Whatever happened to Bob Scrutt as a consequence would be self-defense, no matter how grievous.

Jackie folded up the roadmap. She listened to the sounds of Elwyn showering. He was singing. He dropped the soap a lot. She guessed it was harder to maneuver with one arm out of action. She wondered how a bullet wound felt. She wondered if he could manage a weapon. She'd never handled a gun, until the day she took delivery of John F.'s pistol and ammunition boxes. He'd kept them in his front desk drawer. In all his years at the motel, he never actually had to shoot anybody.

Better safe than sorry, he used to say. She could hear his voice saying it in her head. *Better safe than sorry.* Dead hypocrite.

Jackie sat up and turned on the television. The news was on. The Armz logo glittered. They were showing highlights from the Terror Wars again. Men in suits, men in robes, men in uniforms, men waving flags, men shooting guns, men guarding doors, men making speeches, men driving tanks, men answering questions and explaining things, men shaking hands for the flash of cameras. Explosions. The LeizureScape logo burst like fireworks across the screen. They were showing her new husband's removal for emergency surgery. Footage of him being wheeled out. Gaps. Blanks. Unanswered questions. Nurse Mitzy's guilt-free face and well washed hands. Jackie clapped. She had bought a top-class act.

There were heads talking about celebrity health risks. Anatomical diagrams. A picture of the Dallas Morgue in its sea of flowers. Protesters and their banners. *Armz For Life. Stop the Terror Wars. Stop Reall Life.* Footage of herself throwing the handset and screaming, leaving the house in Fresno, wearing her white protection suit. Media satellite trucks all down the road. Reporters in prime viewing positions on her neighbors' lawns and rooftops—they had paid thousands of dollars for the best spots. Pictures of the dogs. The dogs! Officer 1122 was looking after the K-9 Corps. Did they miss her? It was too unbearable to think about. The dogs had always loved her without any questions, comforted her.

Jackie switched channels. They were showing old pictures of the press. Scrabbling crowds of men with notebooks and cameras. Press men pressing. Men pressing.

Then there was a salesman in a suit, standing in the middle of a freeway, holding a microphone, talking at her, raising his voice, not stopping for breath—

First time around, extra crews poured in to fill the papers and the airwaves with the terrible news as fast as they could. But it wasn't fast enough! Never before had we wanted so much TV! And the rest of the world watched American TV by relay . . . from Communist China . . . to Iron Curtain Russia . . . to Secret Japan . . . to Old Europe.

First time around, the networks lost $40 million in canceled ads. Yes, forty million dollars! Think about that in today's value. Not this time! History teaches us lessons. In the modern era, valuable advertising is auctioned. And on the Big Day, we even auctioned lots in the auction!

We've been breaking all the records for viewing periods, power surges, downloads and streaming, sales of snacking, memorabilia and other related products . . . Just take a look at some of the bestselling items you've been buying . . . LeizureScape software and hardware! Retro-styled AutoCorp vehicles! Reall Life games that break all the rules! Every kind of Armz! And don't you love these Limited Edition Collectable Drinx?

Plus, viewers, there's more to come on Election Day. Everybody's calling it HyperFriday. Don't miss it! If the Big Day was big, HyperFriday will be even bigger! Millions of Americans will exercise their constitutional right to vote—regardless of color, faith, status, mobility, penitentiary or lifestyle choice. All you need is a screen or handset! This is the ultimate in Remote Control! What on this planet could be more democratic than that?

And viewers, don't forget: there'll be people right across the world who'll be watching us with envy! Yes, even in non-democratic countries from Latin America to Africa to the Middle East and the Far East, they'll be crying out for their right to vote too. HyperFriday promises to be the greatest landmark election event ever! The countdown got started on the Big Day, folks. 96% of all viewers say this is the most important election of their lifetimes and every poll in the land shows it's going to be a nail-biting cliff-hanger! On HyperFriday, the eyes of the whole wide world will be upon us!

News anchorman Walter Cronkite appeared on TV in black and white. He was young, taking off his glasses and wiping his eye. He was announcing the President's death. A lonesome guitar was playing. Jackie kept the volume on low. A black shield hovered in the top right corner of the screen. It was the Reall Life logo with a historic date: November 22, 1963. That logo made her stomach go tight.

The picture was a photo of Lyndon B. Johnson being sworn in. A title appeared above his head: *36th President.* He towered over a squat lady in polka dots. A word obscured her head: *Judge.* People pressed in from behind. More words: *Secret Service.* The letters faded. The picture shifted to the right, revealing Jacqueline Kennedy standing by LBJ's side. Then the word *Jackie* appeared in great big letters.

Fresno Jackie felt haunted, like they were broadcasting her own name. She wondered, not for the first time, why John F. had fallen for her. So often he'd made jokes about it, calling her his First Lady, saying that the people loved her, that she was his high-class aristocrat. And then other times he had berated her for not playing her part, for not helping him in his career, for sticking with hers. She was nobody.

The screen filled with Jackie Kennedy's picture. Electric white circles drew themselves on her suit. Arrows pointed in at her body. She was surrounded by arrows. More words appeared: *JFK's blood.*

The program went so quiet Fresno Jackie wasn't sure she could hear it anymore. She turned up the volume as the voice-over began: *She was still wearing her blood-stained suit.* It was an LBJ soundalike, for anyone who remembered what LBJ sounded like. Fresno Jackie remembered. John F. had made her watch all the presidential documentaries. It

73

sounded like LBJ talking to children, or like the voices they always used at election time, as kind and friendly as Walt Disney.

Someone suggested Jackie ought to change her outfit. And you know what she said?

There was a pause.

She said: 'Let them see what they have done.'

Fresno Jackie felt herself shudder. She repeated the line. 'Let them see what they have done.'

She breathed out heavily and sank back into her pillow.

Jackie Kennedy certainly knew a thing or two about grooming.

The music lingered, but the archive picture dissolved into a moving Jackie in color, wearing a bright pink woolen suit. She faced the camera, dabbed at her eyes, turned away, stroked her hair, looked back at the camera. Her name appeared in an information strip: *Wilma Moorman, cosmetic scientist and today's Jackie in Lubbock, Texas.* When she finally spoke, her voice kept catching.

He was like your best friend. I felt real special with him by my side. No one ever made me feel that way before.

It was impossible to know whether she was talking about John F. or Elwyn.

The lookalike flicked her hair away from the camera, the way models did in shampoo ads to demonstrate bounce, shine, freedom from tangles, freedom. No one ever moved like that in real life without whacking someone or getting whiplash.

Jackie glanced at the bathroom door. Elwyn was still showering. He was singing. *Free at last, free at last.* She wanted to see his body, to touch his wounds. She wanted to feel him next to her, warm in her bed. Damaged. Protective. Faithful. Why was he single after all these years? Was it fear of commitment or fear of betrayal? Jackie knew stray men were turning up at the morgue, and women, all claiming to be exes, too many of them to be authentic, like splinters of the True Cross. People would say anything just to get an audience.

The Texan Jackie spoke some more.

I don't know what we're all supposed to do now. The whole world is looking awful sad. And kinda pointless. I tell you what, I'm not taking off this suit. Not ever! Let 'em see what they done.

The way she said it sounded wrong. It wasn't just the accent. *Let 'em see what they done.* The picture froze on her open mouth.

Was she the one who had sat next to John F.? Fresno Jackie searched for signs on the woman's suit. How would it have been to sit next to a warm-blooded man one minute, and then . . . Had John F. cried out in anguish, like Jesus or the Governor? Jackie wondered, but then she remembered his silent face. The starry look in his eyes as the first shot found him. No words. No fear. Just soft gratefulness, radiant and shining as a climax.

How could they do this to us? A retired colonel was saying. He was Warren O. Couch from the Tennessee Army National Guard. *They want to destroy the West. They love death more than we love life.* He was wearing a vacation shirt. Pineapples and parakeets, *FLORIDA* across his chest. He was standing on a public street. Jackie wondered if Florida might be a good place to go. It was full of outsiders and runaways. Sunshine and oranges as good as Fresno.

Next, a teacher named Fidel Santos was talking to an interviewer in Santa Barbara. Where he lived, they had dog bowls outside all the stores. Jackie liked that about Santa Barbara. They even had a dog delicatessen and a dog gift store. She was missing the pups, all the dogs, but especially the pups.

This is a tragic strike against humanity, not just America. Who's behind this one? The Government? Big brands? Islamic fundamentalists? The media corporations? Maybe all of them together.

'It was Bob Scrutt,' Fresno Jackie answered the teacher out loud.

But the real question is why? Fidel asked.

'Because he had to kill the faithless bastard who stole his wife from right under his nose,' Jackie answered. 'While the whole damn world watched.'

Then a pretty girl called Marina Church Garrison appeared on the screen. She was platinum blond, professionally styled, and big chested. She wore a low-slung satin dress like she was ready for the Oscars. No bra. The information strip said she was a call operator from Bismarck, North Dakota, but Jackie wasn't convinced. What kind of call operator needed to put on evening wear? Why did everyone want to be like Marilyn Monroe? Why did John F. have to sleep nationwide with a Marilyn Monroe? Jackie felt a catch in her throat.

The people of my generation never had anything to beat this, the bombshell said. *It's our Vietnam.*

Jackie heard the shower turn off. She checked the time. She had given Elwyn half an hour. He had fifteen more minutes alone. Then it would be time to dress her president. He had slept with the bombshell too. He had betrayed her, disgraced her, on national TV. She gulped to hold down the anger but it rose like a burning liquid from deep inside of her.

The camera cut to one Harvey Marcello, a car salesman from Flint, Michigan. He might have been an actor. It was impossible to tell. He acted natural enough. He even cried a little.

Jackie wiped away a tear.

I'll never forget that day. We all stopped work. We were glued to our screens. We saw it all in real time. No one said a thing. And then we all broke down. Even the men. We've lost our innocence.

'We keep doing that,' Jackie snapped back.

Those who cannot remember the past are condemned to repeat it, a LeizureScape voice said.

Jackie was thinking about Mardie Monroe straddling her panting husband.

I'd just said my line. I was more nervous than I'd ever been in my whole life. He was looking so pleased with me. I had no idea it would all come to this. We weren't the first re-enactment in that same place, by no means. I thought it was safe. So many have been before us.

This Miss Lee Rubenstein was the actress who'd played Nellie Connally the Governor's Wife in the motorcade. One of the two. The information strip said she came from a place called Providence. Jackie snorted at the name. It was the only Providence anyone was going to get from Reall Life. Everything in Reall Life was planned.

But who had planned for Fresno Jackie? She would show them all.

It was a car full of yellow roses, red roses and blood, and it was all over us, said one Nellie Connally. She was older, much older than Miss Rubenstein. She might have been her mother. She was holding up a pink suit on a hanger in dry-cleaner plastic. She had kept it all these years, she was saying. She was the last person alive who'd been in that car.

Jackie knew the feeling. She had kept her wedding dress. It was protected in plastic, with bug-killer in the lining and tissue inside the sleeves. She would never let go of it, even if she had been talking about divorce. It was beautifully made, from another time, when her waist was slender, when Daddy was alive, when John F. only had eyes for her, when they thought they would have children, one, two, three, maybe even four children, two girls and two boys, in the days before John F. got really serious about being like the President.

Jackie got under the blankets and pulled the old-fashioned cotton sheets up to her neck.

I've often said one could understand assassination in a poor, impoverished country. Jackie had never heard of Senator Dirksen. He was in Washington, DC. He was in 1963. *But it is almost impossible to understand it in a free country where every man can find some form to express himself.*

'Tell that to Bob Scrutt!' Jackie said out loud.

What did they expect? A young student called Glenn Czolgosz was asking. *They set up this whole circus. Don't tell me they didn't know what was coming! Point a camera at anyone and they'll act just like they're on TV. It's exploitation. Nothing's too cheap anymore. Not even real life—I can't even say that phrase anymore—they stole the words from us.*

People were always saying things like that. Everything was a conspiracy and that's how Jackie was going to play it in public, but as far as she was concerned in private there was just one prime suspect. He was the one man she wanted to find before anyone else did. His name was Bob Scrutt and he lived in Detroit. He was the angry husband of dead Mardie from Bird-in-Hand. He was a corporate security guard who used to be in the army. He'd got himself the fancy job of sitting on a vintage motorbike in the Big Day motorcade, playing a police officer, pretending to guard her trusting husband. Bob Scrutt was less than ten feet from John F. when the blood exploded. Jackie had heard about concealed weapon action. He was the snake in the grass. There were supposed to be lots of suspects, but she only needed one.

And there was John F. on the TV, all caught up with Mardie's body, writhing around under the grand piano like it was happening all over again right there in front of Jackie's eyes. He was moaning like a stranger. He was moaning and moaning. And Jackie started moaning inside without a sound as she watched her presidential husband thrusting and moaning like a man having a nervous breakdown. Something inside her broke—she felt it happening all over again— only this time it was worse. She clutched at the sheet, and stroked it and pulled it with two hands. She hadn't slept for weeks, not real sleeping, not for months, not since Reall Life was thrust upon her and got inside her and made her do things. She missed John F. She wanted him. She closed her eyes and stroked and pulled the sheet at her neck. She hadn't worked things out because she was broken. She couldn't work things out. She hurt. She hurt. She hurt. She hated John F. even more than Reall Life. It was all his fault. Everything was his fault. He started it. He wanted to be President. He hurt. She hated him and Mardie Scrutt and Bob Scrutt and Elwyn Barter and Reall Life and *The Big Dealey* and everything. She was moaning on the inside without a sound, hating and hurting. They had broken her and the crack was filling up with moans like silent liquid silently pouring and forcing the crack so wide it felt like splitting. The hurt was bigger than Dealey Plaza. Bigger than Dallas or California.

Jack in the Box

Elwyn stared at his in-room TV. It was very old, like the rest of Amanita's furniture, almost quaint. The screen was smeared with fingerprints. Bits were missing. Somebody had scratched their initials on the side.

Elwyn watched himself on the screen's surface, his reflection distorted. He was wearing his neck-brace and his bullet wound was on show. He was in pain, constant pain. He looked like somebody else, not JFK, not himself—could he be somebody else?

He held the remote. All he had to do was press a button and the TV would turn on. He would be able to see himself on the Big Day and before. Coconut carving. Making speeches. Sex with Mardie. He would see the Other One living his life with Fresno Jackie. He would see what other viewers could see: firing lines, body jerks, blood and chaos. But maybe he would look at it differently, perhaps he'd be the one to solve the crime. Who had tried to kill him? He stared into his own eyes. Even in the murky reflection, his eyes were haunted. Tired and fearful. He was too scared to call his own mother—Reall Life would be intercepting her calls. They'd track him down in no time. Too scared to go out on the street looking like Elwyn. Too scared to go to Detroit or anywhere that had a name.

His arm throbbed. He needed Drugz. He stared at the television and watched his face trapped in the box. Disapproving of himself, hating himself. The box was menacing. It was a device from outer space, sent by cruel aliens, endlessly receiving and transmitting. No wonder people heard messages.

Elwyn was too scared to turn it on. He would not turn it on. He vowed never to turn on a television again.

The Big Dealey—Today's Bets

> 'RUBY IN THE DUST' 1-WAY BET
> Suspect: Jacob 'Sparky' Mannlicher
> Firing Line: The DalTex Building
> No. of bullets: 1
> Motive: Mold Enthusiasm
> Odds at 12:30 p.m. CST: 11/21
> Total no. of bets placed on all suspects: 3,639,800
> *Can you believe it? Only 3 days until HyperFriday—*
> *and then it's no more bets!!!*

It's 6:45 a.m. Sparky steps out of his red front door and squints at the world. He's got a towel wrapped around his middle and his pigeon chest is bare. His rifle is slung over his shoulder. The strap chafes his skin and catches the short tight curls of hair above his nipple. He's had an uninterrupted night's sleep—still not a hint of law enforcement. Downtown Dallas stares back at him and the warm November sunshine strip-searches the road. The sidewalks are empty. The nearby parking lot is empty, except for one gold-colored SUV and one tramp in a shopping cart down the far end by some kind of hippie-painted warehouse called Amanita's Inn. No one seems to be living around here except the men who sleep on the streets.

Sparky's at his ninth address in so many days and he's beginning to miss Chicago, his home. But he's not homeless. He's parked his motor home on the street, facing the wrong direction. It's a white clapboard house with an iron roof, one bedroom and drapes on the windows, sitting on a trailer hooked up to a truck. He's parked it by the sign that says *No Parking ANY TIME* with a picture of a car being towed. Sparky's truck is begging for a fine. Or the house is. He's just waiting for a ticket to be slapped on his windshield or his front door. But the cops around here are too important or something—there's hardly a rush on parking. Maybe they're too short to reach up to the door.

Sparky adjusts his towel, locks up his house and crosses the street, missing the crosswalk by yards. He takes a detour to catch his first and favorite CCTV around the corner of a deserted office block. Here is a big black glass eyeball with a white eyelid, hanging off a droopy stalk like some alien sprout with 360-degree vision.

'You're just a ball of fluff!' he mouths at it. No need to waste his voice. This kind of camera can't hear. 'A wannabe never was!'

He knows to focus on the spot where his own eyes are reflected in the curve of the lens. It makes his smarting off more personal. Then he unslings his rifle and cocks it, takes aim, fires and jerks back. It's only a crime simulation. He doesn't want to waste a bullet. He's got to save his ammunition for the real live cops when they come. But they sure are taking their time!

Sparky slips round the corner like he's ready to shoot again, SWAT style. This time he's caught by the long squared-off twin-pivot camera with the Armz logo down the side. He has two angles to play with. He has been acting suspicious for hundreds, maybe thousands, of remote controllers and off-site security guards. He wonders when they're going to start talking to each other. He rips off his towel, and his cock dances with his jumping—this must be an offense. But then he notices the dust on the sidewalk, and the dust on his fallen towel. He shakes it clean and girds his loins again. He crosses his fingers there'll be a really serious crime before or after his. The law enforcers' path to him has got to be complicated and interesting, worthy of a documentary.

Sparky ducks into his lobby. He has given himself a vacant skyscraper, twenty stories free of charge, crow-barred the wooden planks off the entrance in full view of a crop of cameras and found himself a cute pink ladies' bathroom on Level 2. He doesn't mind the mice, and the florets of mildew between the tiles make him feel right at home. Sparky's a mold enthusiast. That's why he came to Dallas, to help the right man win, to secure his place in history.

There's not much light in there, and no camera, so he washes in the dark.

Dressed in classic businessman's attire, with his rifle inside the golf-club bag hanging off his shoulder, Sparky Jack the Jew puts in an appearance at The Lone Star Christian Soup Kitchen run by Brother Pecora. They've got dusty old pumpkins in the window and there's trash all over the floor. Sparky is the only white man, unless the preaching Latino counts, and he stands out a mile in the pews. There's nowhere else around here for fresh coffee and donuts. After the sermon, the Brother asks no questions, except those concerning sugar and creamer.

Sparky takes to preaching on the sidewalk. His audience is busy drinking and chewing and smoking and coughing and cursing, but they listen.

'My name is Jacob Mannlicher. Some folks call me Jack but I prefer Sparky.'

He lays down his golf-club bag. He places himself strategically below a CCTV. It's protected by a wall-mounted cage which is rusty and beaten up, but the little red light is on inside to show that God is home.

Sparky clears his throat. 'I'm still kind of surprised at how the world looks,' he says. 'There are cameras and ID-readers everywhere. There weren't so many on the outside before. The outside world has changed. Feels like being in jail all over again, only it's not so safe, not so . . . individualistic.'

'Individualistic?' an old man asks. He is wearing a T-shirt that says *I bought my timeshare from LeizureScape.*

'Inside, you knew you were being looked at. By someone. A person who knew your name, where you slept, how you scanned and sequenced, and lots more besides. Better still, you knew that person. You could amuse yourself for hours just trying to guess which PC it was—that term refers to a Protective Custodian. You knew their shifts, where they were sitting. The relationship was . . . particularizing. Made you feel real special.'

'You mean you wasn't just some old cliché,' the old man chuckles at his bare feet. '—I mean to say, some old number. Hell, if everybody's special, then nobody is.'

Sparky continues his lecture despite the interruption. He hops onto a block of cement. It gives him an extra six inches. 'After serving my time at Joliet, I wanted to settle down, get myself a nice steady job. The Chicago Mob don't care if you're Italian, Puerto Rican, Jewish, White, Black or Blue. They've got an integrationist policy, they call it diversity and inclusiveness.' Sparky takes a deep breath. 'But you need a degree to get in there these days. You need a fucking PhD. And there's no getting around a . . . gap in the resumé of a . . . businessman.

'Joliet, I said in my first interview, by way of compensation, is a royal castle. They cut the limestone in blocks this big.' Sparky measures out his hands, then takes them wider. The sunshine pours right through.

'Zadafact!' mutters a skinny man with buck teeth. His eyes are yellow. The veins stick out on his hands like worms.

'They had to close the joint after I left. The sparkle . . . just . . . went . . . out of the place.'

Sparky remembers his reception day, the first time he walked into prison. *This is real now*, he'd said to himself. The overpowering stink of 640 half-washed men with not enough underpants and one regulation jumpsuit. The noise of shouting and singing in the galleries. The realization that he would have to shit in public, right there in front of his cellie, or any officer that walked past his bars—no wonder he stayed plugged up for a week. Then he got assigned his own cell. Despite better provisions, it wasn't too good. He still felt shy around the can. He filed for an upgrade to solitary.

'I was the only inmate allowed all kinds of luxuries—to watch the mold grow between the tiles in my cell, to perform regular cleaning duty in the armory where they keep all the Armz, to be both recipient *and* donor of sexual favors.'

Normal guys got beaten up for stuff like that. Not the Man Licker.

'But this kind of experience doesn't win me jobs on the outside. After the first interview, the Goodfellas didn't give me another look. So I do odd jobs.'

One man stamps his foot and says Amen, he knows the feeling. His shoe flaps apart. A grackle takes flight and settles on the empty road.

'I've been selling Drugz for Foodz and Snax. I've been selling Drugz for medical afflictions. The two are connected. I like consistency and I got a clean driver's license.' Sparky thinks for a moment about the dirty Drugz he used to deal on the street. But since Joliet, he's gone 'kosher': he only deals with corporations. He's gotten to know every highway up and down the country. He knows where to stop for Fuelz. He knows where it's Easy On, Easy Off. And he's the last word in gentlemen's clubs. He's a gentleman or he is nothing.

'When Reall Life started with their heritage motorcade,' Sparky says, 'I come to Dallas. I'm an honorary citizen of the Lone Star State. I eat mockingbirds for breakfast!'

No one laughs. The old man with the timeshare shirt looks offended.

'I got Drugz to promote and I got prizes for medical men of all persuasions. I'm not talking puny desk accessories. I'm talking free membership at your favorite LeizureScape resort. A lifetime's supply of Snax. You know what that's worth? I am so sincere about why I'm here I brought my entire *house!*'

Sparky points around the corner to his motor home.

Still not a law enforcement officer in sight.

He checks the CCTV. He searches for signs of appreciative amusement among his audience. A clutch of grackles chuckles on the road, their feathers black and full of rainbows like spilt oil.

A crippled guy starts shuffling towards the corner, gripping the wire mesh fence to get along.

The skinny man's eyes light up. 'Zadyourhouse?' he says. He's picking bits of donut from those jutting teeth.

At this point, Sparky worries about all these bums getting the wrong idea and trying to move into his home. He knows how it feels to crave a bit of security. He raises his voice like a rabbi in top gear. He wishes he was taller. He wishes he had on a fancy robe. At least he's got a weapon. The shuffling escapee stops to listen or have a rest, Sparky can't be sure. The man's back is all he has to go on.

'I figure after all my odd jobs I finally got my calling on the outside. I go to the Dallas Police Headquarters the day before the motorcade and I offer to make sandwiches, but they don't want my sandwiches. You gotta have a degree in fucking sandwich-making to get a foot in there.

'I call up Reall Life. I'm the hero, I say. I should be used for a purpose! I offer to take out that Lee Harvey Oswald, he's so smirky.

84

I can do it all by myself. But they say to me: *There's no Lee Harvey Oswald. So there's no Jack Ruby, if that's what you're playing at. So stop calling us, you keep jamming our lines. There is no job for you with Reall Life.* —What do you make of that? I only phoned them a couple times. But they come on all agitated like I'm some kind of nuisance caller!'

Two of the men are fighting over a cigarette. Sparky turns a little to avoid the sight. One of them has rotten toes—which brings him back to the subject at hand.

'You heard of the Birdman of Alcatraz?'

There is at least some response to this. The odd jobs man says *Yessir* and stamps his foot again. Grackles pecking at donut crumbs scatter and fly off.

Sparky straightens up nice and tall.

'I am the Moldman of Joliet.'

The timeshare man laughs and slaps his knee.

'I know a thing or two about mold. Just like that JFK simulator guy from Manhattan who put smuts on the presidential map. That's why I'm here. I had years in the dark to specialize. I read the mycology society newsletter. I—personally—grew one so special and rare it's not in any books.'

The skinny man wanders away. His donut is finished.

'At Joliet, there's always two of you in solitary. Your cellie is your extra punishment. But I got special treatment on account of my . . . my botanical needs.'

'I was in Stateville once,' squeaks an obese man.

'Me too,' admits Sparky. 'After Joliet.' He remembers his time in the roundhouse. Not a straight line in sight. Too much light. No good for mushrooms.

'Anyone else here from Stateville?'

He's looking to raise a brotherly cheer. A bit of audience participation. There is a general shaking of heads. Sparky figures they're mostly from Texas anyway.

'At Stateville they got broken windows, glass on the floor, a man can get the wrong kind of ideas. And it's like a fucking coliseum. You know what they did at the Coliseum? They put on shows, only at Stateville the show is all round the edges and the audience sits by himself in the middle. Everyone's shouting and doing things. It nearly ran me crazy. I yearned for a solid door. Tiles with cracks, grouting. And water, the bringer of new life. Joliet had given me all that.'

Sparky checks the camera. The light is still on.

'Joliet—God I miss that joint—Joliet gave me everything, everything except this.' He bends over to his golf-club bag and unzips it all the way across. He takes out his rifle, straightens up and shakes it high in the air. He feels a bit light in the head.

The men stand back as one. It's as if they didn't know he had a weapon. The timeshare man frowns and lowers his head. The grackles are hunched all along the eaves of The Lone Star Soup Kitchen, making a line. They're smarting off with their cheeky whoop-sighs. One of them is perched on top of the CCTV.

'This is what you call an SLR.' Sparky is speaking very quietly for a change. He lowers the weapon a little. He looks each man in the face. 'Do you know what that stands for?'

No one answers.

'Does anybody know what SLR stands for?' Sparky is getting angry.

The old man shakes his head again. 'Self Loading Rifle,' he says, without lifting his gaze, behaving like a prisoner before the Board.

'No, no, no, no!' Sparky replies. He laughs for effect. In prison he forgot how to use his laughing muscles. He's still out of practice. 'That is a common misconception! The term refers to Single Lens Reflex. So what you see through the viewfinder is what you get. Perfect framing, memories for a lifetime!'

There is a space in time when everything goes deaf and dumb and slow. The sun is too warm on Sparky's head. His suit feels hot and sticky. He screws up his eyes.

He butts the rifle against his shoulder and takes aim. The barrel is pointing at the old man. There is hardly any distance between them. Sparky can read *timeshare* through the sights.

The target shudders but doesn't move out of the way. It's like he wants to die.

Sparky can see praying words on moving lips.

He swings the rifle around and says, 'This is for you, Pascillo! Come and get me! I'm your man! What kinda cop are you? How long you gonna take? How many clues I gotta give you?' Sparky takes aim at the CCTV. Fires. Jerks back. He's getting better and better at this. He turns again to his audience.

'See that? They say they're preventing crime.' Sparky laughs again. 'They're just recording it for posterity!'

He swings and plugs his audience with invisible bullets. He sees the cripple at the street corner clinging on to the fence. He fires at the nape of his neck. Further on, around the corner, the skinny man is rattling the doorknob on the red front door of his motor home, trying to get in.

Sparky pokes his rifle through a hole in the wire mesh fence, takes aim and fires. He jumps off his cement block. He's laughing—the muscles are working better now. The old man is crumpled up on the ground like a dead thing just by his feet, LeizureScape bold as day on his shirt.

Jackie's Jack

Elwyn was sitting on his bed, wearing boxer shorts. His arm was freshly bandaged. He'd showered, done his hair.

Jackie was leaning against the bathroom door, scrutinizing him, top to toe. She was wearing a sweatsuit, olive green velveteen, slim. She looked impatient. Her face was tight and strange. Perhaps she had been crying or exfoliating.

'What about our deal, then?' she said.

'What about our deal,' he said.

'I got you out,' she said. 'I saved you.'

'So I'll stay with you. But only until the election's over. Things get too messy after that.'

'What things?'

'Think about it, Jackie: the police, dental records—'

'He has no jaw left. His teeth are shot to bits. They can't tell anything.'

There was not enough grief in her.

'There's always DNA testing,' Elwyn said. 'Fingerprints. And Reall Life. If he's dead, that's a crime.'

'You're telling *me* that's a crime.' Jackie scowled.

'Hey, isn't there some kind of murder enquiry? Have they interviewed you? Why hasn't anybody interviewed me yet? I'm a witness.'

'I don't know,' Jackie sighed, glanced heavenward. 'Everybody's a witness.'

'I'll stay with you until HyperFriday. The election's my deadline.'

'If we stick together we can share the prize money, whoever wins,' Jackie said.

Elwyn's head buzzed. He had forgotten about the money. It was safety he wanted, anonymity. But anonymity was going to cost him now. 'You mean half and half? But what if I win?'

Jackie smiled. It wasn't endearing. 'John F.'s one step ahead of you. He gave his life to win.' She stroked the door-frame with her fingers, like she was some friendly neighbor waiting for her cup of sugar, like she would see to it that she got her cup of sugar. 'You'd only win with his extra votes—but not if I change my mind about who it was I saw in that morgue. I could go back there right now and make a scene. I could say what a big mistake I made, you know, because I was losing my mind with sorrow. They'd have all the cameras ready. A tragic scene like that'll tip the balance right over his way. My way.'

Elwyn felt his name slip into the category of leftovers, the also-rans, like all those fungi that didn't fit properly into any group. And then he remembered it wasn't about winning anymore. She was confusing him. He had to hide, get away from Reall Life. He was unwell, he was post-traumatic and this small-town hairdresser was confusing him.

'You know perfectly well,' she said, 'if you lose, I get everything and you don't get a dime.'

He pictured her at a salon desk, wearing a nasty pink smock and cashing out. They were after him, someone was after him. The money did matter. He would need money to get away.

Her face softened. 'If we go fifty-fifty, we both win. It's a low-risk gamble. It's what you call hedging your bets.'

'You think John F. would do that?'

Jackie shook her head. 'No, he wouldn't. It was all or nothing for him.' She wiped her eye. She sniffed. The first apparent sign of grief. Then she pouted like a little girl. It wasn't pretty. 'Do you think you can be like a husband to me, you know, just for a while?'

'Jackie, I'm not the marrying kind.'

'I know. You're a bachelor. You like your independence. I respect that. I do.'

There was no ambiguity in her voice. She had no idea. But didn't she work in a hair salon? He had kept his secret secret—he'd never have come close to presidential otherwise. A Sodomite would have been shot down in the first round. Gay was OK as long as it was cute or broken. He wondered whether to set Jackie straight—

'If you want to get away from Reall Life, we'll have to stay in hotels,' she said. 'Incognito. On the road. Avoid airports.'

'What about the car? Can't they trace it?'

'It's second-hand. I paid cash. False name. It looks new, though, doesn't it?' She seemed proud of that. 'I got another advance for us to live off until the election's over. So we share the prize money, half each. OK?'

It would be more money than he ever earned at the lab, would ever earn in his entire life, enough to start a new life.

'OK.'

'So it doesn't matter who wins,' she said. 'You or him.'

There was a time when Elwyn would have corrected her: nothing else could have mattered more. He'd become addicted to winning. Pain rippled through his arm and shoulder. It didn't matter who won now. Jackie was his only way out. His neck hurt. He didn't want to get shot again. He was afraid of Reall Life. He didn't know what their plan had been.

Jackie was quiet for a time, a long time, without moving from the doorway, staring blankly at him. 'Your hair's not right,' she said at last. 'I thought you'd be better at this.'

Elwyn felt relieved and sheepish all at once. Of course he'd combed and styled his hair in the manner of the dead president a hundred times before today. But she was the hairdo expert, and he only had one good arm.

'It's still wet,' he said. 'And this gel's different from the one I normally use.'

'It's the one John F. used. It's the right one.'

So John F. was the new role model. Elwyn had turned himself into a lookalike. Now he had to look like a lookalike. For the wife. In private. Closeted as a stolen masterpiece.

He put on his JFK voice. 'When I became president, what surprised me most—'

'Don't do that.' Jackie was not amused. 'John F. was no good at putting on the voice. He never did sound like him. He was just a lookalike.'

'He was more than that. He was a livealike.'

'But he didn't sound like him.'

Elwyn had studied the subtle art of impersonation with methodical precision. He was a systematist or he was nothing. No, he'd quit his real job. He was the specimen now, a full-time freak at the other end of the microscope. A wounded, whiplashed, runaway, celebrity freak.

'Talk to me like him,' Jackie said. 'Please.'

He had perfected the historic voice, memorized quotations, inhabited the character, but now he had to put his mind to acting Californian. And yet there was more to it than that: the language of hospitality, the way of the motel manager.

'Welcome to Amanita's Inn, Mrs Kennedy. I'm your captive for today. On behalf of myself, I'd like to thank you in advance for attending to my hair at this time.'

Jackie's face lightened. 'Your voice should be higher,' she said. 'John F.'s voice was higher.'

He tried again. The words turned to gibberish in his mouth. 'On behalf of myself, I'd like to thank you in advance for servicing my hair at this time.'

'That's better, but . . . Anyhow, we can work on that,' she said. 'Hold it right there.' She disappeared into the bathroom and her room beyond. She was back in a moment, hugging a dry-cleaner's suit bag.

'You need to put this on.'

'What is it?' He asked.

'His suit.'

Jackie was wasting no time. Until Friday, she was his passport to obscurity. These next few days would be like a lifetime with Mardie Scrutt. How could he last the distance? After the election, he would be free to be himself again. Grow mushrooms. Grow his hair. Put on a ton of weight and lose the JFK face in the fat. Go on a witness protection program and find himself a good man as rich as Onassis to shield him from the public glare. His head was buzzing again. The money mattered. He had to keep Jackie happy. If he won, he could buy himself all the privacy in the world. But right now he was stuck with her in deepest darkest Dallas, the famous City of Hate, the historic capital of the KKK. *Dallas doesn't love you.* He remembered that ten per cent of Americans hadn't even heard of John F. Kennedy until they saw his funeral on TV.

'You're asking me to put his suit on? Wasn't it destroyed in the—'

'He had spares. And you've lost the accent again.' Jackie stared at him blankly. She was making no attempt at salon charm. 'I want to see you properly. I can do your hair after.'

After what? Elwyn wondered, but there was no further explanation.

He had undressed with anonymous bodies in the dark under bridges, in nameless restrooms and lightless backrooms. He had stripped on national TV with the hapless Mardie. But this was new and difficult. He felt shy. Even modest. His head wasn't right. He needed Drugz.

He slipped off the bed and onto his feet. Gingerly, he reached out with his good hand and took the suit bag from Jackie. Too readily, the zipper slid open with the pressure of his fingers. Slowly he peeled the wrap back and teased the suit out with his bad hand, sending shots of pain through his shoulder.

Jackie did not move to help him but continued to lean, motionless, against the bathroom door.

Elwyn stared back at her unblinking eyes. Gray. Blue. Gray. He was still unable to decide. Friend or foe? —He couldn't be sure.

'Put the shirt on,' Jackie said. Her voice was tight.

He eased the suit off its hanger and let it fall to the floor. He was holding the shirt, the fine triple pinstripe, Commission Exhibit—he didn't remember which number. He dropped the hanger. He felt a shiver on his bare neck, naked without the brace, the tickle of droplets falling from the wet ends of his hair. His heart was beating too fast. He felt sure it bulged through the skin of his chest, but he didn't dare look. Gently, carefully, he slipped into John F.'s shirt. It was a perfect fit. Of course it was. He quivered with pain or excitement, as he fastened the buttons one by one, all the way down to the navel.

'Now the trousers,' Jackie said.

He bent over to pick up the trousers. They were new, starchy, surprisingly unfamiliar. Had John F. worn them at all?

Elwyn put them on, watching as Jackie watched him. He was weak at the knees. He felt a warm tug of arousal as he pictured John F. zipping up his fly. He closed his eyes to visualize his hands, his mouth, lips parted. Like a teasing fingertip, the zipper traced a line of pleasure up his jackhammer. He adjusted the pants, stroked the front smooth, glad of the loose folds that hid him.

'Now the jacket,' Jackie sighed. 'Put it on.'

He exhaled heavily as the jacket settled on his shoulders. He was in John F.'s arms. He closed his eyes and smoothed the fabric down. His hands trembled as he knotted the tie and pulled it tight. So tight it pressed hard against his throat. When at last his feet entered John F.'s tight shoes, he gripped himself, surrendered, groaned and collapsed onto the floor.

There was silence for a while and then the little cricket resumed its song from the pipes. Elwyn stared at his hand.

'John F. would never do that,' Jackie breathed. 'I'll leave you to clean up.'

'I want you to apologize.' Jackie parked herself in his bedroom rocker and rocked.

Elwyn squatted against the wall. He had changed again. A ghastly yellow LeizureScape outfit. John F.'s sneakers. They were too small. He guessed she was talking about the presidential suit.

'I'll get it cleaned,' he said.

'You don't understand. I want you to apologize for, you know, doing it, on national TV.'

Elwyn panic-checked the ceiling for cameras. Were they here too?

'No, I mean with that blond impostor. All this time and you never said sorry.'

'I'm sorry, Jackie.' He was still thinking about the suit.

'You don't sound like you mean it.' Jackie frowned. 'And you don't sound like him.'

Elwyn remembered the glint of lenses in the soft light of the Carlyle Hotel suite. The love Drugz. The improbable coupling. It all seemed so long ago. A lifetime. Now the wife wanted words from the husband that she would never hear otherwise. Perhaps she had reincarnated him just for this purpose. He felt sorry for her.

'I'm sorry, Jackie, really sorry.'

Jackie took a deep breath. 'Call me honey.'

Elwyn's head hurt. Was she demented? Honey was the last thing he wanted to call her. 'I'm sorry. Honey. Things got out of hand. I never expected—'

'Yes you did! You knew all along. Ever since you changed your name. Ever since you got your teeth done. You sleep with hookers and

Mafia molls and actresses like it's just part of some physical therapy program. Admit it! They don't even have names! Admit it! And don't call me honey!'

'But you—'

'You cheat on your wife in public and you call her honey at home?' Her voice had grown shrill. Loud enough for Amanita to hear. 'Is that what presidents do? Is that the behavior of the world leader?'

'Well, yes, actually.'

Jackie stared at him. Her eyes were wild, startled.

What could he say to appease her? 'I had no choice. They made me do it. There was no second prize. You wanted me to win, didn't you?'

'You're sounding like you again,' Jackie said. 'It's no good.'

He felt suddenly tired, shell-shocked and tired. He tried to remember the voice.

'Hi. I'm your husband for today. Thank you for choosing to place your reservation with me above all the others. Your preference means a lot to me.'

She closed her eyes. 'The bastard.'

'I do my best.'

'Your hair is finer than his.'

'And the shoes are too small. They hurt.'

'Less body. You know, everyone's hair is individual. As individual as the person. You can tell what you've been eating, everything. —How long do DNA tests take?'

'I don't know.' Elwyn shrugged. 'Depends what kind of a rush they're in.'

'You promised you'd help me find his killer.'

Elwyn saw the motorcade like an old horror film inside his head, the gunshots like a soundtrack from invisible speakers. First the whiz over his shoulder, a shock wave, past his face, another over his head, behind him, the thundering reports. He ought to have felt fear again. He ought to have felt the pure rush of hormones. Fight or flight. But it all played out like so many special effects. Until one caught his arm. He didn't have the courage to go seeking out his would-be killer. Killers.

Jackie got up from the rocker and adjusted her sweatsuit.

'Which killer?' he asked. 'You think there's just one?'

Jackie paced around the room, picked a ceramic donkey off the dresser, put it down again. 'There's only one. You don't believe all that conspiracy stuff, do you? That's what they're counting on.'

'They?'

Jackie stared into the bin. 'There wouldn't be any money in it if they admitted there was one lone gunman.' She started pacing again. 'Take a look at *The Big Dealey*. The bigger the conspiracy, *the bigger the dealey*! Last time I tuned in they had bets going on maybe eleven bullets. Six guns. Eight different firing lines. I don't remember how many wounds or misses. And that's just a betting show. Then there's all the election programs. And there's *KrimeTime* with that TV Detective. They're looking for all the usual suspects. Criminals. Dropouts. Nuts.'

Elwyn was relieved. She was sounding normal again.

'It means the real culprit gets kind of lost in a muddle and everyone else is kind of guilty,' Jackie said. 'You think Lee Harvey Oswald was innocent? He wasn't. He was the lone gunman, the only one.'

'He never spoke out against the President. He's the only "assassin" ever who denied being one.'

'Who says you've got to do assassinations the one way? Everyone's individual. It's not like there's a formula.'

'So who do you think is the real culprit?' Elwyn asked.

'Bob Scrutt. Mardie's husband. He had a gun and he knew how to use it. He wanted revenge. You slept with his wife. Then she died.'

'That was suicide.'

'Or homicide. But in a way you killed her. And Bob Scrutt was, you know, right there on the Big Day.' Jackie stopped pacing and sat herself on the bed. She swung her legs like a little girl. 'He had the means, the motive and the opportunity.'

She sounded like she'd been watching too many cop shows. Elwyn's head was spinning. 'They said they filtered out all the undesirables.'

'Who said that?' she jeered. 'Reall Life? What's their idea of no-good? Bob Scrutt's a kind of hero. A war vet. He does a crummy job. You made a fool of him in front of everyone. His wife died for *The TV President*. He's not an actor. On the Big Day they gave him best tickets in the house: front row behind your limo—I mean, your limos, you know, dressed up as a special security guard on one of those official motorbikes.'

'You know that?'

'I saw the footage. With my own eyes. But I didn't need to see it to believe it.'

Elwyn shuddered as he tried to picture the man who had wanted him dead. A shady character in a law enforcement officer's uniform, hiding his eyes behind dark glasses and a visor. A man with a gun in the pay of Reall Life.

'You saw him shoot?' he asked.

'I saw his face. And he jerked.'

'At the right time?'

Jackie nodded. 'Concealed weapon action.'

'You're certain it was him?'

She nodded again. 'John F. got some emails.'

'You mean from Mardie,' Elwyn said. 'She sent me some too.'

'No, I found some other emails. From Bob. The address was different. I think he was blackmailing John F. or something. I'm no private eye, but it all adds up.'

'Jackie, if you're so sure he's the killer, why don't you just go to the police?'

'Like go to Pascillo, the friendly face from *KrimeTime*?' Jackie ran her fingers along the fringe of the poncho hooked onto the wall behind the bed. 'And say what? That I'm convinced this vet from Detroit blackmailed my husband, then killed him, only my dead husband's alive and well? Reall Life wouldn't let us out of their sights a second time. We'd be prisoners again. Anyway I want Bob to confess. To me. Face to face. I want him to look me in the eyes and say what he's done. Let him say what's he's done!'

Another one, thought Elwyn. *Another confession.* 'You're going to Detroit?'

'*We* are going to Detroit.'

Elwyn tried to shake his head, but it hurt too much. 'I'm not going to Detroit.'

'Yes you are.'

'The nut tried to kill me.'

'We made a deal. You promised.'

There was not enough feeling in her. But what could he do? Reall Life terrified him. He was helpless. He had no money, no ID, nothing. He couldn't get far by himself. He would think of something clever after Dallas, before Detroit, on the road. First, they had to get out of Dallas. He had to play along with her for now.

'Let me show you the emails,' said Jackie.

Dear Jack

From: blondebombshell@leizurescape.com
To: johnf@kennedyoffresno.com
Subject: Dear Jack

> I luv to call you Jack dear
> After all we went thru
> My hart is split in two
> Pasion had no shield
> Rubber is to blame
> Every one shared our luv
> Growing famouse inside of me
> Nobody yet but somebody someday
> Almost a president of the US of A
> Now is the time for you to be great and
> Take us under your eagle wing!

From: blondebombshell@leizurescape.com
To: johnf@kennedyoffresno.com
Subject: Dear Jack

> As I have not heard from you in response to my poem I am
> wondering if maybe I was to clever about telling you the
> situation with reguard to our situation!? Pls read previouse email
> again by 1st letter initials only. And pls tell me how you can
> help. I'm so confussed! PS Im prepared to move out away from
> here if that the rite thing to do
> LOL ect
> L (J)

From: bobo@leizurescape.com
To: johnf@kennedyoffresno.com
Subject: Dear John

> You know who I am. I know who you are. We have a meeting
> with Destiny. It has been written. It has been broadcast. Haha.
> When you fuck with the Lady you fuck with your life. IOU and
> you owe me

From: blondebombshell@leizurescape.com
To: johnf@kennedyoffresno.com
Subject: Dear Jack

> Your still not answering back! If you use code like me no one
> will be any the wiser beyond you & me. I'm sorry but I'm v
> distracted with the situation and realy need you to reply with
> regards to yr feelings & responsabillities. I was married v young,
> our kids are grownup and left home, my husband was not v hapy
> with me returning to work or this show although I always played
> M.M. from the start coz I allways looked like her, even when we
> 1st met when he was in the Army. If it was up to him, this was
> the last show I ever did. Or not even this one! But M.M. said
> All of us are stars and desserve the right to twinkle. I am
> prepared to make a new start with you & twinkle! for the sake
> of our *** but only if your willing!!!
> Yours ect
> :)
>
> This is my adress if youd prefur to post: 35 Manning Ave
> Dearborn Detroit MI

From: bobo@leizurescape.com
To: johnf@kennedyoffresno.com
Subject: Dear John

> Check received. Await next. In the military it's not the
> individual that counts. Haha. Bet you're having second
> thoughts. The one who comes first doesn't have second
> thoughts.

From: bobo@leizurescape.com
To: johnf@kennedyoffresno.com
Subject: Dear John

> No more checks? Are you trying to get me angry? Maybe
> you forgot who you're dealing with.

From: blondebombshell@leizurescape.com
To: johnf@kennedyoffresno.com
Subject: Dear Jack

> No more twinkle

From: bobo@leizurescape.com
To: johnf@kennedyoffresno.com
Subject: Dear John

> Well, it's all over now.

From: bobo@leizurescape.com
To: johnf@kennedyoffresno.com
Subject: Dear John

> See you soon. Same time, same station. Haha.
> Everybody will know who I am then.

Power Jackie

Jackie and Elwyn sat like honeymooners at the breakfast table. They had not slept at all yet. They'd agreed to say nothing much so that Amanita would have less to overhear, and less to tell if pressed at a later date. Jackie wasn't feeling broken inside anymore. It had been a long and dramatic night, what with the great escape and all the negotiations coming to a head.

Amanita was by the stove, cooking eggs. Her radio was on, people talking too much as usual. She whistled through the talk, as though she was following a tune.

Everyone's a celebrity at the present time, y'understand. It's like there's this production line and they're all just waiting to come off. And I tell you what, it's valueless. We'll look back and we won't remember anyone from today at all.

Jackie studied Elwyn. He was still wearing John F.'s LeizureScape tracksuit. It was old, but the fabric had kept its comforting crisp swish-swish and bright canary yellow color. It didn't suit Elwyn so well, which puzzled her. It made him look sickly and kind of bruised in the face. Perhaps because he was still recuperating from his assassination—he was wearing that ugly neck-brace. Or maybe her two husbands just had different complexions. John F. used to take special vitamin tablets to make his skin yellow—the old JFK had some kind of secret discoloring disease which got passed off as wartime malaria. Maybe Elwyn hadn't bothered about that detail. Jackie knew he had only played the role on the outside, not lived it from inside. She liked that about him.

The daylight was brightening. The sounds of traffic outside were louder. Dallas was waking up.

Until this week Jackie had never been anywhere much. She and John F. had been home bodies. They didn't have passports or people to visit. And leaving home was an expensive business, especially now since she'd become famous. Jackie knew no one else paid Amanita the kind of room-rate that she had counted out in cash the day before.

It was silence money, with extra for the early start and the other rooms kept empty. Amanita had been happy enough to accommodate her guest's irregular desires. Jackie was beginning to understand that every kind of person became helpful with money. The more money you had in your purse to give them, the more helpful they became. *Look at Mitzy Muchmore*, she thought. *And look at my new re-formed husband here, good as gold.* Jackie's head felt light. With half the prize money coming her way for certain now, she was guaranteed all the helpfulness she could desire, before and after HyperFriday.

Amanita stopped whistling as the radio announcer spoke up.

. . . the latest freak accident in the Terror Wars. They were carrying a heart for an emergency transplant operation. The airplane crashed into the mountainside as soon as they got there. The pilot was killed. And so was the heart.

Jackie pulled her cloth napkin out of its wooden ring and smoothed it over her lap.

Amanita glanced over. 'We used to have our names sewn on the corner,' she said. 'If you got tomato sauce on it on a Monday you were still looking at it on a Friday. It taught you how to eat!'

Elwyn smiled and snorted.

Jackie was not sure why. She didn't mind. She didn't mind about the stained suit, either. She could buy another one. She could buy twenty more if she wanted. Thanks to her, they would both be millionaires in a matter of days. His fortune was in her hands. And, with Bob Scrutt on his knees begging for mercy, she would have her cake and eat it too.

Jackie suddenly felt so hungry her stomach ached. She couldn't remember the last time she ate.

'Eat up. You need your strength, honey,' she said cheerfully across the table.

'You too,' Elwyn nodded. He scratched his forehead. 'Honey.' He was behaving, even if he wasn't eating.

She ate everything. Peaches with sugar syrup. Orange juice. Eggs and ribs and tomato gravy. Buttermilk biscuits. Jam. Toast. Coffee. She chewed and sliced and forked and mopped. When she'd finished her food, she helped herself to all the food he'd left.

She would sleep all day and start driving at sundown. She hoped Elwyn could drive. She suspected some New Yorkers didn't even have cars. They probably only knew how to catch taxis. It was a long, long way to Detroit.

'You can drive, can't you?' she said.

'Jackie, I don't think I can come with you.' Elwyn's voice was soft.

'What in God's name do you mean?'

'To see your . . . er, friend . . . Bob.' Elwyn glanced at Amanita. She was whistling along with the radio and clattering dishes in the sink. He whispered. 'Jackie, he tried to kill me. What if he still wants me dead?'

Jackie drained the last of her coffee and held out her mug to be filled. Elwyn obliged. She knew he would. He used his good arm.

'Besides, I'm injured,' he said. 'I can't drive.'

She drank some more coffee. Her heart was thumping. How much of her plan could she tell him? She had to keep him on her side. She couldn't go alone. She needed him for Bob Scrutt. And the prize money. They couldn't split up, not now.

'Our friend Bob won't recognize us,' she said at last.

'And why is that?'

'Because we'll be . . . Nobody will recognize us.'

Elwyn sniffed.

'We'll be dressed up to look special,' she said. 'More fancy than Sunday best.'

'I've thrown out my moustache. And you could never be Mexican.'

He was mocking her. She didn't like that.

Amanita returned to their table and started to clear dishes. 'Well, someone likes my cooking,' she said to Jackie. 'That's how my mama cooked, and her ma before her. You know they say you can take the girl outta Louisiana, but you can't take Louisiana outta the girl.'

'And Fresno is downright unextractable.' Elwyn said it like he was telling a joke, but he wasn't smiling.

'That where y'all from?' Amanita asked.

'Yes,' Jackie said.

'No,' Elwyn said.

When Amanita was at a safe distance again, Jackie spoke. 'He won't bother you, because he won't know it's you.'

'I don't think I can . . .'

Jackie panicked. How could he even think of wrecking her plans after they'd made a deal—after everything she'd done for him? Traitor.

'You try getting out of Dallas by yourself now,' she said. 'Reall Life knows you're here. The place is crawling with cameras and spies. Think about it. I'm your only way out.'

Black Jackie

Fresno Jackie was holding up a big black cloth thing for him to see. He couldn't work it out. There was a lot of fabric. Folds and folds of it. She couldn't hold it high enough to clear the floor. She poked her hand through a hole and wiggled her fingers. It was a game. At some humorless level she was enjoying herself.

'What is it?' he asked at last. 'Forgive me if the answer's obvious.'

Jackie smiled. It still wasn't endearing. 'You have to guess.'

They were in her room now. He had slept all day in her dead husband's LeizureScape tracksuit. He'd had dreams about creatures creeping into his bed and extracting his teeth. He was convalescing and he wasn't in the mood for guessing games.

'Why?' he asked, unable to mask the weariness in his voice.

'Because I say so.'

'OK then. It's a photographer's blackout.'

'What do you mean?' She looked genuinely puzzled.

'Clearly not the right answer then. It's a Halloween costume. Dracula's cape. A motorbike cover.'

'No and no and no.'

'It's . . . a magic cloak. From a tale. About fairies.'

She paused.

'People have been saying things about you,' she said. 'At the morgue. Men. Men claiming to be . . .'

'Claiming to be what?'

'I don't know. Intimate. They're offering to identify you. On TV.'

Elwyn felt his stomach tighten. *Which men?* How would they know him? He couldn't remember any names—how would they know his? He could hardly remember their faces. Apart from a high-school obsession and a broken heart, he'd never had a steady relationship. The last time he'd had sex, apart from Mardie, he was so overweight he looked like someone else altogether. At the lab they called him the Puffball. None of them knew he was gay. It was none of their business. *Which men?* What would Jackie do if he was exposed before the election? Would she turn him over to Reall Life and clear off with his payment? Or turn him over to Bob Scrutt?

'We're like magnets, Jackie.'

'I don't follow you.' She was turning the black cloth over and over.

'Or flames. Those men . . . and those women too . . . they're like moths to the candle.' Why did she bring out the soap opera in him? 'Everyone wants to feel the glow. We're famous.'

'I knew you'd say that,' Jackie sighed. 'John F. said the same thing. He said so many people claimed to be at the grassy knoll the first time there wasn't enough room to fit in a sniper!'

'Exactly.' For a moment Elwyn felt relieved. But there were too many troubling questions. How long would it take to sort the dead from the living? How long before they got his mother to view the corpse? And when would they have John F.'s DNA results?

'Come on,' Jackie grinned. She held the cloth up high.

Elwyn couldn't bear it. He just wanted to sleep, to heal. 'A rug for the drive-in. With holes for your hands so you can hold onto your Snax and Drinx.'

'Getting warmer,' she said. 'Put it on.'

He didn't move. He couldn't bring himself to move.

She was positively triumphant. He was her doll and she was playing dress-ups with him. He took the costume from her and crushed the material in his fist. It didn't crease.

'Here. Let me help you,' Jackie said. 'You've got your injury to worry about.'

He surrendered. He couldn't bear the thought of his wound bursting open, or her making a scene. The cloth weighed heavily on his head, caught on his neck-brace. It rubbed against his eyelashes. Black netting across his eyes mottled his vision.

Jackie fiddled and pulled and adjusted until she was satisfied.

'Thank the Lord it's the right length! You're not a regular size,' she said, squatting at his ankles and tugging at his hems. 'Now look.'

Elwyn went over to the mirror and held his good arm out wide. Through dark blurs he saw himself as a giant black sting-ray. Then he noticed a yellow tracksuit cuff poking out of his cape sleeve. It was some time before he understood his reflection. A Muslim woman was staring back at him. At over six feet in height, she was too tall. Her hands gave her away as a transvestite.

'I got you some gloves,' Jackie said, as if reading his mind. 'For me too. We'll be sisters.'

'This is a joke, right?' His breath felt hot inside his mask.

'I saw them on TV. You know, a documentary. Islam-o-bad, the Bible lands, someplace like that.'

Elwyn stifled a laugh.

Jackie was undeterred. 'No one can talk to you or touch you or take photos or anything. No one can tell what you look like. It makes you invisible.'

'What Drugz are you on?' Elwyn said.

'I got you out of that hospital, didn't I? I thought about a biological isolation suit, but I've done that already, so it stands out. They'd be after us in no time. This way you're nobody. Just some poor quiet foreign lady. Like Mexican gardeners, they're sort of all over the place but sort of invisible.'

Elwyn was feeling hot and claustrophobic, and he was disturbed by his reflection. Could he pass for a woman? How many gay men had asked that very question? Was he just another man in drag?

'I can't do this, Jackie. It's ridiculous. There's a world out there full of creeps.'

'It was hard to get your size but I hunted for it. John F. always said I was a good shopper. It's an under-rated skill.'

'I'm sure you could get a diploma in it.'

'You can get anything you want if you look hard enough. Especially with my credit.'

Elwyn flapped his arm at the mirror like a wounded bat. Her credit. The prize money. How long after polling before the cash came through? There he was, thinking about the prize money again. If he upset her, she would abandon and denounce him. She'd fly off into the sunset with all the high-ratings tragedy and all the money. Reall Life would tie him up for target practice like live bait. If they'd hired a lone assassin before, they'd be sponsoring homophobes by the hundred. It would be open season, a whole new sports show. He was bound to Jackie for the time being. At least she could get him out of Dallas. That's all that mattered now, to escape. He'd think of a get-out clause before Detroit.

'Thank God for burqahs,' Jackie said.

Car Jackies

Elwyn and Jackie loaded up the SUV as efficiently as they could, awkward and heavy in their burqahs.

'It's like water aerobics,' Jackie said, heaving bags into the trunk.

Blinking, still adjusting to the black mesh pressing against his eyes, Elwyn surveyed the scene. It was sundown. The lot was empty, as it had been in the morning, except for a couple of parked cars too far away to identify. Beyond the streets of decaying, empty buildings, a few newer glassy towers scraped the sky. A Fuelz icon leaped up one sheer facade like a huge fridge magnet. The XMart cart was in a new position by the wall of Amanita's Inn. The tramp seemed still to be asleep.

'When do you think that cart moved?' Elwyn asked Jackie. His heart felt irregular. 'And how?'

Jackie was leaning into the trunk of the car. Her shoulders shrugged beneath the black tent of her burqah.

Elwyn figured that his room, and hers, were just the other side of the wall where the cart was. He noticed external pipes for plumbing—a perfect listening post. Was this man genuinely homeless? Or was he engaged in covert operations?

Elwyn's energy surged as he made his way noiselessly towards his suspect. *Fight or flight,* he thought. Adrenaline. Noradrenaline. Yard by yard, the smell of death became stronger. He would die fighting against Reall Life, or he would go mad. He stopped close by the cart, panting, flummoxed. Through black mesh he squinted at the sleeping bag and clothes stuffed in below the slumped torso. They were too clean and new. The agent snored and turned over—exactly the sort of amateur dramatics the CIA got up to. Elwyn caught a glimpse of a black vinyl pouch for a camera or audio surveillance device. He held his breath as he reached out his gloved hand to take it.

The agent's eyes popped open. Then he began to whimper, staring all the while at Elwyn's black leather fingers.

'Spare me,' he wailed. He had one tooth. Discolored gums.

Convincing enough. 'You the chee-chee bird from Hell? Oh, spare me!'

Elwyn jumped at the sound of shouting from behind. With no peripheral vision, he had to turn his entire body around. Hundreds of yards away at the far end of the lot, the Lone Star Soup Kitchen was coughing out a straggle of men, black against the evening sun. One of them was calling to the XMart Man. Elwyn spun back round to see the sleeper climb off his bedding and fall to the ground, stumble onto his feet and grab the hand-bar of his cart. Elwyn turned to watch him push his goods across the blacktop like a crazy shopper staggering down the widest XMart aisle in the universe.

Elwyn looked for cameras. Two CCTVs peered down at the parking lot from tall poles. Now he saw a white vehicle on the sidewalk surrounded by red cones: high up on a crane was a box with dark windows, mirror glass. Someone had to be inside, observing, recording, following his every move and transmitting his whereabouts to every viewer in the land. Reall Life was toying with him. Playing with their prey before coming in for the kill. He was their dead man walking. Performing.

He was anonymous in his burqah, but he was not invisible. The sudden realization shocked him. He felt hot and cold at once. He headed back to the car in a panic. It felt like wading. Swathes of fabric clutched at his thighs, caught the toes of his sneakers. His sneakers hurt. His arm hurt. It was like trying to escape in an anxiety dream.

Jackie was waiting. She was a big black shuttlecock in the SUV. The passenger door was open.

He realized she was the only person in the world he could trust. The only one whose fate was bound up equally with his. With Jackie he was safe. For a moment, he was overwhelmed by a rush of love, grateful and devoted as a rescued puppy. He wanted to hide in the folds of her burqah.

'Come on,' she said, her words muffled by cloth. 'You're making a spectacle of yourself.'

Elwyn lifted his skirts to climb in. She was right. His ankles flashed tracksuit yellow.

Jackie started the engine.

'Are you sure you're allowed to drive?' he said.

'Hurry. We haven't got time for jokes or anything. I don't like the look of those bums down there.'

'Did you see that white unit on a crane?'

Jackie nodded. 'I don't know what it is. Surveillance or something. But this morning there was a house by there. A whole house on wheels. Like it came straight from a residential area. In the dark. Or a movie set. I don't know what they're playing at. They're trying to upset us. Typical. They're sadists.'

She was right.

Elwyn turned to look again, but his neck was too sore. 'I can't see left or right in this thing. Isn't it dangerous to drive?'

'The longer we stay anywhere, the quicker they'll find us. They'll piece the bits together like they do on *KrimeTime*. We've got to get moving. And keep moving.'

Jackie released the hand-brake and revved.

He had escaped once. He just needed to figure out how to do it again.

The Big Dealey—Today's Bets

'CALIFORNIA DREAMING' 4-WAY BET
Suspect: Patsy Addison
Firing Line: The Bryan Pergola
No. of bullets: 1 or 2 or 3 or 4
Motive: Political Belief
Odds at 12:30 p.m. CST: 7/1
Total no. of bets placed on all suspects: 7,777,777
Only 2 more days—then the game's up!

When Patsy Addison checks out of the Hotel Adolphus, she notices an odd kind of fellow sitting in a lobby chair. It's not that he has odd features. It's more that he has an odd way of looking at her.

No one looks at Patsy Addison. She is 77 years old and she knows she has nice enough features, but she was never a beauty and men didn't pay much attention even when she was in her prime.

In her prime. She hates that phrase. It makes her think of meat. Patsy Addison has cancer. There are so many things that make her think of meat these days.

The woman behind the front desk gives her a hotel smile. Pinched in the face, unfulfilled. Patsy christens her Minsk, just for the sound of it.

'Did you enjoy your suite?' Minsk asks.

'Of course,' says Patsy. 'My suite was real sweet.'

Minsk smiles indulgently. She has her script to get through.

'Anything from the in-room bar today?'

'Well, you should know that,' says Patsy, just to be friendly. She can feel the odd fellow's eyes burning holes in her back. She thinks of radiotherapy. He is sitting on a rococo chair with red plush upholstery and polished bone-colored cabriolet legs. Is he someone famous? She resists turning around to have herself another look.

'Matter of fact, I'm a friend of Bill's,' she says to Minsk. It's just a hunch, but the words clearly mean nothing. The desk clerk does not go to meetings for alcoholics.

Patsy is unflustered. 'My friend Bill has me on a strict program. No liquor. No sugar, no salt, no killer whites.'

Minsk acts perplexed.

Patsy signs the receipt. *Patsy Addison III.* She pretends not to balk at the total. And of course she's not the third of anything.

'But no limits on the luxury. I mean, you've had the Queen of England up there, plumping up cushions and admiring the view. I'd say my suite was up to her standards. I liked the kitchenette, the balcony—you Dallasites have marvellous weather in November. And all those doors to choose from. I especially liked my salon for receiving guests.' She pauses. 'Not that I had any.'

Minsk continues with her repertoire. She's onto valet parking.

That's one service Patsy has not used. She has enjoyed signature dishes, floral art, afternoon tea, beauty treatments and breakfast in the boudoir. She has taken limousines to the gun-range most days and kept them waiting outside while she trained.

You sure you never . . .? I don't think you realize what you just done, her personal instructor said after her first round on her first day. His name was Sam. His wide eyes scanned her gnarled fingers, her stringy arms. She'd put bullets through the same paper hole, the number seven, one after the other, despite shaking with shock after the violence exploded from her hands. She had never held a firearm before, not even touched one.

'I do yoga,' she told Sam. 'It gives me peace of mind and body focus.'

Now, she resists turning to scrutinize the face of the man in the rococo chair. Is he a police officer? A spy? Names come into her head. Sherlock Holmes. Romanzki. Vespucci. They all have dark hair. Hawkish noses.

Minsk folds up the receipt papers and passes them to Patsy as if they are a special gift.

What next? The flight to San Francisco? Return to the condo? *Is that all there is?* Patsy hears an old song in her head. Circus tunes, an ironic voice, a name she can't recall. She's always forgetting things these days. She starts to hum. She thinks of the Santa Cruz dogs' home, the noise of barking that sends her to sleep nights. The silence of the crematorium. The scratching of the stray tom at her patio door. Then she remembers the beach. Her beach. The endless space of it. The wild seals that come to visit sometimes. The feel of cold ocean water on her old skin. The waiting room at the clinic—

She takes her receipt and presses it into her purse. She feels like some kind of heroine: even without the Dallas trip, Patsy Addison is a prodigious addition to the GDP, a positive boost to the national economy. All cancer patients are.

She asks Minsk to order her one last limousine. She picks up her pink vinyl case—it is too light and small for a place this grand, more Gidget than aristocrat—and turns to face the music. But the odd dark-haired detective fellow has gone. Patsy is not concerned. He will reappear, she feels certain. She knows it in her bones, deep in her bones.

We don't get many . . . Sam the shooting instructor couldn't finish his sentence, so Patsy did it for him.

'Old ladies?' she said. 'Hell, it's never too late to learn. I'm going to be dead before next Thanksgiving.'

After that he gave her extra time for free. He found the most comfortable handgun for her. It wasn't the obvious choice. Not a favorite with the ladies.

People think shooting is for nuts and wackos, Sam said. *But it's much more fun than tennis.* He confided in her as a mother. He liked shooting groundhogs and rabbits the most. Small animals were his target preference. He didn't ask what hers might be. She sensed it was a matter of etiquette. She liked his honesty.

Patsy steps out into Commerce Street and smells the pollution. She can breathe in all the fumes she likes. There is no need to worry about lung damage or free radicals—she wonders if the scientists who chose that name were knee-jerk conservatives. Patsy Addison used to be a free radical when she was a young thing. She used to think of herself as a gas, when most other people were liquids, or even solids. She experimented, chained herself to things, broke the law. That was before she lost her nerve and sold out. She can't think of anyone who sold their entire soul for a regular job in marketing. There are all those books and films about people who sell their souls for something grand.

The street is full of SUVs and combat cars. Vehicles designed for military frontiers have been in fashion ever since the Terror Wars, although *The TV President* has kick-started a wave of retro AutoCorp designs. Patsy Addison is indifferent to cars and she opposes wars. These days she can't even watch TV. She knows that she does not share the majority view.

At last she sees her limo.

'Could you take me to the Texas School Book Depository, please, driver?' she says. In the back seat she makes herself comfortable.

Comfort is a word Sam uses all the time. *Shoot in comfort. Whatever feels comfortable.* Sam finds comfort in guns.

The driver turns to look at Patsy as if she has lost her wits.

'I mean, the Sixth Floor Museum,' she says.

She reads his ID.

Earl Roberts

'They got lines up there goin' round the corner an' halfway down Main Street,' says Earl. He is exaggerating. 'That there was an official crime scene till a couple days ago. A no-go area. President done got shot again, but you musta knowed that.'

'Of course.' Patsy has seen the commentators and cameramen crawling all over Dealey Plaza and the blocks nearby, police officers and barriers to keep crowds of bystanders under control. They don't seem to have moved a thing since the Big Day. But the rest of Dallas looks empty.

'You musta seen it on the TV.'

Patsy is tempted to say that she saw it for herself in real life. As close as a harmless old white woman can get, which is very close. The security people did not stop her, search her or scan her. In fact, they did not appear to notice her at all. She was wearing a rosette that said *Hooray for JFK*. She'd had her hair done at the Adolphus salon. Lots of hairspray. And she carried a letter from the oncologist forecasting her last tenuous months of life.

'You can take me up to the entrance of the museum. I'll see what I can do about that line,' says Patsy to Earl. She has nothing to lose. She is feeling well.

She steps out of the car and asks Earl to wait. She goes straight to the guard at the top of the line and shows him her medical letter and plane ticket. Everything seems strangely quiet. The sky looks ready for thunder, but Patsy concentrates on the man's face. She has learned that she can do anything, get away with anything, because she doesn't care anymore. That's what those con-artist types do. And warrior types. The world loves a front.

When did she lose her nerve? Was it after the death of her first husband? When she got married to give her kids another father—or when he divorced her? It happened sometime early on, before all those years hawking soda, a lifetime pushing pop to the people from the comfort of her desk. Her prime.

For her long career marketing Drinx, Patsy feels sorry. The security guard wipes his eye and lets her through, ahead of the line. There is not a rustle of complaint from the patient parade of people, every age and every color. They wait their turn.

Earl waits in the limousine.

Patsy feels like a VIP. She doesn't care.

On the door the official signs forbid smoking, firearms and photography, in that order.

Patsy is in the lobby, by the brochures. She sees a photo of her personal instructor Sam, smiling and holding a full-auto sub-machine gun and inviting everybody to come along and shoot in comfort all year round. There are other gun-ranges in Dallas, and other things to do. Quilt Mania. Boot City. Petting Zoo. Calf Scramble. Baseball Museum. Trophy Hunting. The JFK Ultimate Ride Experience with a chauffeur handsome as Sidney Poitier. Every kind of casino and every kind of shopping. But that's not why she's here. She wants to pay her respects one more time.

Patsy Addison loves John Fitzgerald Kennedy. The real one. She doesn't like the way people are picking over his remains and making mischief. She likes the Sixth Floor Museum. It has a sense of decorum. It places him in context.

She lines up for the airport-style security scanner. The guards are wearing black mourning bands on their sleeves. *Who for?* she wonders. She hands over her purse. It is floral and cheerful, what her mother used to call gay. They feed it through the machine. The rubberized belt stops. There is a low conference between the uniforms. An awkward shuffling. They peep at her and back again, like guilty kids.

She is dressed in an elegant dove-gray dress, a tailored jacket, a chiffon neckscarf—bright blue to match her old-woman eyes. She is wearing gloves. Her handgun is clean of fingerprints. All she is missing is a hat, but she has her Hotel Adolphus hairstyle to compensate.

'I'm sorry, ma'am, but there's no firearms allowed,' the white guard says softly into her ear. 'We're going to have to confiscate your weapon until you return to collect it after the exhibition.'

'I understand. It's just, you know, a woman my age has got to be ready to defend herself. Look what they did to our favorite president.'

'Yes, ma'am.' He bows his head a moment.

Without pistol, with purse, Patsy buys her senior citizen's reduced-rate ticket to the show. The place is even more crowded than when she visited the first time. There are students, mourners, locals, foreigners, bodies filled to every curve and corner like cake-mix in a baking tin. Patsy feels a wave of nausea. It's hot. She takes the elevator to the top. It's full of feet and sweating fat. She struggles to find a space between the bodies that shuffle among the exhibits. Other people's soft tissue and cartilage press against hers. Bones rub against bones. Patsy strains to see above the crowd. She can hear the voice of John Fitzgerald Kennedy, talking to another time, a younger her. She was so innocent then, so fearless. He spoke for youthfulness, for world peace, for change, for culture. The exhibit soundtrack is on a loop. Patsy can't bear all these goggle-eyed jostling people. They're in the way, sightseers trampling a monument. Consumers consuming. Focus groups. She feels another wave of nausea. She takes the elevator down again. She goes straight into the bookstore, through the crush, and out onto the street where the visitors' line winds its way around the block—and Earl is waiting.

'I paid my respects,' she says as she steps into the car.

Earl nods, probably out of politeness.

'Where to, ma'am?' he says via the rear-view mirror. His eyes are big and brown and young. Such clarity. Such firm flesh.

Patsy feels a twinge of envy. 'Take me to the airport, please, driver.'

'There was some kinda fellow here looking for you, ma'am.'

Patsy sings, just for the hell of it. 'All my exes live in Texas.'

Earl smiles. 'I sent him inside.'

'Did he have on a badge?'

'He had some kinda badge he flashed, but he left you his calling card.' Earl passes it over.

Detective Oscar Pascillo

Her hunter has a Hotline Number. It's toll-free.

Call 2–4–1–KRIMETIME

The Reall Life logo is on the back of the card.

'Thank you, Earl. Let's go to the airport.'

Patsy is not bothered. The detective is a shadow, just like cancer. She could go mad jumping to lose her shadow, but she knows that he will always be attached to her. So she will walk calmly, quickly, gracefully, to her grave. She will not undergo further treatment, radio, bio, chemo or otherwise. Why drag her kids through extra misery on her account? They have their own lives, their own kids. Patsy Addison has found her nerve.

She feels well. For a moment she thinks her diagnosis might be some elaborate joke. That she is not sick at all. That she will outlive everyone. They have mixed up her tests. Some other Patsy Addison is deluded. The healthy Patsy Addison will go back to the condo and there will be bills to pay, item by item of her Dallas extravaganza. And that moody detective will call on her, rifle through her recycling bin, disturb the neighbors, talk hintingly about how long life is in a penitentiary. That's a word she likes. A place to be penitent. She will defend herself in the name of the original authentic genuine real honest-to-goodness no-artificial-additives President.

Earl is speeding down the freeway. There are XMart outlets and LeizureScape stores on both sides. 'Swedish' and 'Japanese' bath-houses. Churches. Gun-ranges. AutoCorp yards.

You heard of canned hunting? Shooting Sam asked her one time when they took a break together in the fluorescent twilight of the climate-controlled lounge. On the big screen she watched advertisements for the forthcoming Big Day. They made her so furious she felt young again. Determined. She had purchased her favorite handgun, an Armz pistol. She could never remember what model number or caliber it was. Sam was always reminding her, like it mattered. It didn't cost a lot—she couldn't remember that figure either. Sam gave her a senior discount and the holster was half price. By this stage, she had progressed to one-handed distance shooting but moving targets were not so easy. She knew that the stress of a real shooting situation would interfere with her aim. She knew the laws about carrying a concealed firearm. But she didn't know what canned hunting was.

Sam told her about ranches filled with exotic animals—African lions, Russian boars, Australian kangaroos, Arabian oryxes and the like—some of them drugged, all of them fenced in and waiting to be shot, safari-style.

It's like hunting in a zoo. There's no skill in that. It's too easy. Sam called it Shopping for Soft Trophies. His clarity made Patsy feel well.

Now the signs are for the airport and Earl is changing lanes and Patsy is thinking of the TV Presidents propped up in their twin cars like twin rabbits, just waiting to be shot by some wacko. Would Sam call them Soft Trophies? She doesn't know. She doesn't care. She was mad at the media people, not the stooges. She was mad at their TVs.

After the Big Day, she has not returned to the gun-range. There is no need.

Earl drives into the drop-off area in front of her terminal. That's another word with a different meaning. He unloads her case from the trunk, her one small case, made of pale pink vinyl, full of dresses and soft things. She thinks of nerves and skin.

After check-in, she wanders along corridors and looks at objects—people, merchandise, signs, flooring—knowing that she will not see them again. The airport is like a city, an ant farm in glass. Artificial light. Synthetic fibers. False smiles. Fake tans. She is seeing through everything, all the pretense, with a fresh kind of clarity. Perhaps the moody detective is somewhere within the labyrinth, tunneling his way through evidence. But he has other suspects to chase. She fingers his card in her pocket. She passes an interfaith chapel, where a wild-looking old priest is saying mass to a congregation of two. She stops to watch. He seems familiar, she can't think why. There is something about him that makes her wonder if he too is terminally ill. She thinks about an afterlife, but she is not tempted by the promise. She is a free radical again. A volatile gas. The words *Catholic Service* are printed on a card stuck to the open door. Underneath, a ballpoint scrawl says *Father Paine*. Patsy trails her manicured and gloved fingernails along the wall and wanders on.

Hooray for JFK, she thinks. *Hooray for Patsy. That's all there is.*

She feels like she has forgotten something—there always seems to be something she's got wrong or forgotten these days—but she can't think what it might be, until she approaches the security scanners and hands over her pistol-free gay floral purse.

Hijackie

Proceed along Commerce Street for three more blocks. The in-car navigator spoke from the dashboard screen as calmly and knowingly as an air hostess. The glowing street map shifted from block to block as Jackie drove. She had wanted to be an air hostess when she was little. But then she discovered other people's eyebrows and nail polish and hair.

Driving away from Amanita's Inn in the green-gold light of dusk, she felt a mounting sense of anticipation, like when she was a little girl on Christmas eve and she couldn't wait for the next morning. The day after tomorrow was HyperFriday, but that's not what made her heart skittish. Today she had Elwyn in her pocket. He was behaving. The day after tomorrow she would meet Bob Scrutt face to face in Detroit. She would make him confess. She would be his confessor. And then, with Elwyn's help, she would mete out Bob's punishment. *Expiation*—she remembered that from Sunday School. She played with the syllables on her tongue, with her lips, in a whisper behind her veil, over and over until the cloth became hot and moist. She turned the air-conditioning up a degree.

Elwyn was not able to see or hear her, she didn't have to check. He was in his own wrap. Her hearing was muffled, her sight was blurred, she couldn't see anything except blackness out of the corner of her eyes. She strained a little to make out other vehicles on the road straight ahead, and so she drove slowly. She switched on her headlights.

At a red traffic signal, she turned to look at the car next to her. It was another SUV. There was nothing unusual about that. Dallas was full of combat vehicles. But every face inside, pale and luminous, stared. Their mouths hung open in some kind of horror.

'I've seen that look before,' Jackie said.

'What? Where? Have they caught us?' Elwyn twisted from left to right.

'No, no, no. Relax. It's just, you know, familiar. It reminds me of something . . . I don't know. I can't remember.'

Elwyn's shoulders relaxed beneath his burqah. 'You'd think they'd never seen a foreigner before. Give them a weekend in New York.'

Jackie thought she heard him sigh.

'That's how people look when they stop at an accident,' he said. 'They don't do anything. They just stare.'

'I know, I know! It's the look customers get when they see themselves in the mirror for the first time after a treatment's gone wrong. You take off the foil, or the hood, or whatever, and it's too late. Instead of soft natural waves—you know, like a bit of extra body for the poor girl with dead-straight hair and a serious volume problem—she's got friz in a big ball like, you know, a microphone head. The *look* on their faces!'

Elwyn was deadly quiet for a while, but then he started to laugh. Jackie liked that. He was laughing at her funny story. She was laughing now and she felt the fabric of her head-cover suck into her mouth as she breathed in. Thank God she was not wearing lipstick or her face would be a mess. She gripped the steering wheel with her leather gloved hands and let her head roll forwards into a helpless giggle. She was about to tell the story of the customer who came out like a sheep, when someone behind her honked their horn. The lights were green and might have been for some time. She hit the gas and took off with a lurch.

'I can't even make a face at them,' Elwyn said.

'Why not?'

'They can't see my face.'

'I forgot! I forgot! So you can't see I'm blushing dumb red.'

'No, but you have got steam coming out of your eye-vent.'

Jackie felt sure she could see a smile underneath Elwyn's burqah. It made her giggle. He was turning out to be more fun than she'd expected.

Turn slight left to take I-45 South ramp for 180 yards toward I-30.

'That computer's voice gives me the creeps,' said Elwyn. 'It's like AutoCorp's idea of Mother—which is no one's.'

'I know what you mean! Like flesh-color bandages. They never match anyone's skin.'

When the in-car navigator told her she was merging onto Interstate 30 East, Jackie felt her spirits soar. The road got emptier. Faster. She had never driven outside of California before, but she decided that all highways must be the same. Big and mostly straight. Same old LeizureScape and Fuelz outlets. The same choices of Foodz, Drinx and Snax. Just different place names and numbers. Along the edges, workers on bright-lit cranes were installing giant cameras on top of tall poles. One after another for miles. It was 320 miles to Little Rock via New Boston, Texarkana, Hope and Arkadelphia, without changing highways. Then 125 more miles on the one road turning away just before Memphis. She would never have to set foot in Dealey Plaza or Parkland Hospital or Love Field or any other of those upsetting places again.

'I want to know when they'll ask your mom to go to the morgue,' she said out loud. Any mother would be able to tell her son's body from an impostor, she felt sure of that. 'I guess they'll show it on the news when it happens. Mind you, they have had two days since—'

'How are you meant to drive and watch TV at the same time?' Elwyn covered the navigator's map with his black gloved hand. Colored light poured through the spaces between his fingers.

Jackie felt like he was ignoring her but she had to get things straight. 'Will she give the game away?'

'Who?'

'Your mom.'

The road was wet and shiny now, and sheets of white rain drove at the windshield through the evening gloom. Jackie turned the wipers on. Lights ahead shattered, wiped clean, shattered. She could not see too well. She caught glimpses of a white sedan car in the rear-view mirror, its front grille smashed into a crooked snarl.

Elwyn took a while to answer. 'My mother disapproved of Reall Life. She thought *The TV President* was for trailer trash. They'll have to chip her out of her apartment. She hasn't left the Upper East Side since . . . since Arabia.'

'She went to Arabia?'

'My father died in Arabia,' Elwyn said.

Jackie slowed down. The white sedan slowed down.

'Oh I am sorry.' She felt her eyes prickle. She always cried at war movies. 'So far from home!'

'Actually, it wasn't all that far, it was a restaurant in Brooklyn.'

He was tricking her, being smart and snickering. At least he wasn't quoting JFK anymore. And how smart was it to sign your self away to Reall Life? It was the dumbest thing John F. ever did—apart from Mardie. She felt her throat catch. She felt another one of those upsets getting ready to rise up inside her.

She changed lanes to pass a trailer.

Suddenly there was a huge silver truck veering away from her, back and to the left, honking the horn and flashing its lights. The noise was terrifying. Her SUV felt low and small. The truck speeded up, passed her, cut back across her lane in a cloud of blinding backspray. She slammed the brake pedal down. The car skidded.

'I've got to pull over.' Jackie was shaking. Her heart was speeding. She couldn't breathe in enough air. 'This is no good. I can't see properly.' She gasped. 'He nearly killed us. Just to make a point. I've got to. Take this thing off. There's a rest area. Coming up.'

'Me too, I can't wait to—'

'But you can't.' She wanted to curse him, punish him for being the adulterer that he was, for getting her into this situation. 'You're the one everyone will recognize.'

She swung into the rest area. There was no one behind her now, and no other vehicles there. It had gotten dark enough, so it would be safe. She turned the engine off. She breathed deliberately, counting slowly, trying to calm herself down. The navigator screen glowed in the dark, casting a lime-green light like an outline along Elwyn's shapeless silhouette. She tried to think of distracting things to settle her emotions.

Burqah. Abiyah. Buknuk. Dishdash. She'd written down all the names. There were so many products on the internet, so many ethnic disguises to choose from. *Billowy elegance. Total cover.* She had compared fabrics, colors, delivery times. In the end, she had opted for the deluxe all-in-one head-to-toe robe and face veil. There were no nose-strings to worry about, no head ties or elastic straps. She couldn't imagine a man fussing with pins or complicated fabric-folding techniques. Men liked things easy.

Sisters can see out but prying eyes cannot see in. Super sizes for extra-tall and voluptuous sisters available from stock . . .

Calmer now, Jackie turned to Elwyn and tried to focus on the gleam of his eyes. She spoke firmly.

'You're a liability. You must wear Hi-jab.' She wasn't sure how to pronounce it. The internet was full of *hijab*. She made it sound like *hijack*—which was suddenly hilarious.

'Hi Jack!' she said out loud and giggled. She smacked the steering wheel. 'Get it? Hi Jack! I've never thought of that before.'

Elwyn said nothing, but she heard him inhale.

Country Jackies

Elwyn woke up with a jolt. The car had stopped, but the engine was still running. His arm itched and hurt at the same time. He wondered if that was a good sign. Perhaps the bullet wound was starting to heal. He had no idea how long they had been driving. The navigator was turned off.

'Where are we?' he asked.

'Hope!' Jackie replied.

Somehow the word sounded like a taunt.

'Arkansas, birthplace of William J. Clinton.' She sounded pleased with herself, like a low-rent tour-guide.

In the darkness Elwyn could see a line of Fuelz and Foodz outlets, side by side in near-empty blocks. He did a security check. One damaged white sedan car, stationary; one old truck, parked; one black motorbike; four cameras in close range. No humans, no life. It was hard to believe that the worldly ex-president first showed up on planet Earth at this particular spot.

'We need gas,' Jackie said, pulling down her head cover.

'And I need a washroom.'

Jackie eased the car into the space by a gas pump. 'Don't forget you're going to the ladies'. Goes without saying that you keep your face hidden.'

'If it goes without saying, you don't need to say it,' Elwyn snapped. He couldn't help it.

Jackie got out and peered at the pump for instructions. A sticker said: *Smile! You're on camera!* She jacked the pump lever up, pressed a few buttons, untwisted the gas cap, stuck the nozzle in, squeezed the trigger and waited. Nothing happened. The numbers did not turn over.

Another SUV pulled up at the pump behind and a huge woman heaved herself out of the driver's seat. She started crossing herself and staring so hard at the two burqahs, she tripped over a step and crashed against a trashcan, yelping like a seal.

'I'll leave you to it,' Elwyn said.

'Thanks.' Jackie clicked the fuel handle again.

Inside the station, the light was so harsh it pierced through the burqah's little mesh holes. The air smelled of frying and coffee. Watching a mini-screen, an enormous woman sat behind a glass barrier at the cash desk, her body like piles of white ice cream melting in every direction.

Elwyn wondered if he would have to get that big to be himself again. He had no choice. A beard would not be enough. He couldn't face surgery.

The cashier was studded with enamel badges: *God Is On Our Side*, *Fight Terror*, *Armz For Life*. She stopped watching her screen.

He walked as nonchalantly as he could, past her staring eyes, past a security camera, and straight into the restroom. His burqah handling had improved.

When he came out, the woman was still staring. She hadn't moved, but two cooks in Foodz outfits stood near her. They reeked of hamburger fat and body odor. They stared. One of them chewed a piece of wood, maybe a toothpick, playing it over between his teeth and tongue. Elwyn felt other eyes on him from behind a shelving unit stacked high with Snax. A casual shopper or a spy from Reall Life? Or that *KrimeTime* detective Jackie had talked about?

He shuffled as fast as he could toward the door, smiling nervously through his veil, hoping that the people of Hope could feel a smile just as a person on the phone could hear one.

'Y'all got stuck on Halloween?' the cashier called out as he reached the exit. Her face was unsmiling.

'Trick or treat,' Elwyn said in his best female voice.

The door swung open and he jumped in fright. Jackie pushed past him and marched straight over to the cash desk.

'Pump number—'

'I know which number,' the woman interrupted. She was getting bolder by the minute. 'I can't be lettin' y'all pay outside, or after y'all filled up already, unless you show your face.'

'Then I'll pay inside and now,' said Jackie firmly.

The cashier's mouth curled into a pout. 'We'll be getting eye-scanners soon.' She pretended to be watching her mini-screen again. A loud LeizureScape voice was inviting her to bet on *The Big Dealey*.

The Foodz men sidled closer to Jackie.

'How long's your hair?' asked one, snickering.

'I'll bet you got pretty long hair,' said the other one, still chewing wood.

Elwyn knew grinning simpletons could turn nasty without warning, but Jackie seemed to be ignoring them.

Unique heirlooms from the Big Day! the LeizureScape voice said.

Elwyn waited by the door. He couldn't speak further without giving himself away. He wanted to warn Jackie about the person behind the Snax. *Someone is watching us*, he wanted to say. But he was wounded, powerless, voiceless. He wanted to quit Hope—he couldn't leave Jackie. Not yet. They had no gas. He could see the soft green velveteen of her sweatsuit, the pale flesh of her ankles. Her robe was too short on one side, as if she had something very heavy in her pocket on the other side.

Limited edition collectable packs! the LeizureScape voice said.

Elwyn watched as Jackie reached for a monstrous bag of bright blue and pink cotton candy. It was labeled *FAT FREE!* in giant letters. She seemed to be moving in slow motion, browsing rows of *Drinx in Suspect Flavors*. She picked up a pack of smokeless tobacco, peered closely at it, and put it back. She grabbed a box of juice-style pop. A family-sized bag of porkskins. She counted out the dollars, her fist full of bills, too slow, too many, too public.

'And coffee. Two coffees to go,' she added.

'Where you ladies from?' the first cook asked, getting closer.

Elwyn realized that he and Jackie had not worked out a story. He held his breath.

'Islam-o-phobia,' she said with confidence.

Elwyn didn't know whether to laugh or groan.

Still mouthing his toothpick, the second cook leaned over and put out his hand for a handshake.

'Pleased to be makin' your acquaintance, lady. Nobody told us Florence of Arabia was a-comin' to town!'

'Excuse me!' Jackie turned her back on him as sharp as a slap in the face.

He spat his toothpick to the floor. 'And she's none too friendly, is she.'

The other cook tutted. 'Aw, she done missed seein' ya cause a that rag on her head.'

Elwyn was convinced that the man would jump at Jackie and rip off her veil, or worse. He imagined the surly cashier heaving off her stool and out of her booth to join in. He glanced towards the security camera suspended from the ceiling. Then back to the shelving where the hidden eyes were watching.

Exciting sniper action! Your own history-making avatars! the Leizure-Scape voice said.

'I've just been visiting my husband in jail, you know, at Texarkana,' said Jackie, smooth as honey. 'We're meeting up with his friends—you know, the ones that got a pardon—just down the road here. They're expecting us real soon.'

She was a better actress than he had thought.

'That right?' said the cocky cook, not so sure now.

The cashier stroked one of her badges and grunted.

'Thank you so much,' Jackie said with extra enthusiasm. 'You know which pump I'm at.'

Watch out for the suspects—available soon!

Rain seemed to be coming at them from everywhere. The sky was deepest dark, without the borrowed glow of a town or city. Sometimes solitary bright lights shattered high across the sky in blinks like alien spacecraft. Elwyn strained to see a few yards ahead of the car's headlights. He was glad not to be behind the wheel. Sometimes they drove along low bridges. It was impossible to tell if they were going over water, or valleys, or empty river beds. The highway was a stream of stripes, yellow and white and wet black. Straight. Flat. Smooth.

He checked the time. It was just 8:30. It felt much later. Jackie was driving slowly.

'You pass me something to eat?' she said.

The smell of fried fat came off the Snax packets, emanated from the Drinx box, filled the car with Hope. The odor made Elwyn feel queasy.

'Do you like this stuff?' he asked.

'I just grabbed the first thing handy. Those Foodz guys were giving me the creeps. And there was somebody hiding behind the Snax. I just wanted to act normal and get out.'

'Normal? How many Muslim visitors buy porkskins, do you think?'

'Why? What do you mean?'

Jackie didn't seem to know. There were so many things she didn't know. She was in costume, but she hadn't learned her part yet. He opened the pack of cotton candy and placed a sticky pink and blue handful in her outstretched hand. He wondered how many calories. At least the sugar would keep her awake.

'Muslims don't eat pork,' he said.

'Not ever? You mean, like Jews?'

'Yes, like Jews, and no.' Elwyn stared out at the darkness beyond the highway's edge. Where could he escape to? He sensed the emptiness. The flatness. Where could he hide and live? They were hours from anywhere. Perhaps they had given Reall Life the slip after all.

'And they don't approve of alcohol either,' he said.

'Like Baptists?'

'Just like our simple, teetotaling, yodeling, wood-choppin' locals.'

'You think everybody's simple, don't you?' Jackie said.

Yes, he thought—no, not quite everybody. Most people were concerned to eat and sleep, get paid, get laid, and multiply their kind in the biological drive to superabundance. No different to any other organic being. As simple as smuts and molds.

They passed a lonely sign advertising the Little Rock Presidential Center. Elwyn remembered Clinton's heirloom sneakers were in a Little Rock museum. Size 13. Why did he remember useless information like that? He was going to be the TV President, that's why, and people were destined to remember useless information about him too. He would have his own Presidential Center. No he wouldn't. He was a cheap imitation of a dead man. His shoes didn't even fit. John F. had gone further, beaten him in the race to oblivion. Elwyn realized he didn't lust for him anymore. He didn't lust for anything now, except to sleep, sleep like a free man, like a simple thing in the dark, undisturbed.

A road sign pointed to Little Rock ahead. Little Rock was where the Clanswomen had kept their headquarters. Another City of Hate. Not too far from Dallas. Not far enough. His bullet wound throbbed. He needed Drugz.

'I wish you could drive,' Jackie sighed. 'My eyes are getting sore.'

REMEMBER LOT'S WIFE, a mysterious road sign said.

WANNA ESCAPE TV? FOLLOW THE SIGNS!

★ ★ ★ ★ ★ ★ ★ ★ ★ ★ ★ ★ ★ ★ ★ ★

ELECTION CHAOS

As viewers nationwide prepare to cast their vote, chaos and confusion look set to dog the election. And it's not just the usual themes of voter suppression, intimidation, miscounting, fraud, corruption, ballot errors or redistricting.

Advertisements continue to show the two presidential candidates in selected highlights from Conviction Tests held in recent months. Viewers are encouraged to choose their favorite leader—but it's not so easy! Swing voters have little to go on, because the two candidates look so similar. There are no obvious differences in facial expression, makeup, hairstyle, sweating behavior, manner or attire. Both men appear at exactly the same camera angle and, according to most polls, they are equally appealing, photogenic and trustworthy.

Voters hoping to back a sure winner must confront the 50/50 probabilities of post-election blues and day-after triumphalism. Doubters have expressed misgivings about mold on the one hand, and Catholicism on the other. And support is split right down the middle in 'blind tests' where focus groups are shown photographs of the two candidates without captions or assassination details.

'Regular TV viewers are in the best position to judge because they can evaluate all the data, including voice,' commented one behavioral analyst. 'Accent and speech-patterns tell us a lot about the candidate's potential as a world leader. And regionality—east/west, urban/rural—plays a major part in any election. This one is no exception. Last but not least, there is the assassination.'

Cosmetic scientists tend to favor New Yorker Elwyn Barter for his successful use of weight loss products and sophisticated demeanor. He appears to be a less divisive figure on emotive issues such as impersonation skills and 'Marilyn'. Phrenologists detect greater leadership and liberalism in his cheeks and chin, as well as a closer physiognomic similarity to the 35th President. But John F. of Fresno displays more trust in his golden complexion and less disturbance in his eyes, an interpretation which has been officially endorsed by the Society of Iridologists. The Californian's surgically enhanced nose and mouth have the people's touch—a welcome ease with the common man—no doubt reinforced by his years in the hospitality business.

Deeper public turmoil has been provoked by a new billboard campaign from Reall Life. Appearing nationwide shortly after the Big Day motorcade, posters depict the TV President with bleeding wounds to the head and stirring headlines such as 'Terror Strikes Home' or 'He died so that you might vote.'

Charity workers and mental health practitioners have reported a surge in emergency calls across the country.

'Callers appear to be re-living the trauma they felt in 1963,' explained insurance analyst Dr Mark Weiner. 'Trauma plays out like a fugue. It is more powerful than memory. When the experience returns, it may feel just as vivid and real as the first time.' As for *The Big Dealey*, Dr Weiner commented: 'Like the stock market, gambling is a zero-sum operation. If someone is winning, someone else is losing.'

The Detective Oscar Pascillo Hotline is likewise beset by confusion. Call center operators are urging members of the public to think twice before calling the 2–4–1–KRIMETIME toll-free number.

'This is a criminal murder investigation, but people are calling us to cast votes or place bets,' stated one operator. 'The lines are jammed. We only want to hear from witnesses with information regarding the assassination. What happens on *The Big Dealey* or HyperFriday is incidental to us at this time.'

WITNESSES! Call 2–4–1–KRIMETIME if you have any information regarding the assassination and attempted assassination of our presidents. And, if you have any information about the criminal damage perpetrated on AutoCorp motorcade vehicles or other private property, call 2–4–1–KRIMETIME, toll-free.

★ ★ ★ ★ ★ ★ ★ ★ ★ ★ ★ ★ ★ ★ ★

Jack-o-Lantern

He had dozed off again. They'd stopped. He'd been having nightmares, being chased and chased, getting attacked by jungle animals in slow motion from all sides. His burqah was damp with sweat. His neck-brace chafed.

She was rubbing her eyes and blinking at the windshield. Her burqah was stuffed in a pile on the seat between them. He remembered: she had unveiled after Hope. Her pale skin looked blue. Her flame-red hair shone purple where it caught the motel sign light.

WANNA ESCAPE TV? TRY LODGING WITH THE LOT!

Up and down the road he could see wire fences and warehouses and AutoCorp yards. Everything was closed. A few night signs glowed feebly against the sky.

Ernie's Farm Machinery
Fireworks, Lottery, Cigarettes
Don't Take Your Organs to Heaven!

Jackie pointed at the navigator. 'Look at the great big varicose vein east of here.'

They were in North Little Rock. *The wrong side of the track,* he thought. A song. He gazed at the twists and turns of the Mississippi on the map until his eyes lost focus. 'Always makes me think of cranial sutures.'

'Excuse me?'

'The wiggling lines you see on skulls.' He tried to draw with his gloved finger in mid air. Sometimes parasites created similar paths on the caps of fungi. But maybe he oughtn't talk about wiggling or skulls. Her husband's head had been shot to pieces.

'Sorry.' He squinted at the neon. He was feeling drugged.

WANNA ESCAPE TV? TRY LODGING WITH THE LOT!

'It's past eleven,' he said. 'Can you live without TV tonight?'

'We don't want TV, John—Elwyn, because we don't want to be recognized.' She was speaking extra carefully, as if he was a child. She was patronizing him—he couldn't stand it.

But he bit his tongue. 'I always seem to be sleeping these days,' he said. 'Or waking up.'

'You're wounded. You're healing.'

NO TV. NO SEEING MACHINES. VACANCIES.

'I think they must be, you know, fundamentalists or something,' Jackie said. 'They had signs coming here about Lot's Wife.'

'Lot's Wife.' Elwyn shivered. 'Remind me.'

'I forget her name. She turned back to look at Sodom. The city got wiped out by brimstone or something, and she turned into a pillar of salt.'

Brimstone. Sodom. Lot's wife. They were words from another time and place. Elwyn clenched his teeth. He'd always joked that America wasn't representative of New York. How would The Lot feel about a gay transvestite Muslim? He looked for security cameras, but couldn't see any.

Jackie said, 'They don't have TV so I'm hoping they won't know who we are.'

'Maybe they read the papers.'

'That's why we can't drop our disguise—'

'What do you call that?' Elwyn pointed at the illuminated sign. 'Isn't that a seeing machine?'

'I don't know. Look, everybody else has TV. I couldn't believe my eyes when I saw the signs. This is a godsend.'

'Just like those plagues of frogs. They were sent by God.' He was trying to be humorous. But religion wasn't humorous. Religious men always seemed to hate men who loved men.

'All I know is, I don't want to wake up to find that detective poking his big fat nose in my window,' Jackie gathered up her burqah and eased it onto her head. She pulled the layers down over her shoulders and smoothed out the folds. She was a parakeet under its night blanket, but she carried on talking. 'Do you think that was his car back there?'

'What car?'

'The beat-up white car with the dark windows. I thought he was following us.'

Elwyn felt jittery again. 'I didn't see it.'

'He's onto all the suspects. A Black Guy. A Pinko. Maybe even Bob Scrutt for all I know.'

'So what makes you think you'll—we'll—get to Scrutt before the law does?'

'They're not arresting anybody yet.'

'Who says?'

'I heard it on the radio. You were sleeping.'

'Why aren't they?'

'I don't know,' Jackie shook her veiled head. 'It's like a game. Like cat and mouse. They're still asking people to bet. And collect stuff. Makes me sick. Come on. I need to rest. We've got to get up early. We've got all day on the road tomorrow.'

Elwyn might have suggested sleeping in the SUV, but his body was aching all over. The prospect of a real bed was too tempting. And there would be no TV.

He could just make out trompe l'oeil blocks of stone painted on concrete walls that blotted out too much of the night sky. It might have been a fantasy fortress courtesy of LeizureScape—with all the lights turned off and everybody gone home. He hated theme parks, now more than ever. His wounded arm was hot and itching. He tried to calculate the time: five days since the injury.

Jackie was carrying most of the luggage. She seemed to be taking the lead as usual. She was probably class president in high school. Or head cheerleader.

At a mean doorway in the fortress wall, Elwyn pressed through a creaky turnstile after her. He hated turnstiles as much as theme parks. Turnstiles only went one way.

By the weak light of flaming braziers hooked to cement posts, too few for comfort, they picked their way through a rock-effect landscape garden. It was like a studio set from *Lost 'n' Space*. Elwyn kept tripping on his trailing hem. Jackie did too. His sneakers hurt. He was resenting John F. and his small feet. Resenting his vile yellow tracksuit. Resenting his kidnapper wife. He tripped on his burqah and nearly fell face-first onto an outcrop of artificial rocks. It was all he could do to stop himself swearing.

'Talk about the blind leading the blind,' he said.

'Shut up, will you!' Jackie gestured at him wildly. 'You'll give yourself away!'

He stood still. He heard the creak of the turnstile behind him as it swung an inch in the wind. The sound of highway traffic was already a distant drone.

'Oh,' said Jackie. 'This isn't what I expected.'

There was no light pouring from a welcoming hotel lobby, no hospitable glow from its windows. The building was unnaturally dark. Its front door was made of white plastic, molded into wood-effect panels and covered in stickers.

'So kind of them to list the extras,' Elwyn said.

This is a lens-free zone

No Cameras

No Binoculars

No Flashlights

No Unmarried Couples

No Microscopes

No Sodomites

No Magnifying Glasses

No Computers

No TV

No Security

'Welcome to VacationLand's premier resort!' Elwyn said. 'Otherwise known as the last resort.'

Jackie may have been scowling at him through her veil. Still holding the bags, she turned around and pushed the door open with her back. Elwyn tripped at the threshold and stumbled in after her. A little bell rang. It made him jump. It was an old-fashioned sound.

The lobby was sparse and plain. Everything was probably white, but it was hard to tell in the flickering candlelight. Elwyn felt like a great black crow, standing next to another in the gloom. There was nothing to sit on. And no windows. Just a high paneled counter fixed into a corner like a booth. He guessed it was the front desk. There was a stooped man sitting behind it. Elwyn dropped his bag to the floor and stood rigid as a suspect before a judge.

But the desk-clerk kept his head bowed. He raised his head a little. He seemed to be frowning at his lap, and winking rapidly. He wore a kaftan with a bulky cartridge belt and a double-barrelled shotgun broken open over his arm. To the left of his long beard there was a plastic badge that said in curly gold letters: *Hi! My name is Ammon!*

Elwyn couldn't decide whether the man looked more like a prophet or a hippie or a terrorist—no, he was too big and broad. In another life, he might have been a bouncer.

Ammon snapped his weapon closed, and stood it upright on the desk, his fist clamped around the shaft.

Elwyn flinched like a rabbit, even though the barrels pointed up at the ceiling. Could he ever get used to guns? He would never get used to the people who owned them.

'That's what you call transitioning from prop to firearm,' Ammon muttered by way of welcome. 'And there's no sights. Just so y'all know the security situation.'

'We'd like a double room please,' Jackie said, projecting boldly through her veil. She was to do all the talking. At least she sounded like a woman.

One room? Elwyn thought. *Sharing? Why not two rooms?* Why couldn't they just sleep in the car? They could have parked anywhere.

'Did y'all read the signs?' Ammon said, thumping the big book before him with the shotgun's wooden butt.

Elwyn softened his knees to make himself shorter. He really was too tall. The floor seemed to glitter, ever so slightly. It took him some time to work out that the entire lobby area was sprinkled with salt.

'The sign said you have vacancies.' Jackie's voice was forced.

Ammon kept his head bowed low, despite the strength in his shoulders.

'And we want to escape TV,' Jackie continued, too cheerfully.

Elwyn could tell she was trying to sound assertive, but she was losing her nerve. He looked up to the wall behind Ammon. There was an oversized sampler-effect print in a frame.

And they smote the men that were at the door of the house with blindness.

Elwyn glanced at the door. Were there other Ammons lurking

behind other doors? Were they all armed and winking and mad? If he wanted to escape, would he get past the one-way turnstile?

'All we need is a room for tonight. Is there a problem?' Her voice quivered ever so slightly.

'What's wrong with your friend?' Ammon turned toward Elwyn, keeping his head low. 'Cat got your tongue?' He started fiddling with the trigger of his shotgun. He squeezed it lightly, flicking it repeatedly like a plaything.

Jackie pulled a wad of bills out of her purse. Then she pulled out some more.

'What's the room rate?' she said, placing the cash carefully on the counter. 'Here's extra for your charity work.'

Elwyn tried to add it up, so much money. Mitzy, Amanita, silence money, the car—Jackie was spending thousands before they'd won a cent. There was no need to throw her money around here. She was drawing attention to herself.

Ammon reached out and took the cash. He leaned the shotgun on his shoulder, hunching it under his jaw to free up his right hand. The barrels pointed toward the sampler on the wall behind him. He frisked the bills between his fingers, neat as a bank clerk, and put them to one side. Still he was not pleased.

'Y'all are not man and wife,' he grumbled, gazing downward. He resumed his trigger-flicking. In the dim light his eyebrows looked like two hairy caterpillars mating.

Elwyn felt his stomach tighten. How fast could he run in this gear? And where to? He thought how absorbent salt was, how ready to take blood.

'Y'all are sisters?' Ammon said.

Elwyn glanced sideways at Jackie. Through the mesh, he could see the surprise in her eyes. Or perhaps he was imagining it.

'Yes,' she said. 'Sisters. We grew up so close we're almost twins.'

Ammon hung his head, rocking it from side to side. His breathing was irregular.

'Sisters in blood also? And sisters in God! So rare!' His language switched from Arkansas to Ark. 'Are ye the firstborn and ye the younger?

'Yes,' said Jackie. 'I am the firstborn.' Her speed was impressive.

'E'en though ye be the shorter and ye be the taller?'

'Yes,' she said. 'That's right. I am the shorter.'

'And y'all—ye be women of the cloth?'

'Yes,' Jackie lied effortlessly. 'Nuns. Sisters in the service of God.'

Elwyn was amazed. She was faster than mercury.

'Y'all have not known man?' Ammon stopped playing with his trigger.

'That's right,' Jackie said, without a hint of dishonesty.

Elwyn nodded with as much conviction as he could muster. It was pathetic. His neck hurt, despite the brace.

'That's why we have to sleep in the same room together,' Jackie added.

Ammon sighed with such force his reading candle sputtered. An ecstasy had descended upon his face. He broke open his weapon and spoke again, trembling a little.

'We are honored to have thee, twice-sisters. Blessed and honored! A blessing and a sign. Thanks be to the Lord.'

There was too much zeal in the man's voice, but Elwyn exhaled and realized he had been holding his breath.

'There's a Bible in y'all's—thy drawers. Here be thy light. And thy bags of salt.' Ammon handed over an old-fashioned lantern, candles, matches and two motel-style sachets. 'And remember, sisters: no scopes, no lenses, no security. May thine eye not offend thee, firstborn. May thine eye not offend thee, younger one. May the eye of the Lord bear witness.'

Elwyn held up the lantern with his good arm. Their room was just as sparse as the lobby. Four whitewashed walls, a door leading to a bathroom, a huge air-conditioning unit that hummed, a white plastic patio table with matching chairs. There was a double mattress, made up with a white comforter, on the floor. No windows, no lighting, no adornment except a sampler-effect framed print on the wall.

And if thine eye offend thee, pluck it out, and cast it from thee.

'Nice,' said Elwyn, putting the lantern down by the foot of the bed.

Jackie closed the door. 'Dammit, there's no lock.' She looked miserable.

'Old Ahab said there was no security.'

'I thought he meant no cameras or scanners.' She pressed their bags hard against the door to make a barricade. 'Or generally, you know, like in this life, there's no security. I guess keyholes are bad. I guess keyholes are like seeing machines.'

'How much did you pay old Mammon?'

She looked around the room. 'At least it's clean. John F. would approve.'

'Jackie, how much did you pay?'

'Enough to make him helpful. It's a drop in the ocean.' Jackie pulled off her burqah and let it fall to the floor. The black fabric was instantly iced with salt. 'I need the bathroom.'

Elwyn stood in the middle of the room. His mind felt fuzzy. The bed looked so inviting. He wanted to sleep. He didn't know whether to undress or sneak off quietly while Jackie was out of the way. He'd have to move the barricade. He could do that with his good arm. Ammon stood between him and the front door. He'd have to speak to him, say something. He could put on a woman's voice. It wasn't so hard—

'Do you think this place is going to be safe enough?' Jackie asked, suddenly back.

How long had he been standing there?

She threw herself across the bed, a green velveteen silhouette on the white comforter. Her feet stuck out: mottled pink ankles and sneakers with fluorescent reflectors. She stared at the ceiling.

Elwyn felt drugged, tired enough to lie down and sleep for days. 'He thinks we're sisters. We're probably safer here than anywhere else in the entire country.' He glanced at the two pillows. 'He thinks we're going to share the bed.'

'We are.' Jackie was using that firm voice again, although it sounded different horizontal.

Elwyn pulled off his gloves and dropped them on the floor. He couldn't afford to offend her. She had the power to protect him, or to turn him over. He looked like a husband to this hairdresser from the suburbs. She wanted to share a bed with him and he wanted to laugh at her. This was going to be harder than telling his own mother.

'Jackie, you know how Mammon back there asked if "ye had not known man", and you lied and said yes—I mean, you have known man?'

Jackie stared at him. Her gray-blue eyes were road-weary. She fixed him with her gaze. She said nothing.

He was a black butterfly in a white box, pins of pain in his wounded muscles. He perched at the end of the bed.

'Jackie, I lied when you lied: I have known man and I expect to know more. It's about as optional to me as my shoe size.' He snorted—John F.'s sneakers were pinching—he was wearing a woman's dress—he didn't know whether to laugh or cry. 'I have known woman too, but it's never been my chosen route. So to speak. No offense.'

Jackie kept staring, motionless.

Why was she not responding? He was handing over the power, everything—and her face was blank.

'I can't be John F. for you any longer.' He was speaking lines from a soap opera again.

'You never were John F.,' she said. 'I gave up on him a long time ago. Nothing was going to happen in bed.' Her voice was quiet. 'You think I'm really stupid, don't you?'

Yes, he thought. *And no.* 'I think you're major. And I'm minor.'

'What's that supposed to mean?'

'You're tougher than I am, you're an oak. You're like marching tunes and neat endings. You're a rational number.'

'Why do you have to talk in circles all the time?'

'I'm gay, Jackie.'

Was she offended? Disappointed? Disgusted? He studied her for signals. Maybe she was mad. Mad crazy, or mad at him. He still didn't know how to read her.

'You ought to know something about that, Jackie, you're a hairdresser.'

A tear fell out of the corner of her eye. She didn't wipe it off.

Crying was the last thing he expected her to do. It made no sense. Was she thinking of John F. again?

'You're always putting me down!' She gulped. 'You and Reall Life and John F. and—you think, after all this—after my husband—and that woman—and the morgue—and I got you—' She turned over on her side and curled up, facing the wall. Her shoulders shuddered, but she was silent.

Elwyn felt sorry, tired and sorry. He lay down behind her and held her like a sister, stroked her shoulder with his bad arm, stroked her wild orange hair, the sleeves of her sweatsuit, the back of her pale freckled hand.

He was lying in a rocky place. They had kidnapped him and trapped him in a sack. Hot. He struggled to move. They would throw him in the river. But first there was the snake, larger than an anaconda.

Sisters, sisters! hissed the snake.

He was struggling in his sack. His feet were caught.

Sisters, sisters! The snake had been drinking blood and the blood had turned to wine. It hissed and the smell was all of liquor.

. . .and he went up out of Zoar, and dwelt in a cave, with his two daughters . . .

Elwyn opened his eyes and could not see. He didn't know where he was. Amanita's Inn. Hospital. Home. The rocky place. The cameras were hissing at him. He was in the snake's cage at the zoo and the snake had wrapped itself around him. He could not see. He was blind in the blackness. He was waking up and there was a voice behind him.

. . .and the firstborn said unto the younger, our father is old, and there is not a man in the earth to come in unto us . . .

'What's that?' Jackie's voice whispered. 'Who said that?'

. . .let us make our father drink wine, and we will lie with him, to preserve the seed of the father . . .

Elwyn was still wearing his robe. And shoes. He was holding Jackie. She was wearing her sweatsuit. She was tapping his hand in the dark. Her fingers felt warm. The snake was hissing behind him.

. . .and they made their father drink wine, and the firstborn lay with her father, and the younger arose, and lay with him . . .

Elwyn felt the snake behind him. It was lifting his skirts up, rubbing his thighs.

Behold, she's a furry sister! Come, furry little peach, and lie with daddy! Come to me, daughter! Are ye the firstborn or the younger?

The snake was sporting a gun, cold and hard. Reciting words, sounding feverish. 'Thus were both the horny daughters of Lot with child by their father . . . the father of the children of Ammon unto this day—that's me, daughter. Come, part thy peach for me.'

Elwyn felt the horror rise to his throat. There was no light. Ammon was on the mattress behind him, grasping him by the buttocks and tugging at his pants, maneuvering himself into position.

'Come, firstborn, part thy peach for me.' Ammon belched, hot alcoholic air.

'But I am the firstborn!' Jackie shrieked in the darkness.

Where was she? How could she see anything?

'The furry one's the younger,' Jackie said. 'I am the firstborn. You know my voice.'

Ammon stopped fiddling with Elwyn's clothes and struggled to stand.

'Ah yes, my sister-daughter. Come to me, my horny little virgin. We gotta preserve the seed of Lot.'

'Over here,' said Jackie. 'Are you standing?'

'Yes, my angel, where are you? I can hear your sexy little voice, but I can't see you! Oh, you wicked little cock-teasing firstborn! Come to daddy and feel his action!'

'Step over the younger sister. I'm here. You must do the coming.'

Ammon groped at Elwyn's body and stumbled over him towards Jackie's voice. The rifle swung loose against Elwyn's wounded arm. He yelped with the pain, squeezed his eyes shut in the darkness, braced himself for gunfire.

'I'm coming, little sister darling.'

'I'm waiting for you. I'm waiting for you right here.' Jackie's voice squeaked a little.

'Now we're gonna lift your skirt and part your peach, cos we got some Moab to—'

There was a crack, like a pie dish breaking, and then silence.

Another sound, this time more of a thudding crack. Something fell to the bed.

The silence was so heavy and hard it pressed in on Elwyn's ears like a solid.

'The filthy bastard,' Jackie said at last.

Elwyn's heart was punching at his ribs.

'The filthy—dirty—'

Elwyn rummaged around for the lantern and the matches. Everything seemed to take hours. His fingers were shaking. He dropped things as soon as he held them. Eventually there was light, weak and glimmering in the stark room.

Jackie was standing against the words on the wall, her face pearly white and shiny. Her bloodied top was caught in her bra on one side. The reflectors on her sneakers flashed half-heartedly in the candlelight. Her knees were wobbling.

Ammon lay sprawled across the bed, his kaftan hitched up around his waist, erection frozen in mid air. His shotgun was lying across one arm. There was blood all over his head, streaked and clotting. Blood on the whiteness of the comforter.

The silence was a buzzing now, deep inside Elwyn's skull.

'He had a fall or something,' Jackie said. 'On the rocks out there.'

'He's wounded.'

'He struck his head. It's not a crime.'

'Seriously wounded.'

'He's not dead. He's just drunk.' She crossed herself. 'Besides, he tried to—' She gulped. 'Both of us. The bastard's got a gun.'

'You can talk,' Elwyn said, looking at the pistol gripped in her hand.

★ ★ ★ ★ ★ ★ ★ ★ ★ ★ ★ ★ ★ ★ ★ ★

CONSPIRACY COVER-UP

Rumors that Fresno Jackie is traveling cross-country dressed as a Mexican are unconfirmed. It is also unknown whether she is traveling alone, or with her wounded husband survivor. In several states, anti-mask statutes forbid the wearing of a disguise in public, and offenses are punishable by financial penalties or incarceration. Anti-mask laws are believed to owe their existence to efforts to curb the activities of extremist group Ku Klux Klan, but this doesn't mean other citizens are exempt.

'Anti-mask statutes variously ban the use of a hood, mask, false whiskers or other personal disguise,' stated Jerrol Cheek of the Alabama Institute of Law.

He commented further: 'The possibility of a felony arises if an individual is disguised for the purposes of evading or escaping discovery, recognition or identification, and/or concealment, flight or escape in connection with a public offense, or during the commission of another felony. Impersonation can be an offense also.'

Rumors still persist in some quarters that the two presidential candidates have been swapped, which muddies the election picture and threatens to harm Reall Life revenues. Results of DNA tests and other identification procedures performed at the Dallas Morgue are yet to be made public, owing to a 'Special Situations' hushing order imposed by LeizureScape lawyers.

'This is a matter that concerns the rights to privacy of the individual,' Legal Affairs Spokesman Bradley Clay-Gaudet II said in a press statement yesterday. 'The law will not be sold into the service of conspiracy.'

Independent eye witnesses claim to have seen the mother of the deceased leave her apartment in New York's well-heeled Upper East Side. Reports indicate that the grieving Mrs Ruth Barter was only persuaded to go with police protection. 'This is too much sorrow for one small family,' she said. Her husband, zoologist Irwin Barter, years ago died in a Middle Eastern restaurant when a suspected animal rights campaigner allegedly poisoned his food.

VIEWERS! What will you have to show your grandchildren? Look forward to heirloom memories you will cherish for a lifetime. Reall Life brings you unique gifting ideas throughout the voting season. Look out for amazing special offers while stocks last.

★ ★ ★ ★ ★ ★ ★ ★ ★ ★ ★ ★ ★ ★ ★ ★

Jackie Be Quick

Jackie stared at Ammon, loathing him. The stain on the comforter around his head was like a rooster's crest, red and wavy. Why was there so much blood? What could they do with him? How long would it take for another one of The Lot to find him? His lust was on display, like a big finger pointing out his guilt. How long would it stay like that? Surely his naked shame would be enough to silence him and his brothers. How many brothers were there? Why was there so much blood?

There was blood on the pistol gripped tight in her hand.

'Where the—Jackie, where did that come from?' Elwyn was mad at her.

'It's John F.'s,' she said.

'You can put it down now.'

There were sticky blood-red spatters on her green sweatsuit. She smoothed it down. Her knees were shaking.

'I can't.'

'Jackie, put it down.'

She shook her head. She leaned against the wall.

'Better safe than sorry,' she said, repeating what John F. used to say. It always sounded right, but everything felt wrong now. Her marriage, her life since Reall Life, this bleeding creep, this horrible place in the middle of nowhere.

And then tears started. For the second time in front of Elwyn. She hated that. The way women cried in front of men in the movies, in shopping malls, in the privacy of their own homes. The way homemakers cried when they won a prize on a quiz show. She was crying like some stupid girl in front of some stupid boy. She knew Elwyn cried too. She had seen it on TV. And John F. had cried for all the nation to see. But men hardly ever cried. Men only cried when they were scared of losing something.

Jackie sank to her knees and squatted on the pillows. She was hot and cold at the same time. Her eyes were streaming.

John F. would have melted, but Elwyn did not move to comfort her. 'We should call the police,' he said.

'We can take him with us,' Jackie said, wiping her face on her sleeve, calming herself down. 'Or we can lock him up here—but there are no locks! He'll be out in no time. We've got to stall things until the election's over.'

Was it dark or light outside? Impossible to tell. She checked her watch. Nearly five o'clock. 'There'll be a morning shift.'

'I'm going to call the police,' Elwyn said.

'And get caught? And give up now?'

'I'm going to call the police,' Elwyn said again. He ripped off his burqah. The fabric got twisted up and caught. He peeled off his neck-brace and let it fall. 'I didn't—I wouldn't have—what the hell are you doing with a gun? I don't want to be—it was self-defense. Look at him. It's proof. The police can see that as well as anybody. I'm going to call the police—have you got a phone?'

She blew her nose. Dried her eyes. She was not about to give Elwyn her phone. It was turned off and she didn't want Reall Life to track them down. She didn't want Elwyn to call anybody.

'If you call the police you'll lose everything.'

'In prison you lose everything anyway, Jackie.'

'You'll lose everything. They'll find you out.'

'And how will they do that?'

Would she really give him away? What would they make of her traveling interstate with a sad gay man in a burqah pretending to be her husband—her lawfully wedded husband who was so recently, so tragically taken from her? How mad could her grief be? The election would get messed up. Maybe they would cancel it. She would lose everything, and never mind Detroit. She had to keep him on her side, even if he was a homosexual.

She said, 'They'll put you in a cage for deviants and watch you get shot. Worse than a duck derby.'

Elwyn took hold of Ammon's wrist to test his pulse. He retched and turned away from the bloodied head, still holding on to the wrist.

Jackie had run out of plans. It was HyperFriday the day after tomorrow and she was losing control. Instead of being invisible she was leaving a trail of clues for that Detective Pascillo to follow. She thought she had seen him on the highway. Shadowing her in his beat-up car with the tinted windows. Sitting pretty just yards behind the SUV, taking his time, hiding in the rainstorms. For all she knew he was already parked outside, waiting to analyze her sweatsuit for blood. Him and the entire county police force. Waiting to lift Elwyn's veil and expose him for what he was—a fake. All they needed was a snip of John F.'s hair for the DNA. She was about to lose everything—

'He hasn't actually seen us,' Elwyn said. He was still holding Ammon by the wrist.

She felt her body go soft. It was like in the movies when a storm was over, and the drama was coming to an end. The candle flame fluttered. The air-conditioning unit whined.

'He avoids eye contact and he's sure we're both women. So he's a very unreliable witness.' Elwyn sounded tired. 'We know he hasn't seen our faces.'

'Stuff like this happens all the time in the hospitality business. And look at his—' Jackie couldn't say the word. All of a sudden, she wanted to laugh out loud. Ammon's penis looked preposterous.

Elwyn spoke quietly. 'I think his pulse is OK. We could call a paramedic and just leave.'

'They might think he was up to no good with a call-girl or something. All kinds of stuff happens in hotels. You know, with people like—John F. called them transients and hourly guests. Even religious types.'

Jackie stared at Elwyn kneeling beside her in John F.'s yellow tracksuit, acting squeamish. He was so unlike her husband—she was seeing the differences now more than the similarities.

Elwyn sat down at the end of the bed, his back to her. 'So who's going to call the paramedics?'

'The manager who finds the . . . the problem. Or another guest.' Jackie was thinking of TV. *KrimeTime*. *Vespucci*. *My Little Eye*.

John F. had protected her from the harsh realities of his work. He always said she'd be shocked at what went on. He took the line that every motel was a no-tell motel. No place for a lady. Certainly not his First, and Only, Lady. She gulped.

Elwyn stood up. 'No, I mean, it has to be you on the phone because Ammon thinks we're both women.' He sat down again. 'I don't feel too good.'

Jackie sat next to him. 'Why don't you go out to the car? I'll bring the bags. I'll call the doctors from the lobby. Then we can get away from here.' She rubbed her tired eyes.

'Jackie, are you OK to drive?'

She was exhausted. She needed to sleep some more. But she was whirring, on edge. He was on her side again. She pictured the long straight road ahead of them. She'd never sat close to a gay man before. She didn't like the idea, but at least he would keep his hands to himself.

'We need food,' she said.

'What if he wakes up?'

She realized she was still holding on to the pistol. She tried to loosen her grip, and her fingers stuck. It felt as if she was leaving her skin behind, never mind fingerprints.

'He won't wake up yet,' she said.

'I thought you were the Blusher,' he said. 'But maybe you're the Destroying Angel.'

'What are you talking about?'

'They're fungus names.'

'What about you? What mushroom are you?'

He was very earnest. 'I'm Fried Chicken.'

Jackie felt suddenly hilarious, worse than being in church at a funeral. She choked back her laughter until it burst out of her, and then she couldn't stop. She pointed over her shoulder at Ammon's erection. 'You got a hat for that? That there resurrection needs a hat!' She fell against Elwyn's arm.

'Not that arm!' He jumped.

'I'm sorry. I forgot.'

'I'm getting out of here.'

He grasped his wounded arm, stood up slowly and shuffled toward the door.

Jackie wanted to tell him everything. About her childhood, Irish Grandma Jackie, her favorite Snax, her life in Fresno, her secret personal identification numbers, everything. She realized she had never had a best friend. Not the sort of person she could tell things to. Not the private giggles. Or the tears. Everybody seemed to think that hairdressers talked to everybody. They were wrong. She wasn't like the others at Mane Event. She got worried every time they organized an after-work social. She'd always kept herself to herself.

'You forgot something,' she said.

Elwyn stopped at the door.

She dug into her pocket and held up the car keys. She wondered for a moment whether she could trust him. What if he just drove away? What would she do?

He turned around. His face was so tired, so weak and sickly. Poor wounded gay president. He couldn't drive if he tried. He'd said so himself.

'Your burqah,' she added.

Besides, they were getting on so well. Just like Bonnie and Clyde.

Jackie watched as Ammon's beefy chest rose and fell ever so slightly. Rose and fell, rose and fell. The blood streaks down his face were lipstick stripes, dark and clotted in his bushy eyebrows. He had split ends in his beard, she couldn't help noticing.

She picked herself up off the bed and went over to the baggage by the door. There was a great swipe in the salt where her barricade had been pushed open. And footprints from John F.'s sneakers. She recognized the tread. Without putting the gun down, she unzipped the side pocket of her bag and fished out her portable hairdressing kit.

'Trim, trim,' she said, as she leaned over Ammon. She cut off his beard, close to the chin, nicking him occasionally, catching his skin with the points of her scissors, causing new blood to leak. She used the gun instead of a comb to lift the hair for cutting. It was hard to cut straight, but she didn't care. The hair was like the fuzzy stuff that gathered behind sofas and fridges. She let it fall onto the bloody comforter in a dark cloud around the man's head. So many split ends! Such bad condition!

She considered the hair on his scalp.

She glanced toward the door.

'Trim, trim,' she sang softly to herself as she cut off Ammon's long hair. It was so much fun to make a bad man bald. She didn't mind the way his skin caught the tips of her blades every now and then. She felt young again. Happier than when she was twelve. All her dolls had haircuts. All her dolls had Jackie bangs and Jackie bobs.

When she got to the head-wounds, she sniffed with disgust and moved on. The hair stayed longer there.

She checked the door again. No sign of Elwyn or the morning shift.

'I'm not a beautician,' she said quietly to Ammon in her best salon voice. 'But I can sort you out there too if you like.' As she pointed at his pubic hair with her pistol and scissors, his erection got in the way. She saw a little line of blood appear, finer than a thread.

She snipped lightly at the penis with the tips of her scissors, making more blood, little cuts.

'Criss-cross,' she said.

She was cross. No, she was angry. At him and all his brothers, the dirty men who hid in holy robes, the creeps that hung around swimming pools and shopping malls, exposing themselves, molesting girls, the men who laughed at her when her pants split open on TV.

'Trim, trim,' she said, sing-song.

The Big Dealey—Today's Bets

'RADICAL ALI' 2-WAY BET
Suspect: Ali Mohammad Saad
Firing Line: Military Helicopter OR Media Helicopter
No. of bullets: X ('wild number')
Motive: Contractual Duty
Odds at 12:30 p.m. CST: 11/9
Total no. of bets placed on all suspects: 9,112,001
Time's running out! Get your bets in before HyperFriday!

Ali needs a trim again. He sits at his desk, keeping his head down, running his hand through his strawberry-blond hair. He can feel his body filling with the pus of corruption. Things have not calmed down since the motorcade. The Polytheists keep talking about *The TV President*. They stand by the water-cooler, distracting him with their chatter.

'Which one are you voting for? I heard the dead one's not dead, that it's all some kind of trick, just like *Kandid Kam* or *Say Cheez*, only the joke's on the viewers.'

Ali knows that non-Muslims will not fail to do their best to corrupt him. They desire to harm him severely. It says so in the Qur'an. He remembers to be grateful to Allah for these struggles. The Disbelievers gather with plastic cups in their hands, at the corner by the photocopiers where the carpet tiles are curled up and taped down. There is no natural light here. At AutoCorp only the directors and presidents get natural light. The walls are pale brown. The air is cold and conditioned. Some of the carpet tiles are missing and there is old black glue on the underfloor. It catches dirt and fuzz.

The Unbelievers carry on and Ali listens.

'Something rotten's going on behind the scenes, just like in 1963, same as 9/11. They've got information coming out of their ears. You telling me all those databanks don't talk to each other? I'm getting to be so cynical, I can't even believe the weather girl anymore!'

When the photocopiers finish their loads, when the water cups have been drained, the Unbelievers are still talking. Engineers, programmers, technicians, administrators—still talking on company time, distracting Ali from his work and his hair.

'And what about the Terror Wars? I didn't hear one peep out of them about that. Either of them! What president doesn't have a Terror Policy?'

Ali can't stand it any longer. There are too many opinions in the world. Opinions make him sick. Too much idleness, drinking and partying—it is the capitalist ideology. He goes to sit in the simulator lab and closes the air-sealed door behind him. He is at peace here. The shelves are full of environmentally hardened mini-computers that are fully operational, years ahead of their real use. They hold the code to his life in this world. Like him, they must be able to withstand a hostile environment: extreme temperature variation, vibration, moisture, radio frequency signals, huge electrical loads, noise, more noise, and the general pressures of a motor.

Ali is at home with software. All the new stuff works, he likes to say, but necessarily it breaks everything that came before. That is the way of new systems. He pretends he's dipped his mind into epoxy goop to protect himself from the hostile environment. He imagines his receptors are wrapped in nickel tape. He has to endure all the tests:

Television.

Liquor.

Bacon.

Prejudice.

Halloween.

Birthdays.

Pornography.

Christmas—his grandmother keeps leaving him messages about it. He can't join her for turkey. He won't be wishing her a happy Christmas. The sin of Shirk vexes him, because Shirk is sly.

Major Shirk is polytheism—a sin Allah will not forgive without total repentance and abstinence—that much is clear to Ali and he's not about to sin that bad. But Minor Shirk is slippery. Minor Shirk is showing off or seeking fame. *It is as inconspicuous as a black ant moving on a black stone in the darkness of night.* It is as subtle as praying at a higher standard, knowing that others are watching. But sometimes it is more conspicuous.

When Ali was still Eugene and in the first grade, his grandmother made him kneel in front of the TV. Dolan Brading was on, the guy who'd helped her to be born again—he called himself God's midwife. *Now put your hands on the TV and pray!* Little Eugene had obeyed, but he was sure it was wrong. It was Major Shirk, although he didn't have that name to use yet. He was a Muslim before he knew it. He was getting ready, years before he was called.

And then along came *The TV President*—a riot, a surge of Shirk. Total Shirk-out. Shirk Overload.

Ali looks through the glass in the door. The group by the water-cooler has disbanded. He quits the simulator lab and returns to his desk. The office is quiet again. Nothing but the hum of fluorescent tubes and the clicking of keyboards. Ali has a double cubicle. It makes him feel proud—but pride is a trait of the people of the hell-fire, so he checks himself. Most of the other cubicles around him are empty. Ali has observed wave after wave of restructuring and downscaling. Where people have cleared up and gone, there are a few personal items left, still pinned to the dividers. Ali has defaced a girl wearing a scanty bikini on a postcard from Florida. She belongs to one of the disappeared. The dividers are padded and covered in heavy cloth. They block the view but they don't block the sound. Ali hears everything. Footsteps. Doors. Now two guys from the garage are standing in the middle of the departmental walkway, talking, distracting him.

'They musta done DNA tests on the corpse. Hell, any jerk with a couple dollars can get his kids tested for paternity. How long's it take? A couple days? We have a right to know for sure which one got taken out and why. But they're keeping it quiet.'

Ali checks the time on his computer screen. Five minutes pass and the garage guys are still talking.

It's idle hypocrites like these who object to Muslim employees taking time to pray.

Ali can't stand it anymore. He packs his things and takes the elevator downstairs. As he comes out the back door to the parking lot, there's a huddle of workers standing around smoking, blowing clouds into the fresh air, arguing about the details of the latest episode, or maybe today's news, as if it matters.

'—They got over the state line dressed in some foreign disguise. The hospital nurses are all under arrest. I'm votin' for the one that escaped. Those nurses musta known something we don't. And there's no point havin' a dead president.'

'—They're set on digging up everyone's graves. Marilyn Monroe. JFK. RFK. Lee Harvey Oswald. Even Princess Diana. Live on air.'

'—I put a month's salary on Radical Ali for *The Big Dealey*. It's always them. Anywhere in the world there's trouble, and there's them, they're the ones behind the trouble.'

Ali feels like butting in. It's his spiritual obligation to speak out, not to remain silent or integrate. Just last week servers in the canteen complained that halal meat was the thin end of the wedge. In today's staff newsletter, another Unbeliever is objecting to Muslims having their own public holidays. It is a kind of persecution. Ali remembers to be grateful for these struggles. He is going to have a haircut, by Allah's will.

'Back so soon?' Mohammad says.

'Yes.' Last time Ali had his hair cut was just before the Big Day. It's only been a week.

'Same as last time?'

'Shorter.'

Ali's barber holds the scissors up high, draws a stream of hair between his expert fingers and snips.

Snip, snip.

Mohammad's shop is in the Arabian Mall, between the café with the hookah-smokers on the sidewalk and the Halal Pizza Pie Co. Reassuringly, every one of the barber's signs are in Arabic, except for the words *HAIR ELEGANCE* and *GEL*. Ali doesn't know what the rest of them say but he wants his haircut to be halal like the pizzas next door.

'The place where I work is full of Shirkers,' Ali says to Mohammad in the mirror. 'They talk about TV all day.'

The barber nods but says nothing.

Snip, snip. Snip, snip.

The sound is satisfying. A ticking of time. Ali wants his hair short as possible, but not so short it resembles an Unbeliever's fashion style. *The one who takes on the look of a certain people becomes one of them.* The last thing Ali wants to look like is an ordinary American. He is not an American Muslim. He is a Muslim in America. He would like his scalp shaved, but he's saving that for Mecca, maybe next year.

There's a 3D iridescent picture of Mecca on Mohammad's wall. Metallic red, green, blue, gold and silver. The colors switch around when Ali moves his head, like colors do on oil slicks. He's got the same picture hanging up at home, only his is bigger and it has a striking gold frame.

Ali's strawberry-blond hair stands out at the mosque, which worries him because it feels like an act of Minor Shirk, but he's not 100% sure. He has to ask the Imam.

Ali's attention-seeking hair slips between the barber's fingers and falls away at the snip. The roots appear to be darker these days. More strawberry than blond. Good.

Maybe his hair is meant to be an invitation, which is Dawah, just like a lady's modest dress. Anyone can see a Muslima coming a mile off with her hijab. It gives her the chance to bear witness, which can catalyze an Unbeliever's conversion to the world's No.1 religion. Ali should not call it conversion, even when he's thinking. Islam came first, long before the times of ignorance, no matter what the Jews or Christians say. *Reversion*, he says to himself. *Reversion*. Hoping that his outstanding hair will have the hijab-effect, he wants the Unbelievers to see him coming out of the mosque, notice his coloring and ask him questions. He has been reading books, guides, manuals, step by step. He is geared up to explain the one and only path to Paradise.

But Unbelievers don't hang around outside the mosque. They park by their own church or drive by, and when Ali is at a mall or downtown he just looks like any other white guy getting in and out of his car.

158

Most people don't even recognize him from *The Big Dealey* because of the scarf he wrapped around his head and face for the official mugshot. If he's honest with himself, he's got to admit he envies women their cloaks and veils. It gives them honor. Marks them out. He's had a beard since his reversion but recently someone called him a garden gnome, which defeats his purpose.

Snip, snip.

At the slightest touch of Mohammad's fingertip, Ali knows to lean to the left, to the right, or straighten up again. His fair hair falls away like dust.

There's one other white Revert that he can think of at the mosque, but he's Hispanic and blessed with near-black hair and a sun-kissed complexion. Ali can't get a tan to save his life. The African-American Reverts blend like wallpaper, not that there is wallpaper.

Some of the brothers avoid Ali. He knows that. They don't want him to marry their sisters. There are four reasons he can isolate:

1) He is relatively new to Islam, which is true; that's something he can't help.

2) He does not belong to an ethnic minority. (Although in Detroit, technically he does.)

3) The brothers say he takes things too seriously.

4) His Arabic isn't up to scratch and he gets it wrong, although he practices so often that his English is beginning to sound foreign, and these days he can recite the prayers without the disks, and when he answers the phone, even at work, he says *assalamu alaikum* like it was written into his DNA—it's not the protocol at AutoCorp but they can't fire a man for his right to practice his faith, although that struggle would be of interest if Allah willed it.

Now Ali starts repeating his prayers, silently, while the barber sweeps his fingers through each layer of hair and snips with his silver scissors.

Ali likes to think his hair is the color of the mosque's domes. The Ummah need more money. More money for more mosques. He is so proud of the gold-roofed Masjid, one of the biggest mosques in America, rising like a shining beacon on Ford Road. Some buildings come down, others go up. Empires too. That's the way of the world.

Ever since 9/11, Ali has been gradually coming awake and opening his eyes.

The Tuesday when Allah created darkness, Ali was sick in bed and missing high school. He watched the falling bodies. They were specks in the air, just blurs, but they were made of blood and fear. He stayed home all day all night all week. He heard the crashes and cries and phone calls a hundred times, more than a hundred times, looking for answers. He didn't eat. He didn't sleep. His acne got worse. The more he watched, the more he realized he had no answers. Everything in this world was empty. Nothing stood forever. He was no one and he stood for nothing.

Slowly, slowly, out of the black smoke and ash another tower rose up for him. It was indestructible. Hard. Defiant, afraid of nothing. It was the tower of Islam. He couldn't turn away from it. When he started work at AutoCorp, he was still Eugene McVickar by name—he had not yet taken his Shahada. There was nothing different to see from the outside, but he was already different inside. Not everyone felt the same way he did, which is why the Imam said to be prepared for negative reactions.

Snip, snip, snip.

Mohammad is working around the back and Ali leans his head forward, bowing to the mirror. He can feel the hair-dust slip like silk down his neck. It is forbidden to wear silk. The barber's chair is comfortable. Ali feels happy and at peace. Happier even than inside the simulator lab. Mohammad says nothing. Nothing to distract from his hand movements, deft, caressing, combing, cutting.

Ali keeps his head down so that the barber has an easier time dealing with his neck. *Snip, snip.* He wonders if he should ask Mohammad to color his hair. Black dye is haram but henna is halal, so he could go brown, even though his eyebrows and eyelashes will always be golden. And what about facial hair?

Mohammad gently tilts Ali's head up again and sweeps him with a feathery brush. The bristles flick over Ali's ear and tickle. The brush caresses his other ear and strokes his neck. He gets a special sensation, deep in his gut. It's as if somebody is stroking his soul. If he moves too much, the feeling will evaporate. The brush touches his face, lighter than fingertips. His eyelids flutter and blink. If he ever finds himself a wife he will get her to brush and stroke him every day.

Mohammad stands back to survey his handiwork before returning to clip Ali's moustache. This is part of his duty to Allah, and Allah knows best, but Ali still is vexed by the helicopter pilot who called him a garden gnome.

'They're all going to hell in a handbasket,' Ali mutters.

The barber gives a wordless nod and continues clipping. He moves to Ali's strawberry-blond beard. He pauses and speaks: 'Like a shave?'

Ali can't resist. He wants to prolong the feeling in his gut. He nods and shuts his eyes. He feels the cool slap on his cheeks as Mohammad lathers him up and shaves his acne-scarred cheeks, avoiding his main beard. It's a fine art knowing where to draw the line, but this guy's a pro.

Ali tries to concentrate on the physical sensation but his mind keeps going back to work where the fluorescent lighting above his cubicle flickers. On. Off. The next light along doesn't function. He could reach the ceiling without too much trouble because it's low, but he has to wait for some union guy to change the tube. Same with the photocopier, unless he fills the paper-tray after-hours when no one from the union is there to see—Ali likes to work late anyway.

'If I win on *The Big Dealey*,' Mohammad says, 'I'm gonna buy—'

'But gambling is Shirk!' Ali's eyes pop open. He is scandalized. 'You're not saying you gamble?'

Mohammad shakes his head as if to say no. Not one hair, shiny black and full of gel, moves. 'Alhamdulillah,' he says. 'Praise be to Allah.'

But there is no need to translate. Ali knows that one.

'Alhamdulillah,' he replies in his best accent. But what is his best accent? Middle Eastern like the Imam? Pakistani like the other engineers? North African like the guys at the sidewalk cafe? 'One day we will, insha'Allah, be the first, the biggest, religion in the country. In the meantime, brother, pagans, Jews, Christians and hypocrites will do their best to corrupt you. Their desire is to harm you severely—and that's a quote.'

The nice feeling has gone from his gut, so he closes his eyes and lets Mohammad finish his job. *Islam is perfect*, he reminds himself, but *Muslims are not.*

Ali feels guilty because he is a suspect on *The Big Dealey*, the gaming program created by LeizureScape. He himself is not betting or smooth-talking or seeking fame but he is provoking others to commit Shirk.

Viewers gamble on the likelihood that:

a) he is a militant extremist fundamentalist Islamist terrorist who is an American citizen working from inside the system just as a virus sleeps within software;

b) he is the only suspect who has been commissioned: he has accepted a fee for assassination services rendered under contract;

c) he has shot at the presidential motorcade from inside a helicopter which, unlike the others in the sky that day, bore no logo but appeared to be a military vehicle courtesy of Armz, and yet may have been a media one courtesy of Reall Life;

d) he personally operated the mounted weapon, no bigger than a rolled-up prayer mat; and

e) he aimed with surgical precision at the eloquent political candidate whose charming speech translated lies into the semblance of truth, stirring hearts and leading minds to false worship (Shirk, Shirk, Shirk, Shirk).

Ali stares at the mirror and tries to see his own face as if he's never seen it before. Is he photogenic? Good looking? His grandmother always said he was like a famous actor but she never did say which one. How does he appear to strangers seeing him on TV for the first time? Can they actually see he is a Believer, despite his blond eyes above the scarf-line? Is he recognizable? Can they see his acne scars?

Since the Big Day, the LeizureScape statisticians have been claiming Radical Ali is the most popular bet for both Muslims and Jews, because of his 'classic credentials'. Christians in their millions are betting on him too. The truly faithful Ummah, who rightly do not gamble, have been caught on camera, cheering on city streets in every single continent. Young kids wear T-shirts printed with Ali's name, demonstrators shake placards of his anonymous scarf-wrapped face at TV crews, or burn flags of the Reall Life logo.

This is not the outcome Ali imagined when he signed his contract with the undercover agents. He had been invited to fight Shirk! By the word and by the sword. He didn't need to ask too many questions. It was meant to be. His payment was his reward. Ali Mohammad Saad would fund another new mosque, bigger, more gold, more faithful, and Allah was willing. Accepting orders from anyone but God was idol worship.

Ali judges himself in the mirror. Mirrors do not lie. They show and tell the hard facts.

'Now that I am a minor celebrity, have I committed Shirk?' he wonders out loud. He must ask the Imam. Shirk is as inconspicuous as a black ant crawling on a black stone in the darkness of night, but Ali is as conspicuous as a white—

'By cutting your hair, I also played my part,' says Mohammad quietly. He is looking at him through the mirror. He has stopped working. 'People are betting on you.'

Ali's ears are tricking him. 'What did you say?'

'Don't let them exploit you,' says Mohammad. 'It is finished. The hair is finished.'

Ali studies his own reflection and all he can see is a garden gnome with a very short haircut. He wishes he could wear hijab, but he knows the Prophet curses men who dress like women. They're as doomed as women who dress like men. He wishes he could wrap his whole head in a scarf like he did for *The Big Dealey* mugshot but a man can't go around Detroit looking like a famous terrorist.

He gets up out of the comfortable chair and follows Mohammad to the cash desk. He is suddenly aware of a rock anthem playing in the background. Through the singer's voice, he can hear female moaning, deep-bellied drums, and strings sharp as a nest of rodents.

'Music is the instrument of Satan, brother, you should know that.'

Mohammad is awkward as he turns the sound system off. He takes his payment and gives Ali his change.

'Have a nice day,' he says.

'Insha'Allah,' says Ali. 'Insha'Allah.'

When he steps out onto Warren, Ali feels the cool Michigan wind on his chafed cheeks and newly cut beard. The traffic melts away the sound of music. He walks past the hookah smokers, searching for a familiar face from the mosque. The guys are hanging out. Watching programs on hand-held screens. One of them returns his nod and half a smile, but Ali's not too sure.

At the corner by the stop lights, Ali looks up and down the street. He loves Detroit and he loves Dearborn most of all. This is where he lives and shops and drives and prays with his Ummah. From bakeries to books, this is Halal City. The Halal Zone.

The streets are wide and open. The sky is big. All the motor vehicles are packed with Muslim brothers and sisters enjoying the life-enhancing software that he, Ali Mohammad Saad, has provided for them. His sensors, navigators and controllers are quietly going about their business recognizing voices, translating for each other, transmitting secret data, avoiding collisions, solving problems. And soon they will be guiding every faithful driver to a new strawberry-blond mosque—

Nobody approaches Ali for his autograph, which is fine. Less trouble. Being masked on TV was a good idea, and mascots mean more than individuals, he knows that. Nobody seems to be wearing the T-shirt printed with his photo—it's early winter after all. He grins at the clouded sky and feels the white wind on his face. He is at the epicenter of the world's motor industry: the home of mass production, the first-ever parking lot, the city that drove out public transportation. This is the capital of AutoCorp, one of the greatest companies on the planet, like Fuelz and Armz. Ali takes a deep breath. One of the greatest.

He walks a few yards to his car outside the new Islamic Academic Center. Two ladies step out of the SUV parked in front of him. He wonders what they look like. They are as mysterious to him as he is to his international supporters. He can only tell that one of the ladies is tall and one is short. They are covered head to toe in black. Gloves, eyes, the whole package. Ali loves that. More and more sisters are doing it. More and more sisters everywhere are refusing to show off. He averts his gaze as he is meant to do.

He wonders if he can stipulate on matters of dress when it comes to placing an advertisement for his wife. Of course he can. He gets into his car, and starts dictating the ad. The voice-recognition system is listening.

'Maker of Mosques . . . Destroyer of Shirk . . . High-paid High-level Software Engineer . . . SEEKS Prayer-loving . . . Fertile . . . Modest . . . Muslima . . . for Marriage, Children and Non-corrupt Lifestyle in Dearborn. Full Hijab Essential. Religious Innovators need Not Apply.'

★ ★ ★ ★ ★ ★ ★ ★ ★ ★ ★ ★ ★ ★ ★ ★

REIGN OF VIOLENCE

Crowds of protesters representing different minority interests continue to gather outside national and regional headquarters of entertainment giant LeizureScape. Fearful television staff have been prevented from entering or exiting Reall Life.

Violent scenes occurred early this morning as angry crowds smashed the world-famous Statue of Liberty at LeizureScape's Las Vegas HQ, injuring several workers. In LA, a man was impaled on LeizureScape security barriers. And in Orlando, Florida, the world's favorite mouse was taken hostage by terror organization Jihad-Joe. This follows yesterday's kidnapping by the same organization of celebrity abortionist Gilberto Heindel.

'You know, that fellow Oswald set something loose in the country,' stated notorious TV Producer Cherry Pickering.

When asked about the protests, Mark Washington, Vice President of Reall Life, quoted the words of Jesus in a rare phone interview: 'He that is not with me is against me.'

Washington was not prepared to comment further.

But a source close to Reall Life confirmed that *The TV President* format has been sold to as many as forty countries eager to emulate the program's success. Big spenders first in line include Chile, India, Pakistan, Egypt and Israel, where assassination is already a tried and tested theme for domestic audiences. Russia and Austria have also come to market, after earlier signs of caution. Italy and Holland have signed deals. And Nepal is thought to have brokered a 'multiple royal assassination' spin-off with the aid of anonymous sponsors, despite low TV ownership levels in that country.

'The serious money is in formats,' stated Wall Street broker Decker Duran. 'Reall Life can take a back seat now. It's growing serious revenue. Just look at the shares. Never mind the jackpot.'

While finances are spiking for Reall Life, an anonymous source alleges that rising star Fresno Jackie has been bankrolled on the basis that she is a multi-millionaire-in-waiting. The former hairdresser from California will be in a position to repay her alleged seven-figure debt

166

if husband John F. wins the election prize money. If not, the camera-shy stylist will likely sign a lifetime contract with LeizureScape worth millions.

'She hates the spotlight, but it'll be her only way out,' commented Mane Event colleague Bertha Alvarado. 'Too bad for her if the mushroom man wins.'

VIEWERS! Not sure which way to vote tomorrow? Relax! It's time for revision!!! All The TV President Trials, Tribulations, Conviction Tests and behind-the-scenes dramas are yours to browse in any language, any time, any place. Plus premium-rate viewers get strictly unedited access to the Big Day's shocking motorcade massacre. Tune in to Reall Life for state-by-state, vote-by-vote, moment-by-moment coverage of HyperFriday . . . LIVE!

VIEWERS! A historic first for Reall Life: vote-counting procedures have been harmonized nationwide! Forget the trouble with electoral college votes, precincts, absentees and provisional ballots! All you need for a fair vote is your TV handset. Choosing the world's No.1 leader has never been easier! Voting begins midnight tonight. Don't miss out. It's your democratic right!

★　★　★　★　★　★　★　★　★　★　★　★　★　★　★　★

Jackie Be Nimble

Still gripping the pistol, Jackie held up her phone and clicked. The flash was shocking. Another photo. Flash. The whole of Ammon, from head to toe. His shotgun, resting across his arm. His ammunition belt with its pouches of red and gold-capped cartridges, bright and festive as Christmas ornaments. Flash, flash, flash. She blew the hair trimmings off, zoomed in on his nicked and shaven face, his shorn and bleeding head. Her phone made the sound of an old-fashioned camera clicking and winding on film. Each flash lit up the room like lightning.

She wasn't sure why she was still holding her pistol. Ammon was not going anywhere just now. She zoomed in on his ghastly erection and snapped again.

'Say Cheez!'

She looked towards the door. Time was short. Elwyn was probably asleep in the car already. He always seemed to be dozy or sleeping. Poor, wounded president. He was healing. That's why it was up to her to organize everything. Costumes, transportation, dramas, everything. She was like a producer these days, like those people from Reall Life, only she was nice.

Jackie took some more souvenir shots, with the bed, the wall sampler, the rest of the room, before saving them in her digital gallery. She had to be quick. The little hour-glass picture spun round and around. So cute. But it took so long!

'Hair by Jackie at Mane Event,' she whispered like a model's voice in a shampoo ad, turning the phone off. She slipped it into her portable salon kit.

She pulled the kaftan down to cover Ammon's private parts. The action made her wince, worse than cleaning dog dirt off the carpet or lancing an abscess, which she had to do sometimes for the pups.

Ammon didn't move.

It was time Jackie did.

At last, she put down her gun. Her head was light. She was hungry.

It was time to wash the Bible man's blood off her hands, to fix her face in a mirror. She probably had blood on her face too. But there was no mirror. No seeing machines. She should have known. And what could she do about the blood on her sweatsuit? Thank Jesus she had a burqah. Those Hi-jabbers knew a thing or two about camouflage.

Hungry Jackies

The light outside was dark and dirty. The air felt more like water, fine rain sifting down in a mist. Jackie looked around her in every direction. There were no other vehicles in the parking lot. She stroked her burqah, hoping the rain would not go through to her sweatsuit and turn the invisible blood into liquid again. She felt a ripple of fear. She wished she had bought a spare outfit. But there hadn't been enough time to think through all the options.

Elwyn was asleep in the car, just as she'd expected. Saliva had gathered on his head-cover in a shiny wet patch.

She threw the bags into the back seat and slammed the door.

'Come on!' she said. 'We've got to get out of here before the morning shift. Ammon's going to wake up and call the police.'

'What about the doctors?' Elwyn said.

'Them too.'

She turned on the navigator, revved the engine, backed out. As she drove away she checked her rear-view mirror.

WANNA ESCAPE TV? the sign said backwards.

The navigator directed her toward I-40 East through North Little Rock. Yellow lights fuzzed in the rain. There wasn't a dog, or a paper boy, or a drunk, in sight. A car here and there, but not a single one with a blue police light. And no suspicious white sedans with tinted windows. Just gloom and closed factory outlets, rows of houses with shabby front yards.

'Someone's scratched the paintwork,' Elwyn said.

Jackie had seen the damage already. The scratches went deep into the shiny gold surface, deep into the honest metal.

'It looks like it says something,' he said. 'IOU. I think it's a threat.'

'It happened back in Hope. When we were inside the Fuelz store. I didn't want to tell you yet.'

'Last night? Are you sure? Why didn't I see it?'

'It's on my side, that's why. Anyway, you're reading things into

170

it.' She tried to sound devil-may-care, but she knew Reall Life was lurking everywhere.

'*IOU*,' Elwyn repeated. 'Maybe it was Bob Scrutt.'

'He's in Detroit. And why would he do a thing like that? Look, people scratch things on cars all the time.'

'So why didn't you tell me?'

She didn't want him to start getting scared again and quit. She had saved him from Reall Life, she had saved him from Ammon. She was sparing his feelings, although he didn't seem to bother about hers. He was as bad as all the others, even if he was gay. It didn't bear thinking about. Of course she'd suspected it all along, even though Elwyn was more secretive than John F. Everybody was more secretive than John F. Her husband had an open face like a pizza pie, no surprises there. Who else would cheat on their wife in front of a whole country? Even the pups had more secrets than John F.

'You're wounded. I didn't want you to get upset.' She turned on the radio.

Six out of seven Americans are going to be victims of violent crime in their lifetime. That could be you or your loved ones. So having the confidence to use Armz against your predator is not just a right, it's a noble cause.

'There, you see?' she said.

But Elwyn changed stations.

Yes I was intimate with him before he died, man to man, right here, under this bridge, it's a well-known spot for . . . Mind you, he looked quite different then, but I recognize his voice, and I recognize—well, they showed EVERYTHING on the—

Elwyn changed stations.

He was lab manager and culture collection curator, but he kept himself apart, acted superior. More like a loner, if you ask me. Then he went on some radical weight loss program and suddenly he was JFK—it was incredible!—and then he was making jokes all the time. If you ask me, it went to his head—

Elwyn switched the radio off. He was clearly upset.

Jackie knew they were talking about him. For a moment she felt sorry for him. It couldn't be easy to hear people saying such things, even if they were right. What would the girls at Mane Event say about her? *She kept herself apart.* Maybe she had more in common with Elwyn than she'd thought.

'Is it true you used to be fat and have a beard and not look like anyone?' she asked.

Elwyn was quiet for a while and then he burst out laughing.

'I'll bet nobody paid you any attention before,' she said. 'Just like me.'

'I can be fat and have a beard again, just you watch.' He sounded a bit crazy. 'I can't wait, Jackie: we can get married and be nobody together. Out of sight, out of mind. Live on Snax. Exercise our right to bear Armz. You can grow a beard too. They won't be able to identify us. We'll be mutants. Polymorphs.'

There he was using foreign words again. She frowned at him through her veil.

'Different shapes and sizes.' He paused. 'What did the medics say?'

'These things happen all the time in hotels.'

'They said that?'

She didn't want to think about Ammon. Her stomach rumbled. She had chewed on a few porkskins before veiling up, but it was not enough. 'We've got to eat or we'll die. Let's stop here. It's a drive-thru.'

A mile further down the road, they parked behind a church and unveiled to eat. Chicken-and-egg waffles, baby-pink milkshakes, multi-story muffins and coffee with French Vanilla non-dairy creamer. The car windows steamed up. Jackie felt satisfied and full, almost happy.

Elwyn stuffed the food into his mouth like a starving man and all the while he didn't say a word. No doubt he felt satisfied and full, just as she did.

After breakfast, they lowered their veils again.

The highway toward Memphis was straight and full of trucks in every lane. Clouds of white backspray jetted out and flooded the windshield worse than any soapy car-wash. Jackie was grateful for the light that penetrated her burqah, even if daytime visibility meant she had to remain under cover. At least she could see.

172

Workers on rain-swept cranes were fitting huge surveillance cameras to the tops of roadside poles.

But there was nothing to see. Just drab land, flat as an XMart hyper-lot. White sky that went all the way down to the green and rusty grass, no trees. Mist everywhere. A dead gray animal on the roadside in a furry hump. Old broken-down tractors and trucks. Trailer homes. Crop sprayers. Truck auction lots. One or two poor-looking houses near the curb. Nothing. Then at last, some trees.

Trees are normal, Jackie thought, *California is full of trees.* She could see Christmas trees, and twiggy trees stripped of their leaves. She wished she knew their names. Elwyn would know, but she didn't dare ask him. She couldn't tell if he was asleep.

The road was down to two lanes. The mist thinned. Farmers' fields stretched out to the horizon on all sides, full of low-cut plants and patches of shiny water. Flooded fields like mirrors.

'Ducks,' Elwyn said. It was the first thing he'd said since breakfast, more than two hours ago. He was awake after all. 'Mallards out there. Sitting ducks in here.' He sounded drunk.

Jackie kept driving, thinking, remembering. Reall Life had turned her into a fairground duck. 'I get mad just thinking about the things they asked us to do.'

'You never had to do the Conviction Tests,' Elwyn said.

'How dare you even start to feel sorry for yourself!' She was furious. If it wasn't for him and John F. being so stupid, so greedy—she never would have . . . 'You had a choice! You wanted the power or something. I wasn't running for President. You chose to do it!'

She bit her lip. She had signed the contract.

'You're right,' Elwyn said. 'I chose to do it.'

She didn't expect him to say a thing like that. Actually, it was the way he said it that made her pay attention. She waited for him to talk some more. She glanced across. His head was bowed. Maybe he was falling asleep again. But then after a while he lifted his head and spoke.

'My mother said it was a show for trailer trash. I don't think she appreciated quite how many people . . . I don't know what happened to me. I quit my job, everything. I'd gotten used to being on the other side of the lens. I started doing those lookalike contests for a joke. Then Reall Life came along and, I don't know, things started to get exciting.'

He pointed at the radio. 'That guy was jealous. He's past his sell-by date and he knows it. He'll never swing a high-profile mold case with a giant payout. He's not going to save crops or lives—and he knows it.'

Elwyn started making funny noises inside his burqah. He might have been crying or laughing. 'Funny thing is, he's on the radio now. My celebrity is going to his head.'

You're not as smart as you think you are, Jackie wanted to say. *You're still thinking about payouts and showing off.*

Elwyn went quiet. Then he spoke some more. 'But he was right: it went to my head.'

He sounded almost sorry. John F. never got that far.

Jackie checked the rear-view mirror. No sign of the creepy white car. 'I always used to think those shows were, you know, natural. Like you just carried on your life as usual, and the TV people just happened to be there recording it. I didn't know they made you do things. Once we'd been fighting and made up, but they made us argue some more, so they could get a different angle. And John F. got angry all over again. Real angry, like I've never seen before. One time, they fitted Clipper with a water-tube to make it look like he was wetting the carpet. Isn't that the cruelest thing you ever heard of?'

Elwyn did not answer.

'And secretly they put a split in my pajamas so when I bent over they could film my—you know. They zoomed right in.'

Elwyn still didn't say a word.

'It's like pornography, that's what. Porno.'

She didn't mention John F. with Mardie, or that channel to get the wife's reactions. She could feel herself getting upset.

'Ammon back there, that was legitimate self-defense,' Elwyn said. 'And you called the medics, right?'

'I said so, didn't I?' Jackie felt a shiver of fear. What if Ammon was dead? She'd been so engrossed in the hairdressing and the photographs she had forgotten just about everything. She turned off the navigator for something to do. 'He's probably groping the nurses right this very minute. —Oh God, look at that sign!'

'The best-paying slots in Tunica—'

'No, no. The other side.'

A close-up of John F.—ten, maybe twenty, feet wide—loomed over the road. A nice smile, one of his best. A headline across the top.

ASSASSINATED IN DALLAS! *He died so that you might vote.*

Jackie felt her stomach turn over. 'They're so cruel! Why are they so cruel?'

They were near Memphis now, skirting the edges a few miles west. The highway was lined with spurs and exit signs and promotions.

Another advertisement showed an African American face, close-up and grainy. He looked familiar.

ASSASSINATED IN MEMPHIS! *Don't miss the museum-experience! Next Exit.*

'Who's that?' she asked.

'Martin Luther King.'

'The King died here too. Poor Elvis. Poor Memphis. I'd love to see his home. He had green carpet on the ceiling. I wish we had time.'

She still felt churned up in the stomach. GET THE WIFE'S REACTIONS! She started to hum to distract herself. *Are you lonely tonight?*

But she could feel the anger rising up inside of her. She turned on the radio again.

As part of Operation Homefront Intelligence, we're putting in Armz security cameras and obviously they can be used for many purposes in the Terror Wars. You can be driving along at 80 miles per hour and those cameras can zoom in on the teeth in your smile—

She switched over to another station. If only she could find a station like The Best of Music.

—which is why we get micro earthquakes in this region every few days—

She and John F. used to love listening to The Best of Music. She could feel the tears choking up her eyes and sinuses. Now there was a woman singing how she'd been to Paradise but she'd never been to Me.

'That's too bad,' Elwyn said, changing stations for her. 'You keep your eyes on the road.'

It was wall-to-wall country-and-western songs with too many stories about people dying and people learning their lesson, which made her uncomfortable, or heavy rock which gave her a headache, or religious people discussing morals and Jesus, which normally she didn't mind, but it made her feel guilty about Ammon and other things, or advertisements for XMart and Foodz and LeizureScape that went on and on with long parts at the end where the announcer spoke so fast it was impossible to understand, just like the small print at the back of a catalog, or the back of her contract with Reall Life.

Elwyn switched over again.

—but eye witnesses have spotted the Kennedys in locations as far apart as Moscow, Idaho, and Melbourne, Florida. Listeners with any information relating to the assassination or the couple's whereabouts, are urged to call 2–4–1–KRIMETIME in confidence. A reward of one million dollars is being offered to witnesses who can lead the authorities to the missing persons.

And breaking news, just in: it has been confirmed today in Dallas, Texas, that the deceased presidential candidate is Elwyn Barter, the super-eligible botanist from New York City whose lifelong dream was to be voted America's No.1. News of the victim's DNA test results put an end to the rumor and confusion which threatened to hijack the election tomorrow, HyperFriday. Reall Life producers, and their sponsors, can breathe a sigh of relief as the ordinary voter's choice becomes clear once more.

In other news—

Jackie hit the radio control with the heel of her hand. She was terrified of what they might say next, what Elwyn would hear.

'They've killed me, men of science have pronounced me dead!' Elwyn reached for the radio.

Jackie slapped at him. Elwyn yelped. The SUV veered, straightened up again. She'd hit his wounded-arm hand.

'Dammit, we're crossing the river,' she said. 'I got so distracted with all those signs and everything. We must have missed our turn.'

They were trapped on the bridge, great struts of aqua-painted iron hanging high over the Mississippi.

She had to keep him in line. 'They're calling my bluff. They plan everything, every single itty bitty thing, but they never counted on changing their plans for Jackie Kennedy of Fresno.'

She remembered the camera left stuck on her television, how they kept on filming her secretly when her part of the contract was over and she was meant to be grieving the death of her husband in the privacy of her own home—but her contract with Reall Life would be valid again! She panicked. She needed time to think things through, but she had to distract Elwyn.

'And you know all those crowds?' she said, like she was making conversation.

'What crowds?'

'You know, fans. Or people mourning. Even those protesters you keep hearing about. How many of them are phonies? They're extras, like friends and family. Reall Life pays for them, you know, to get attention, like that fruit I brought you in hospital. Everything's worked out. Assholes.' It felt good to swear. She did it so rarely.

TENNESSEE

They passed the state line half-way across.

Texas, Arkansas, and now Tennessee, another state under her belt. Four days ago she'd never been outside of California. Maybe one day she would be able to boast she'd been to every state. Ahead, through fine rain, she saw a tall silver pyramid building, a concrete spaghetti junction, cars flying over and beside them every which way. Towering gravel levees. A steamer called The Mississippi Queen. Everything looked jumbled and exciting.

For a moment, Jackie toyed with the idea of stopping in Memphis and forgetting all about Bob Scrutt. Then she remembered Ammon in his pool of blood, still warm, the faintness of his pulse, the phone call she hadn't made. The things she'd hidden from Elwyn. The money she'd borrowed. The money she had to win. The confession she had to hear from the man who'd murdered her weak straying goat of a husband.

'It's a great big khaki monster,' Elwyn said as they crossed the river again. He sounded sad enough to throw himself into it.

ARKANSAS

Soon she would be able to add Missouri, Illinois and Michigan to her tally. Seven states already. Not bad for Fresno Jackie.

Jackie swerved onto the exit for Jericho.

'What are you doing?' Elwyn cried out.

The white car was after them.

'Dammit!' She hit the wheel. 'He's following us.'

'Who?'

'That detective guy. Pascillo. I'm sure it's him. With all these trucks he stands out like a . . . He's been somewhere behind us ever since Memphis—no, earlier!'

Elwyn twisted around.

In her rear-view mirror, Jackie could see the white car clinging low to the blacktop, its damaged grille looking like a snarl behind her. The rain had stopped so the air was clear but she couldn't see past the dark window glass.

'See him?' she said.

'Well, I can see a car.'

'We've got to lose him.' She revved past the speed limit.

For a long time the narrow blue-shield highway ran alongside the interstate, but then they crossed it into back fields and country.

Soon the road was empty behind her and Jackie felt her shoulders relax. She must have been wrong about the detective. There must be so many white cars on the roads, even with damaged fronts. She loosened her grip on the wheel. Slowed down. There were houses here and there, with beaten-up couches on their porches, all sorts of junk. Front walls and roofs patched in with flat metal sheets and corrugated iron. Trailers. Dogs. Funny little churches, just sheds with a steeple on top. Not a single soul in sight. Everything looked very poor, like those foreign places on documentaries.

Elwyn activated the navigator. 'We're near Lepanto, whatever that is.'

'Does it look big enough to get some gas?'

'Maybe. And some healthy food.'

'This time you can guard the car.'

178

'This time no porkskins.'

There were fields and more fields, flat as a lake, with dark low bushes in lines. Stripes of sunlight on a slant, pale yellow and heart-warming after all the bad weather. She eased off the accelerator. She could see shreds of white clinging on for dear life to all the bushes. Cotton! She could see rusty-colored brown stalks now, little green leaves.

'It reminds me of when I used to put John F.'s clothes in the wash without checking the pockets first for tissues. Those little bits of white just got stuck everywhere.' She choked back the sadness.

Elwyn didn't say a word.

Further down the road there were giant blocks of cotton batting, the size of trailers. Some had bright red covers, some green, some blue. She'd never seen cotton bales in real life before.

'I could sleep on top of one of those,' she said. 'I'd be the princess and the pea.'

Not a peep from Elwyn. He'd grown so quiet it was hard to believe it was still him.

She wondered and worried what he was thinking. Was it the news of his death? Would he try to leave her? The thought of him leaving her now was worse than anything she could imagine. And how could she ever return to Fresno without anyone, all alone forever?

WELCOME TO A SUNKEN LANDS TOWN

Lepanto was an old-fashioned place, with a main street straight out of a black-and-white movie. The stores had posts out front, and awnings over the sidewalks. Jackie liked the look of Lepanto. It felt safer than Hope. And there was no trace of that detective or his mean-faced vehicle.

At the gas station, she filled up and left Elwyn sitting inside the car. A sign told her to smile for security—she'd seen that one before. At least there were no eye-scanners or other ID-readers. She decided there were more cameras in the world than she could fret about, even in this cute old town in the middle of nowhere. She couldn't keep worrying about being caught on TV, especially now that she was anonymous. She was getting used to her burqah, moving more easily, feeling warm and cozy, like she was hiding inside a big black blanket.

In fact, the burqah was beginning to make her feel strong—strong as Superwoman, or Batgirl. It didn't matter what she looked like, or who she was, or if her hair was out of condition, or if she had food stuck in her teeth. She was totally invisible.

When the tank was full, she went inside the Fuelz store to pay.

It was a kind of café, with a few farmers and old ladies sitting at plastic-covered tables watching a big screen. There were racks of dimestore products—was that a person lurking behind them?—packs of smokeless tobacco and dry beef strips, Drinx coolers and fried Foodz lit up in a mini-oven.

Jackie scanned a tall unit with a sign on top: *The Latest Heirloom Collectables from Reall Life* . . . There were Jack and Jackie dolls in clear presentation boxes. Jack and Mardie action dolls. Souvenir AutoCorp model cars. Computer games and Holy Bibles from LeizureScape. Limited-edition boxes of Snax.

Jackie toyed with the idea of buying a set of oven mitts, each printed with a different gun—when she realized everything had gone deadly quiet.

She looked around. Everyone stopped whatever they were doing, even though they weren't doing much. They all stared, so bare-faced it was downright offensive. Worse than cameras.

Jackie put the oven mitts back on the shelf and went over to the Foodz oven.

'Are they meat?' she pointed.

The cashier looked at her as if she was speaking Indian.

Jackie positioned herself directly in front of the mini-oven and jabbed at it. 'Are you serving this food?'

The cashier nodded. Her hair was badly bleached, dry and hard like straw. She needed good salon advice.

'Are. They. Meat?' Jackie emphasized each word.

'Yes, ma'am, they're pork. We're all out of catfish.' The cashier broke into an irritating lipsticky smile. Her teeth were chipped and crooked, with bits of pink stuck on the moist enamel. She glanced out in the direction of the table sitters.

'Great,' said Jackie. 'Give me two of them.' She was not going to say please.

180

Slowly, so slowly, the cashier stuffed the fried pork rolls into plastic bags with sauce packets and polystyrene trays and heaps of napkins.

'And what about some beer?' Jackie said. 'Where's the beer?'

'I'm sorry, ma'am, we're too close to the church for that.'

'I see.'

Jackie paid in cash, as usual, and the woman nudged the food forward on the bench without saying a thing. So much for Southern hospitality.

'I hope you won't mind me saying but you've got lipstick on your teeth.' Jackie nearly spat the words out, loud enough for everybody to hear.

Then she turned to face her silent audience: a couple of ugly farmers, two mean old ladies, a fat boy with his mouth hanging open. Someone hiding behind the shelves. A skinny girl standing around with bad skin. All staring. All speechless.

'What's the matter with you stupid people?' Jackie cried out. 'Haven't you ever seen a Muslim before?'

Everything was quiet, but she could hear the sound of a LeizureScape program, a machine somewhere rumbling.

'Matter of fact, ma'am, tell the truth, no we haven't. Except on the news, when they're talking about the Terror Wars.'

The woman spoke as if she had all the time in the world. Still looking Jackie in the eye, she put one slow careful hand under the bench—on an alarm trigger, probably. Or a weapon. And then she spoke some more.

'Now one thing you have showed us today is that all kinds of folks have got a different appreciation of good manners. So thank you, ma'am, for visiting us here and you have yourself a nice day.'

Jack a Dull Boy

Elwyn was in the car, traveling slowly, maybe 10 miles an hour, floating a yard above the ground like a magic carpet. He was smiling behind his burqah, through his veil, loving the sweet people of Lepanto, appealing to their civic pride, winning their votes. He heard fireworks. They were letting off fireworks to celebrate, to release the extravagant emotion of the occasion, too great for their hearts. The car jerked. He jerked. He had practiced, back and to the left. There were helicopters above. There had been helicopters all day. Reall Life was up there. Others too. The police. Media coverage. He saw his giant simulcast face just before the roadside screen shattered and fizzed. The next shots were too loud for his ears. First the whiz over his shoulder, a shock wave, past his cheek, another over his head, behind him, thundering reports. Another screen crashed. *Back and to the left*, he thought. But he lunged forward and to the right. Fresno Jackie screamed and threw her bouquet into the air. She was on the car-floor clutching at his burqah. Shaky orange hair. Demented. Green stretch velveteen. The car was still moving forward. A lynch mob was after them. White burqahs with white pointed hoods and mean little eye-holes. Bullets tore through the upholstery. Bullets clanged off the metal. The SUV was being destroyed. What about the simulations? Had the audio started? It wasn't meant to hurt. It didn't hurt until his arm bounced—

'So much for Southern hospitality!' Jackie threw herself into the driver's seat.

Elwyn was cold and perspiring all over. Nightmare. His mouth was dry. Awake now. Nightmare. Awake.

'I got you some lunch,' she said. 'But it wasn't easy.' She passed him a plastic bag.

It was warm. The odor reminded him of airline food.

'I want to get away from here,' Jackie said. 'We've got to bare our faces to eat, and those people in there are all, you know, kind of crazy and staring at us.' With her lunch on her lap, she started the engine.

'I can't get used to this outfit. People treat you like you're the devil or something.'

Elwyn's head was muddled and jittery. He shivered. He was officially dead. Somehow that represented a coup for Jackie. He had been erased by Reall Life—why? To make the election easy? He and Jackie were flying up Tornado Alley like a couple of unhinged outlaws running from a crime scene, trying to disappear from view. They'd left a wounded man in their wake. And a tell-tale neck-brace. Where did he lose the neck-brace? Disappear? How many burqahs were there in the boondocks?

Outside town, Jackie pulled over, unveiled and tore open her stinking lunch pack.

Didn't she care? She was Californian. All the Californians he knew were health nuts. They advocated fiber and tofu and the death penalty for bad cholesterol. Even their truckstops served espresso and artichokes.

Elwyn was feeling poisoned. He was beginning to fear that there was no real food anywhere at all between the big cities. It was mall-to-mall Foodz, Drinx and Snax. Fat and sugar and salt and plastic. The idea made him panic. Jackie made him panic.

'I'm not hungry. You can have my share. I'm cold. I have to warm up and stretch my legs.' He got out of the car and started walking.

They had stopped near a cemetery. It was matter-of-fact, just a field of gravestones by the road, low and exposed to the sky. There were no walls, not even a pasture fence to contain the spread of the dead.

The ground was soggy. Rich alluvial soil. He looked for signs of fungi. Saprotrophs, consumers of dead organic matter. Keratinophiles, connoisseurs of protein—hair and fingernails. The gravestones were bright green and white and orange with concentric circles, waves, lichen clouds consuming the names of people.

Lichen, tough stuff. The dual organism, a partnership of fungus and alga. Just like him and Jackie, depending on each other for survival. Neither of them could survive on their own. Or could they? She had saved him from Reall Life.

—Or could they?

He was convalescing and she was feeding him junk food, fattening him up, locking him in a car for days on end, driving him straight toward his would-be assassin. What for? A confession, she had said. He was jittery. Or another attempt on his life? Those emails from Bobo were demented. He couldn't think straight. He had to see those emails again. He was exhausted. He was walking. Stumbling. His hems were wet and heavy. Lichen. A mutualistic association. Just like him and Jackie. He imagined the lunch he would like to be eating right now: asparagus yakitori, wild arugola salad, corn-fed poussin, char-grilled polenta with braised porcini. *Boletus edulis.* He yearned for Manhattan, hungered for it. He pictured the market in Union Square. That's where all the fresh produce was, even the farmers. Ironic. He was walking. He was falling. He was walking in a muddy field now. He was back home near his apartment in the Upper West Side. Near his old school. The oldest school. Private not public. If he walked five more blocks he would reach the site of John Lennon's assassination. When was a murder an assassination? How many presidents had been shot dead? Too many. And how many failed attempts? Even among assassins—striving, planning, ambitious assassins—there were those who succeeded, and those who failed, winners and losers. Who had tried to kill him? Was Jackie right about Bob Scrutt? Was Bob the lone gunman or were there others? There were too many bullets. He had to see those emails again. Too many bullets. Too many firing lines. Why was nobody getting arrested? Amazing how unchanged Dealey Plaza was—only they couldn't stop a Texas Live Oak from growing—how so many things were exactly as they had been on that fateful day decades ago. Like *Great Expectations.* Jilted. Frozen. The depository, the railway bridge, the white picket fence—what was a picket? Did it refer to the shape or the wood or the arrangement? Did it have to be a fence? They had tried to kill him. But he was alive and walking, he was walking. Stumbling. Straying. He wasn't used to it. He was panting. He was tempted to keep on walking. The sky was huge. Empty. Clean. He had no money, no ID, nothing, but he had a burqah for a blanket. It was fall. He would forage for macrofungi. Berries. Rabbits. Fish. He'd get lost in the swamps and bayous and bottomland forests. He felt strangely free. He would survive. He would keep on walking.

The first shot sounded like fireworks. But only for a moment. The second shot seemed to come from everywhere at once. The sky was full of echoes. Then he heard the car horn, insistent as an alarm.

Elwyn gathered up his skirts and ran, tripping, staggering back to the SUV. The engine was revving. His heart was revving. She was ready to go. He was safe. The car stank of Foodz. His arm hurt. She accelerated. He was safe.

'Who was it? Did you see them?' he gasped.

They were speeding. She drove through crossroads without stopping, sped past signs so fast he didn't know which towns were near. She checked the rear-view mirror. He turned round to see. His neck hurt.

'Did you see them?'

They cut back under the interstate highway and drove right up to the Mississippi's banks through a town called Osceola. At last she stopped, as if to get her breath back from running. She did a U-turn.

Some black kids were playing ball between old clapboard houses at the end of town huddled up against the levees. Election boards were stuck in the grass, one after the other.

VOTE ELWYN BARTER!
VOTE ELWYN BARTER!
VOTE ELWYN BARTER!
VOTE ELWYN BARTER!

'We've lost him,' she gasped.

'Who?'

'That Asshole Pascillo.'

Elwyn was safe.

Jackie obeyed the speed limit all the way back through Osceola.

On both sides of the road he recognized the same old big brands in their bright plastic building blocks, one after the other, stranded in plains of concrete. He searched their parking lots for a white sedan car.

Was he really safe? Was Jackie imagining things?

They rejoined the interstate highway heading north. The road signs were green again. He couldn't talk and Jackie didn't say a word until they crossed the state line.

'Missouri,' she said. Then she said no more.

The blacktop got rough. They crossed countless little bridges over little rivers, speeding through tawny cropfields and bare-branched woodland. Fall color was long past its peak, but solitary leaves clung onto sycamores, sweetgums, hickory and silver maples. Elwyn drank in the bright red of spicebush berries, the crimson of catkins, the brown of oak leaves. He tried not to think about the gunshots, but he kept hearing them in his head, insistent as a tune he wanted to forget. His head was muddled. He had trespassed onto some bigot's land, provoked a cowpoke. Or strayed too far for the detective's comfort. What was Reall Life's script now? Why didn't Pascillo just arrest them?

When the signs pointed the way to St Louis, they switched highways, reaching Cairo at twilight, where the monster Mississippi kinked and split in two. The light was murky, the vegetation skeletal against the sky.

'My eyes are so sore,' Jackie said. 'Maybe we should stop here. At least I can take this thing off now it's dark.'

But in Cairo they got lost, crossing the rivers again and again, hurtling along narrow iron crib-bridges or high ridges above flood-plains, roads so tight it was impossible to stop or pass. Jackie was driving too fast. The SUV veered, narrowly missed the roadside barriers.

'If we can just find the Interstate again, there's some kind of national forest up ahead,' Elwyn said. Anything to get out of the car, someplace he could think, away from her. She was driving so badly he couldn't think. 'The navigator shows it as green land. Maybe they have lodges. It looks kind of remote. We can stay in Thebes, or Karnak, Lake of Egypt or Vienna.' He began to sing, silly as a canary in a mine. 'One of these things is not like the other—'

'Please don't do that,' Jackie said. 'You're distracting me.'

When he saw the reassuring red and blue I-57 shield, Elwyn felt like shouting for joy. But he knew not to. Jackie was still concentrating. Or sulking. He couldn't tell. At least the road would be straight and wide again. He had to think of a plan to get away before Detroit. His feet were pinched and wet. His arm was hot and pulsing.

It wasn't until Ullin—a nowhere highway-exit place in the national forest, with a Fuelz stop lit up like a shrine in the black night, and a LeizureScape motel full of lone hunters in camouflage lugging crates of firearms back and forth, and a diner next-door serving home-cooked fried catfish, fried okra, hominy, turnip greens and bean stew—that Elwyn had the realization: those shots outside Lepanto had come from Jackie's pistol.

★ ★ ★ ★ ★ ★ ★ ★ ★ ★ ★ ★ ★ ★ ★ ★

HYPERFRIDAY LATEST SHOCK

Fresh controversy springs up in the wake of *The TV President* getaway rumors. Unconfirmed reports that survivor John F. Kennedy of Fresno and his wife Jackie are on the run disguised as Fundamentalist Muslims or Mexicans have led to a series of alleged civil rights abuses in cities and towns all over the country.

'In the last two days alone, we've filed reports on 40 instances of hate crime,' stated FBI media spokesman Tip Truly.

He added: 'The incidents range from aggravated assault, and simple assault, to intimidation such as ethnic slurs and verbal abuses, with strangers in the street lifting face-veils off Muslim females or plucking at the moustaches and head hair of Mexican males.'

Nikita Atsugi of the National Homefront Select Committee for Racial Equality, Inter-Faith Cooperation and Ethnic Affairs (NHSCREIFCEA) commented: 'This development is totally un-American.'

'Naturally, any such act is inexcusable,' was the verdict of Louisiana Kohn, bestselling author of *Home Sweet Home*. 'But let's not forget that these groups, who wish to pursue special victim status, continue to stream into our country, often to escape the tyranny or poverty of their own homelands. You've got to ask the question: where would they rather be?'

My Little Eye host Corliss Claunch said in a press announcement today: 'The time has come for a show of solidarity. I urge all patriotic Americans to take the Spartacus route. All women, and men too, should don the burqah, or the poncho, sombrero and moustache. The authorities can't send us ALL to jail!'

Official responses from the Muslim and Mexican communities have been few and far between. Ali Mohammad Saad, familiar to *The Big Dealey* players as 'Radical Ali', issued a written statement saying: 'The Prophet hates men in drag.' Specialist employment lawyers up and down the land are filing a number of test-cases in which devout women claim to have been fired by their employers simply for wearing the hijab veil to work.

188

Meanwhile, the two fugitives at the heart of *The TV President* drama have not yet been found. Efforts are being made by Operation Homefront Intelligence to trace internet transactions, phone-calls and emails connected with Fresno Jackie. The salon stylist is alleged to be in breach of her contract with Reall Life.

Eye-witnesses claim to have spotted the romantic runaways in locations as far apart as Moscow, Idaho, and Melbourne, Florida. Video security recordings appear to simultaneously locate the couple at a KashKwik outlet in Los Alamos, New Mexico, a Drugz store in Sioux Falls, South Dakota, and an XMart warehouse in Lynchburg, Tennessee.

In other news:

Detectives are investigating an armed robbery earlier today at a gas station in Normal, Illinois, in which two thieves caught on camera got away unidentified, thanks to their unusual choice of disguise. They were not wearing biker helmets or head-stockings, but full-length burqahs normally worn by females. However, 'ear witnesses' present at the crime scene testified that both attackers had male voices. According to one analyst, this may be a new form of copycat crime.

Latest HyperFriday polls show the deceased candidate Elwyn Barter of New York and the living candidate John F. Kennedy of Fresno are neck and neck. Voting numbers look set to reach the highest levels since records began.

★　★　★　★　★　★　★　★　★　★　★　★　★　★　★　★

Jack Frost

Elwyn could detect the edges of unfamiliar objects arranged like obstacles around his bed. Where was he? He was freezing cold, shivering like a whippet. A mean streak of artificial light slipped through the slit where the curtains failed to meet. He could see, he knew what things were, that a table was a table, that a window was a window, but he wasn't making sense of them. He was just a pair of eyes. Where was he?

He remembered that he was in a motel, upstairs, near a highway, stuck in the crotch of a national forest crawling with hunters. There were noises outside. Below. Coming from the SUV or near it. Was that detective breaking in or scratching more words into the paintwork? *IOU.* Was it Jackie who had scratched the paintwork? Elwyn moved as quietly as he could. His arm was hot and painful. His wound was seeping through the dressing. The thought made him feel sick.

Jackie was asleep in her own bed. Her breathing was emphatic, not quite a snore. His bed creaked as he sat up. Her breathing altered. He waited. She turned over and her mouth made rhythmic bubbling sounds like a fish. He stood up. He felt dizzy. He could make out the table more clearly now, the bags on the floor, the chair draped with his burqah and tracksuit. He tiptoed to the window and stuck his head through the gap in the rubberized curtains. The light was gas-pink, the color of all-night parking security. Beyond the motel fence the world was very dark.

A sheen of frost had crazed the golden roof of the SUV. Nobody was breaking into it, and nobody was scratching words on it.

In the next bay, a hunter in full army camouflage was arranging nets and boxes in the back of his pick-up. Releasing catches. Closing doors. Piling up bags of tackle. His body cast stark double shadows between the parking lot lights.

Elwyn gazed down from his safe perch in the darkness, scoured the pick-up with his eyes, felt like a sly monkey hiding in a tree. Shaking. So cold! A bunch of keys rattled and glinted at the hunter's belt.

A few car spaces along, two capped and camouflaged hunters were unloading their pick-up, lifting heavy plastic crates and carrying them purposefully away. Wordless. Their breaths made steam puffs. Some of the containers were long enough to hold rifles and shotguns inside. Others were square and sealed. Elwyn watched, and kept watching, shivering all the while. A cloud appeared on the window-pane where his breath condensed. He was freezing.

What was he to do?

He had not confronted Jackie about the gunshots in Lepanto. Perhaps he was wrong and she really had saved him from a phobic farmer, or that shadowy detective. He didn't know what to think. He had turned in on himself, tried to make himself small and inconspicuous. She didn't seem to notice or care. She was wrapped in her purpose, determined as any hunter.

What was he to do?

He was so cold. She was asleep. He could escape, steal her cash in a second—her purse was on the floor by the bedside table, he had watched for it—but how could he get away? He had no ID. His driver's license was—he had to think hard—when was the last time he was himself? Back in Dallas. In that hotel room. The presidential suite. His driver's license was there, along with his wallet, his credit cards, his clothes, shoes that fit. What would Reall Life do with his belongings now that he was officially dead? Maybe his things were in a bag, ready for his mother to collect. With no ID, car rental was out of the question. Besides, he was in the middle of nowhere and Jackie would wake up long before any rental car showed up.

What was he to do?

With enough cash he could pay somebody. One of the hunters. If he offered them enough money, surely they'd be prepared to miss a day of slinking about and slaughter. What was one day in a season? He would pay for their room, an extra night, as many nights as they wanted—but what was his story? Was he a veiled Muslim woman or a JFK impersonator? Was he a she, escaping the evil sister who wanted to marry her off to a foreigner with unpatriotic—worse still, terrorist—leanings? Or was this the moment to unveil, to bare his famous face? There was a bounty on his head.

191

Which hunter would he pick? He would pick the wacko, of course he would, the small guy with big needs, the marksman who would shoot him accidentally on purpose, deliver him up wriggling and helpless to Detective Oscar Pascillo. The monosyllabic bachelor from rural Notown would swiftly expand to fill the TV vacuum, before returning to his shady hideouts armed with fame, Jackie's cash and a monstrous reward from *KrimeTime*. Reall Life would love the camouflage outfit. They would find blood among the blotches. Deer blood. Barter blood. LeizureScape would release new interactive hunting games before hunting season closed.

The sky had turned a shade lighter, and Elwyn could just make out thick columns of black birds migrating across it. He wondered how long they had been flying. He imagined he could hear the beat of their wings. If only he could fly. He shivered.

He would have to wait until Detroit. A big city would be safer. He could give Jackie the slip, disappear into a neighborhood of Mexicans or Muslims, find himself a doctor—his wound was infected, he was sure of that, his arm was too painful, he was too cold, he had a fever—he had lost his train of thought—where was he? In Detroit, with the Mexicans, in disguise, with the good Muslim doctors, biding his time until he could think of what to do next.

Or he could simply call 2–4–1–KRIMETIME and hand himself in. Reall Life would take charge again. Jackie would be out of his hair. There would be no more hiding, no more running, no more pretending to be someone else. He would be a bona fide American citizen again, in full possession of himself, in full view of the law. He would go back to work at the lab. Commute. Drive to New Jersey every day just like he used to. Or get a new job in Manhattan, ride the subway just like any other strap-hanger. He'd come out. Clear the closet. But the cameras would be on him once more, crawling all over him like bugs, probing his every pore. They would damn him for being gay and presidential. He would burn in the public glare. There'd be a sniper waiting for him around every corner. He was a dead man walking. No, he wasn't ready for Reall Life yet.

What was he to do?

The hunter below pressed his electronic key in mid air. His pick-up beeped and winked, locked.

That was it!

He had been thinking crookedly, stupidly. He didn't need to rent a car or pay a driver. All he had to do was steal Jackie's keys and purse. He would drive to Detroit—no, better still, Chicago. Paris on the Prairie. New York on the Lake. And Jackie would be stuck: no car, no money. The shoe would be on the other foot. He would be rid of her.

He pulled back from the window and scanned the room again. His head was spinning.

She was still asleep, making soft grinding noises, clenching her teeth. His dentist on Broadway could see to that. *Tap tap tap*, he'd say, identifying the offending cusps. *It's showtime! Tap tap tap!*

Broadway, Manhattan, another country.

Elwyn stepped carefully towards the chair and lifted the tracksuit. The pain in his arm made him wince. The fabric rustled and swished. He had to be careful. Synthetic sparks would strike out into the darkness, wake up Jackie and blow his cover. His heart was beating fast, louder than a creaking bed. He held the table to steady himself as he dressed, first one leg, then the other. One sleeve, then the other. He picked up the sneakers. Pain shot through his neck. He took a deep and soundless breath. He slung the burqah over his good arm. It felt heavy.

Jackie turned over. She was fish-lipping again.

Elwyn crept as slowly as he could without losing balance, all the way to the other side of her bed. Her purse was on the floor, the same black purse she had clutched in the hospital when she first appeared in his life and declared him to be her darling husband for all the lenses to see. It was a memory from a long time ago. How many days? He almost felt nostalgic—

'What are you doing?' she said all of a sudden, her voice awake and clear.

He gulped a mouthful of air and coughed. He coughed so hard he thought he would cough up his heart. His stomach was clenched. He wished for her swift cunning, but he couldn't think of a single answer that would satisfy her. He was shaking like a sick dog.

'A picket, what's a picket?' he babbled.

'Are you OK?' Jackie sat up.

He could see the shape of her wild hair against the headboard. He coughed for time.

'Is it the shape or the gap?' he said.

'Poor thing. They shot you. You're still healing,' Jackie said.

Had he said enough? Did she believe him? Did she trust him? He still didn't know how to read her.

'You've been sleep-walking,' she yawned. 'Go back to bed and get some rest.'

He obeyed, meek as a pet, slipping under the covers, closing his eyes, shivering, and biding his time until Detroit.

Jackrabbit

The Illinois landscape swelled and rippled, the road cut through rock, coniferous and deciduous woods, past lakes with rushes, a bright blue private prison, tall water-towers with town-names, bold and bulbous against the rain-washed sky.

Marion

West Frankfort

Salem

We were hooked on pig shows, a man on the radio was saying. *I joined the local pig club,* his wife enthused. *We decided to start a family, have our own pigs.* Their favorite slept on a real bed with heaps of educational toys, heirloom tomatoes and other gourmet food.

Elwyn switched over.

If you have a heart attack, the micro-chip in your clothing uploads your medical history and reports your location. With ubiquitous and invisible intelligence—

Elwyn switched over.

—these guys are sayin' that climate change is the biggest threat facing all of us, bigger and worse even than terrorism—

Yes, we're rocking into HyperFriday, the day we've all been waiting for, the votes are pouring in and, thanks to global-positioning technology, we're getting a state-by-state countdown of the—

—airbrushed color body detail by Drugz. Every single celebrity has a tan! Everyone wants to glow like the stars—

Jackie turned the radio off. 'I wish they had The Best of Music.'

Elwyn preferred it quiet anyway. He had to think. He couldn't think. The news was beginning to frighten him. The advertisements frightened him. He couldn't tell the difference. Infomercial. Advertorial. Docusoap. It was cross-pollination. Miscegenation. Advertainment. He couldn't focus. Jackie frightened him now. The less said, the better. It was easy to withdraw inside his burqah. It made him feel safe, even from Jackie all wrapped up in hers. He could sleep, or pretend to sleep, retreat under his cone of silence. He had to think,

195

and plan, but he couldn't. He gazed at the landscape and his mind drifted. He remembered going to a petting zoo in the country when he was a child, and feeding a horse some hay, but the horse bit him deep in the fat of his hand, and his father kneeled down to prise open his bleeding fist, and Elwyn vomited on his head. His father died just days later, but Elwyn had been too young to understand the crossroads of coincidence.

They sped past shorn cornfields, a shining white plastic crucifix taller than a phone tower, a Bible factory outlet, an Adult outlet. At the university town of Champaign (another sprawl of Fuelz, Foodz, LeizureScape and XMart buildings), Jackie stopped to re-fuel. She kept hold of the keys. Elwyn tried very hard to think and plan, but he dozed off, worrying about champagne and campaigns.

He woke just as Jackie returned to the car, and a woman ran up to her and grabbed her sleeve. She was some of kind of hippie Tinkerbell, all bangles and gauzy layers.

'You have a beautiful body!' she cried out, earnest and shining. 'Don't be ashamed of your body. Show it! Show it!'

Jackie shook her off. 'I'll do what I like with my body!'

She got back inside the SUV and pulled the door shut. 'Damn dropout! Who does she think she is anyway?'

The woman stood in the middle of the forecourt, crestfallen.

Jackie started the engine and drove off, close enough to run over toes. The woman leaped out of the way.

They were back on the highway in minutes. Elwyn felt as if he had been sitting beside Jackie for weeks, years. The road was straight and long, lined with cameras on concrete posts. Lens after lens. He worried about micro-chips in the blacktop, micro-chips in the car.

'We seem to have lost our tail,' she said at last. She seemed happy. Lighthearted, even. It was unnatural.

Elwyn tried to remember how he'd first heard about Pascillo. News, billboards—or just Jackie? He couldn't remember. His mind was fuzzy. Was the detective a figment of her imagination?

'See that? Land of Lincoln!' Jackie pointed at number plates on the trucks in front, blithe as a tourist.

Elwyn said nothing. Kennedy was assassinated in a Lincoln. Both presidents were shot in front of their wives, both buried in conspiracy. Their dates matched. Their stories were crossed and crossed with coincidence. One wrapped around the other. History made circles—like lichen, like tree trunks—not straight lines.

The fields looked groomed, rich and beautiful despite the lack of contour. A hand-painted sign peeked up from the grass by the roadside.

Crooks are many—

Farm buildings were pristine geometric shapes arranged in still-life clusters. Russet barns, white walls, olive roofs, bottle-green, egg-blue roofs, silver towers. There was a stark beauty here. Could he live in a place like this?

Another sign. *Guns are few—*

He felt so cold. Could he hide in a place like this? He could go on a Witness Protection Program. Advise on fungal troubles—crops, soil. Become the local hero. Get found out. Exposed. Mobbed.

Crooks have guns—

A cargo train, rust-red and black, threaded across dirt-gray land, worn gold land, so flat, empty. He was nowhere. For days they had been driving in a straight line through nowhere. There was so much nowhere. Most places were nowhere.

Why can't you?

Where did Jackie hide her pistol? In a holster or the Mexican carry? Did she keep it under her pillow? In her burqah pocket? It was a man's pistol, too big and heavy for her little fingers.

GUNS SAVE LIFE.

He could still see her standing over Ammon, unable to put the weapon down. She was right-handed. Extra weight in the right pocket would explain why her burqah hitched up on the left, the exposed ankles in Hope—would Jackie shoot at him? She had saved him. Twice now. Would she shoot at him? He shuddered. He turned the heating on.

'Jackie, what exactly do you want me to do when you—we meet up with Bob Scrutt?'

'Nothing. I just need a witness, that's all.'

He didn't believe her. His next question was harder. He thought about it for a while. 'What are you going to do with that gun?'

'He'll confess, that's all.'

'That's all you want?'

'Let him say what he's done. But I need a witness, you know, or it's just his word against mine. You know how they go back on themselves and deny everything.'

'So . . .' Elwyn forgot what he was thinking, he pictured his father, thin as a photograph, he pictured himself with all the weight he needed to throw a heavy punch in high school, then he remembered, he remembered what he was going to say and he chose his words with care. 'So it doesn't have to be me.'

'Who else can I trust? Remember what you said? We're like magnets. We're famous. I don't have anybody else.'

He had felt the same way about her. She had saved him. Their fates were bound together until after the election, after the payout. But now she was delivering him faster than vital body parts to his would-be assassin. He was shaking with cold.

'Bob Scrutt wanted to kill me, Jackie. Maybe he still does.'

'You can keep the burqah on. He won't know it's you.'

'I'm six-one. You're supposed to be on the run with your husband. Maybe he'll work it out.'

'He can't see you, you can see him, that's what counts.'

'Jackie, I think my wound's infected. My head—my arm's no good for anything.'

'Haven't you been taking your Drugz?' She was putting on a voice. She was play-acting again, enjoying herself. 'Naughty, wounded president! Soon as we stop.'

It was early evening when the signs for Chicago appeared overhead and the city's great glow reached out from the horizon.

But Jackie turned right without saying a word, without glancing at the navigator or turning on the voice-guide. She knew exactly where they were going. How did she know? Clever, scheming Fresno Jackie. They crossed the Indiana state line, passed over factories and yards, followed four lanes solid with trucks and cars heading east on I-94. The road was flat and straight and full of signs.

Kennedy Avenue, Lincoln Oasis, Phantom Fireworks, Armz from Boom to Zoom.

If you are betting more than you can afford to lose, then you've got a problem.

The signs were talking to Elwyn like voices in a dozing dream.

Character is what you are in the dark, Exit now! Advanced Cosmetic Dermatology.

Winterization.

Welcome to Michigan—home of AUTOCORP! shouted a huge silver wrench by the curb, tall as an office block.

The messages were coming too fast for him to think. He read them all, in different voices inside his head, enthusing, confusing, commanding, berating, taunting him.

U-Pick-Your-Own Sheriff, State Police Exit, Jail, Easy to get to, hard to leave.

LeizureScape Simulators best enjoyed before lunch, Snax, Drinx, Foodz galore!!!

Girls! Girls! Girls! Pipe organ played daily, Sex for life, Christ died for our sins.

The TV President chooses Drugz, Official Tan of the Dallas Cowboy Cheerleaders.

A black-and-white photo of himself—or John F.—hung over the highway. It looked like both of them, and neither of them. How could he not recognize himself anymore? The expression was serious, infinitely meaningful.

DEAD OR ALIVE? Which one do you WANT?

'Detroit City Limit,' Jackie announced.

Insects and rodents holding you hostage?

'Bob Scrutt here we come.' She sounded pleased with herself.

Elwyn tried to picture the man on the motorbike behind him on the Big Day. He couldn't. He remembered the uniforms, epaulets, exhausts, the gleam of vintage parts. *Back and to the left*, he had steeled himself for his last ever Conviction Test. But he had lunged forward and to the right. Like a dance. Not meant to hurt. Weapons above. Weapons below. Reall Life. Security. Coverage. He saw his own face on a giant screen just before it shattered and crashed. The car was still moving forward. Bullet holes in the upholstery. Bullets bouncing off metal. What about the simulations? The car was still moving forward. Heading east toward Mr Mardie Scrutt, the nation's favorite cuckold. Bob Scrutt. The name was the name of his executioner.

The Big Dealey—Today's Bets

'HUMBLE PIE' 1-WAY BET
Suspect: Bob Scrutt
Firing Line: Security Motorbike behind Presidential Limo
No. of bullets: 2
Motive: Revenge
Odds at 12:30 p.m. CST: 6/7
Total no. of bets placed on all suspects: 31,428,571
HyperFriday started at midnight!
This is the last day of the greatest game ever!

Bob Scrutt's TV has no sound and no action. Just pictures of stairwells, lobbies, landings, shafts. Security for every story, every entrance and exit. Now and then, he gets a bit of entertainment: illegals trailing garbage bags on the seventh floor; a civilian couple arguing silently on the street.

As he buffs the screen with his XMart superkloth, Bob whistles. No one is listening. The lobby echoes. Bob likes things clean. He also likes things neatly folded, ironed flat, straight. He doesn't like Reall Life.

Will they get to him before he goes AWOL? Ever since the Big Day there's been a kind of negative energy running through his veins. He's been on edge, shaky and thirsty. He's been wanting liquor again. Tonight he's craving it. He has packed his duffel bag. It's under the front desk. He has a feeling they're coming for him. He's not running scared of Reall Life. He's just prepared. *Bring 'em on*, he's thinking. Bring 'em on. Ready with his service stuff, even his Field Jacket, his favorite photos of Mardie looking beautiful and holding his hand. He misses her, she's an ache in his chest.

On Bob's second TV it's a different story. There's action. Everybody's talking and hysterical. Mouths opening, heads bobbing up and down with the election coverage. It's HyperFriday, and votes have been coming in since midnight.

Nobody has to wait around for the counting because there's none to do. Every vote is instant. The numbers are ticking over, easy as a gas pump.

Bob refuses to vote in this particular election. He's making a stand.

He stops whistling. He wants to hear more but he keeps the volume on low. He knows about respect, even if no one else in Civvy Land gives the word a second thought. There's no respect out there, no gratitude either. It's because of men like him that civilians can sleep at night. He fought in the first of the Terror Wars, although nobody used that name back then. He didn't die in a blaze of glory, didn't get his picture on the front page.

He turns up the volume, carefully, one notch. They're interviewing the Vice President of Reall Life.

Everybody's watching, Mark Washington says. *And everybody's voting. Who in the world hasn't seen the the Big Day Massacre? In pure television terms, this is bigger than the atom bomb, the moon landing, the twin towers.*

'Pure,' Bob Scrutt repeats. He likes to say things over.

Washington wriggles out of questions, talks about the importance of law enforcement. Washington is troubled by the missing candidate, Bob can see that in the cozy civilian eyes.

The bets are on, Cherry Pickering is saying. She reminds Bob of some kind of bird. He doesn't know the names of birds, but he knows she has a beak and the sort of raised round eyes that look backwards and sideways while they're looking straight ahead.

'The bets are on,' Bob Scrutt repeats her words.

He has met Cherry, shaken her hand. She's the one who gave him the job in the motorcade. *We've vetted you*, she said. *The casting people say you're over-qualified! That's why we're offering you the No.1 security position. But we wondered . . . is the role a little bit close to home?*

'Where I live, unemployment is 40 per cent,' Bob says to the lobby. The elevator doors are his audience, and there are two potted plants with absorbent multicolored gravel. The walls echo. Bob is repeating the speech he wrote down very carefully and then memorized, the words he said to Cherry Pickering in his job interview—which she referred to as his audition piece.

'Everything's falling down and broken, bad as places I saw in the Terror Wars. We got a big hole in the heart. We got dollar stores. And immigrants. Kids get shot for their shoes. My wages are low. I'm a security guard, but I got no security. My wife Mardie died. The army used to be my family. They took care of the bills. Fed me. It was them or Mardie. Even after my honorable discharge, I been offering protection to my country. See what happened last time we got the president in a car without a top? It was a security issue. I'm a security guard.'

The Big Dealey is just a spin-off, Cherry Pickering is saying on the TV now. *The election is the main event. Everybody knows that.*

Bob scratches her nose with his big finger. If she was putty he'd be making her look different. Deformed even. But she's not, and she keeps talking to the interviewer with a straight face. Bob cleans off his fingerprint with the XMart superkloth. It looks like he's cleaning her head. He wishes he could rub her out.

The Big Dealey simply gives viewers the opportunity to play poker with wounds, and so on, from the comfort of their own homes.

Everything she says sounds like it has double meanings. Bob can vote for the President, anyone can vote for the President, but he can't bet because he's a Suspect. He's got privileged insider information. He doesn't have to guess what he did and didn't do on the Big Day. He knows. He was there, armed to the teeth, ready to shoot his two enemies dead—he checks his other screen for a moment. The fighting couple are gone; the janitors are dragging their feet.

Cherry still is talking.

Optical and acoustical enhancement products are selling faster than our teams can encrypt them. Sales of games have gone ballistic. We're so lucky to be living in this era—gamers and betters can buy everything they need to make an informed choice. Voters too.

Cherry Pickering. Who has a name like that in real life? Bob figures she chose it specially like a stage name. She's the one who signed up Mardie, took her out of her decent family home and spread her wide, pimped her, coast to coast.

And here's some exciting news: you can bet on the election outcome too, with the all-new tele-concept Dubble-Trubble. Gaming started just hours ago but the bets are already flooding in! People are reaching out in a tidal

*wave of participation. Who said viewers were becoming jaded? It's . . . it's
. . . overwhelming!*

Bob Scrutt refuses to vote, he's making a political point. But now, suddenly, Cherry's saying he can bet on the election outcome. It's a brand new program.

He takes out his phone and stares at it. Tonight he's going AWOL. He's going to drink again. He's going for broke. He calls DUBBLE-TRUBBLE. His fingers are moving slowly but his heart is going fast, like the first time he did target practice, or his first time with a hooker.

He selects ELWYNBARTER and bets 1. He's the dead one in the morgue. The winner has got to die.

He selects JOHNFFRESNO and bets 2.

He selects the margin: 3.1428%.

How much money is he willing to play? There's no limit. When Mardie went back to acting work she said it was for the money. After the army, he never made enough to please her.

Why did she die? There's an answer to that question. It is for Bob to ask why. If he ponders long enough, he's sure to find at least one answer for every question concerning Reall Life.

Bob clears his bank and sends his bet. His fingers are moving in jerks. Now he really has nothing to lose. What's done is done. His heart is beating harder, faster than a dose of combat Drugz. His hand is shaking as he pours himself some milk. Full fat. Mardie always used to buy the no-fat milk. She worried about her weight. She went on diets. She wanted to lose a bunch of weight. But he liked his Mardie lardy. Loved her. Once he caught her cursing at the mirror with no clothes on, when she thought no one was looking. He reminded her Marilyn Monroe was no toothpick. She wouldn't see it his way.

Bob sinks back into his seat. His heart is settling down. In the army, nobody goes around telling their problems to a therapist.

They're showing an old brown newspaper on the TV. It's the *Dallas Morning News* from November 26, 1963. The edges of the paper are ragged and burnt. Words are highlighted in pink. Mardie's favorite color.

We must remove all hatred generated by news media and cut it out of our hearts. As never before, the eyes of the world are upon us—and they will be looking with a critical stare.

Bob turns the TV off.

No, he turns the silence on.

He stares and sees his face in the screen. He dabs the milk off his chin. He is not young and handsome, but he's not old and ugly either. After the army, he kept on taking the combat Drugz—he still does. His brothers in Armz, even Jarheads, the proud and the few, are partial to stimulants. What kind of person doesn't want to improve himself, function better?

You have not become someone else, his wife had cried at him. *There's no one else for you to become! You're just acting like somebody else.*

In the early days, when she was happy, before the horoscopes and goldfish and therapy, Mardie used to call him Private Private. He was bashful and had soft skin. She was prettier than Norma Jean. They'd started their family young, no point waiting. The kids used to call him Sir. They had respect. Those were the days when Mardie liked being an army wife, a military mom.

'Kids get shot for their shoes where I live,' Bob bellows. He misses Mardie more than he can say. Loves her. Repeats her name, over and over.

On Bob's other TV a lone clerk is leaving an office on the sixth floor. A legal firm. They're suing everybody. Everybody's suing somebody. In the army nobody goes round looking for people to sue. Why would anybody enlist if they expected life to be safe and easy?

The moment has come. Bob sweats a little as he slips himself a swig of vodka. This is momentous and subtle. He ought to cough, but he doesn't. The drink hardly feels warm. Even after all this time, it's as natural as air for him, or combat Drugz, or water. That's why he's got it in a soda bottle. He came prepared. He watches himself on screen. Security cameras can only see. Security cameras can't taste or smell. They don't know that Bob Scrutt is drinking liquor again.

But when the alcohol starts to sneak out through Bob's skin, his ankle bracelet will know. His ankle bracelet knows about his past. *Driving while intoxicated. Driving under the influence.* His ankle bracelet can smell his vapors. That's its operational mission. By the time Bob gets home, his remote supervisors will know he's got spirits in his blood. The trackers will know. They'll have his whole life charted in half-hour portions. They'll have his co-ordinates on a real-time computerized map. They'll be after him.

Mardie hated his bracelet, called it a leg-iron.

Outside on the sidewalk, a woman in fur is trying to drop a parcel into the overnight mailbox. Bob can't see her properly on the TV screen but he guesses the parcel's getting jammed in the slot. He wonders if he should help her. The thought crosses his mind that it might be an unexploded device, or a biological weapon, in which case he doesn't want to help her. Or maybe she's a mystery tracker, doing a random check on his location. The parcel falls. She peers in through the window glass, fingers pressing, and then she shifts away, looking behind her, before dissolving into black.

Bob gets out of his seat and heads for the window. His ankle bracelet is bothering him. It goes everywhere he goes, testing him in secret. It's tamper-proof, waterproof, impact-proof. Its sensors weigh against him. Sometimes he wants to cut it off just to see what happens, if what they say is true. Tonight he's going to see what happens.

'Somebody's got to clean that,' he mutters at the window.

When he reaches the plate-glass he sees himself again. His complexion is red, dark red. His eyes have gotten pouchy. He takes the XMart superkloth out of his pocket and wipes the window where the woman was. Nothing happens. Of course nothing happens. Bob is on the wrong side of the glass. He makes his way to the revolving doors, waits for the scanners, and opens the side-door lock. Goes outside where the wind catches him. It's cold, but nothing is cold like the desert at night and Bob's seen action, Bob's been all the way, killed a man in the face, thrown grenades into slitty windows. He can't forget. He wipes the glass clean. Removes evidence of the woman in fur. The cold cuts into his shirt so he goes back inside.

Takes another swig.

He likes working nights, sleeping days. He likes things regular. At home he's got the mugs in rows, with all the handles facing the same direction. He's got the models he constructed—helicopters and Stealth bombers and trucks and boats and submarines and personnel carriers and ambulances and jeeps and missile launchers—lined up to face the same direction on custom-made shelves in every room.

One day Mardie cleared his model vehicles from the bedroom and declared it a No-Fly Zone. He didn't think of any double meanings, not in those days before Reall Life took her hostage, and words started being two-faced. The Terror Wars upset her.

When civilians are taken hostage, how long before insanity begins? Bob asked her once, and answered before she could: *After three seconds, that's all it takes.* Poor Mardie. That's why she went for therapy.

The elevator doors open and the clerk from the sixth story shuffles out, his arms full of files. He looks at the floor. His eyes flick up in Bob's direction as he says good night, but the sound comes out like a cat's sneeze.

'You suing somebody this late?' Bob says.

The clerk's head shakes. It's nearly an answer. The scanners are silent but the door is as loud as thunder rumbling. A wave of cold air rushes in. The potted plants shake. It's HyperFriday and no one has come for him yet. Maybe they never will. Maybe the ankle bracelet doesn't work and they've been conning him all along. But Private Private can't risk that. He needs to be prepared.

He pretends he's holding his M16 in one hand, his cock in the other, just as he was taught. 'This is my weapon and this is my gun. This is for fighting and this is for fun.' It used to make him laugh. Not anymore.

He reaches down to his duffel bag and opens it. He's got weapons in there, pictures of Mardie and the kids, tools. It's the cutters he's after. He's shaking again, but he feels strong. He takes a swig of vodka and coughs. The battle is over. He rolls up his trouser leg and rests his booted foot on the desk, baring his ankle bracelet. He angles the clippers just right and slams them shut. Stabbing pains run up his wrists and elbows, through his chest. His heart is drumming. He hacks again, and again, until the strap falls apart and bounces to the floor. His connection has been cut. The circuit is broken.

They are coming for him, he can sense it now, clean as vodka in his veins. The Detroit Police. The Trackers. The 2–4–1 detective. It's just a matter of time. His connection has been cut. The circuit is broken. HyperFriday will be over soon. And Bob Scrutt is prepared.

Every Man Jackie

Jackie got excited as she drove into the neighborhood where Bob Scrutt lived. Dearborn—what a dear sweet cozy name! Innocent as a soft smooth baby. She felt giddy and girlish, happier than she'd been in years. Every which way she looked, there were veiled women in cars and on the sidewalks. For once she would not stick out. These were her people!

It was evening already. She needed to eat, needed strength for the task ahead. She stopped at a big foreign-looking food store with a parking lot, and led Elwyn inside.

'Look!' she said. 'It's Ali Baba's Cave!' She pointed to shelves of bubble-pipes, golden trinkets, boxes of candy-flavored tobacco and tea. Radical Ali T-shirts and scarves.

She was holding Elwyn's bad arm. She was not letting him go. She couldn't trust him anymore. Because of his pain, she didn't have to exert much pressure. It was like power steering.

A great big golden chandelier glowed in the middle of the store. Multicolored neon strips flashed. In shiny glass displays there were piles of sticky cakes, stacks of Snax and home-made candies. The wall-to-wall coolers were filled with Drinx of every color and creed. Other women were wearing all kinds of head covers. Jackie was in her element. She tried to remember some of those names she'd learned. *Niqab. Jilbab. Buknuk. Dishdash.* For once she could buy food without somebody staring or making comments. It was like a coming-home party. Or a convention.

'Open Sesame!' she said, generally.

Wide screens hung from the ceiling. The vote numbers were going up and up. John F. was ahead in one state, then Elwyn, then John F. She decided to ignore them.

Elwyn said nothing. She was tempted to pinch his bicep just to get a response. Of course, he had to keep his mouth shut in public. But these days he'd gone quiet in private too. He hadn't said a word since the hunters' motel when she caught him acting suspicious and making excuses. That was more than twelve hours ago. Not one word—apart from complaining about his arm. He was scared of Bob Scrutt. But she was man enough to deal with Bobo, or whatever her husband's killer liked to call himself. And she was man enough to deal with Elwyn. He was moping inside his burqah, putting on a long face, she could tell. Amazing how much she could see through it.

There was a dining area to the side of the store. People were sitting down for dinner. She felt so hungry.

'We can eat here! In public!'

Elwyn shook his head. 'It's take-out or nothing.'

'But—'

'Think about it.' He was right.

People were watching TV as they waited in line to be served. Their heads were lifted upwards to the screens where reporters were jumping, grinning, knitting their eyebrows, rattling off theories and statistics. Jackie watched too, despite her best intentions. Suddenly there were grainy surveillance pictures of two veiled characters in black holding up a gas station in Bagdad, Arizona. Then a bank hold-up in a town someplace called Faith—with two robbers wearing burqahs.

The customers and servers in the bakery were distracted. Women with bare faces looked a little upset. Everyone went quiet.

On-screen they showed another robbery—this time Mexicans with big moustaches and sombreros to hide their features. Ponchos over their weapons.

Then there was a picture of Detective Pascillo and his toll-free number.

A list of crime scenes started running along under the detective's chin: Emporia, London, Wounded Knee, Odessa, Council Bluffs, Disappointment, Palestine, Stillwater, Jordan, Blackduck, Delhi, Beardstown, El Dorado, Truth or Consequences, Winnemucca, Famoso, Modesto—

'Hey that's near me!' Jackie said. Once, *The Modesto Bee* had put John F. on the front page.

Turned away from the screen, one customer seemed to be studying Elwyn's hem. Her head was wrapped up tight as an infant in swaddling.

There was a blue chiffon bib tied across her nose. Her eyes in the slit were dark and somehow blank.

'Your burqah's got mud all over it,' Jackie said quietly into Elwyn's ear. 'People notice. See how nice and clean the others are.'

'See how short they are,' he said back. 'I'm a giant here.'

'Excuse me,' the dark-eyed woman addressed Elwyn. 'I hope you don't mind me asking, but where is your burqah from?'

'Islamophobia,' Jackie jumped in. 'In the Bible Lands.'

The woman looked startled, then her eyes creased up. Her head rolled back and she laughed so hard she had to hold her belly. She turned to another customer and told her something in a foreign language. The other woman covered her mouth and snorted.

Jackie thought how rude that was, and decided not to engage in further conversation, even though she was curious to know what had prompted the question. The woman wandered off somewhere anyway.

These were not her people after all.

Someone had spray-painted white letters on the back window of the SUV.

OHI

The I was messy, as if the vandals had gotten distracted. White paint ran down the window, over the spare tire, dribbled onto the bumper.

Jackie was holding a box of pastries, still clutching Elwyn's bad arm.

'Why does anybody have to go and do a thing like that?' she said.

'Because they hate you. And they want you to be scared for your life.' He was putting on the JFK voice, even though he knew it aggravated her. He didn't seem to care about her feelings anymore.

'It stands for something.' Jackie felt sure it was a test. She had to get the answer right. She panic-scanned the parking lot for clues. No sign of the mean white car in the shadows. No sign of any other vandalism either. Was that damned hook-nosed detective in Detroit? If he was, she had to get to Bob Scrutt before he did.

'I know! I know! OHI. Operation Homefront Intelligence!' She pressed Elwyn's arm. 'Is Pascillo working for them too?'

'I don't know,' he said. 'And I don't care.'

Jackie circled the car with Elwyn. Scratches on the side, which did or didn't say IOU, mud, thousands of dead bugs, and now graffiti. They stopped at the front. The bakery lights shone through the rear window.

'It's the other way round,' Elwyn snickered. 'And it's not an I. It's LHO.'

Suddenly he burst into laughter, strange and wicked as a nut. His arm jolted hers. He pulled away, but she held on tight. He yelped. He was hysterical. She couldn't stand him much longer, but it would not be much longer. Soon they would be free. What did LHO mean? Another test. Worse than a quiz show. But she wasn't going to ask him. She had to keep the upper hand.

Driving through downtown Dearborn, Jackie saw store windows painted over in huge letters: *Arabic, Lebanese, Yemeni.* A row of dollar stores. *Islamic Center of America.* Signs for the AutoCorp mega-factory. A dollar store. Another dollar store. *Immigration lawyers. Halal meat.*

The navigator directed Jackie to turn right, then left, then right again. She honked her horn at two leisurely teenage moms who got in the way on a crosswalk. They shouldn't be allowed out so late—it was past seven already. She reached the street where Bob Scrutt lived, slowed to 10 miles an hour around the corner.

Elwyn was silent, hunched and shivering.

The area was not well-lit but Jackie could hear and see everything, sharp as a cat. The SUV crawled along the tree-lined curb. The houses were mostly old and made of brick. Kind of small. There was a screen on in nearly every front room. She caught glimpses of big faces: Elwyn or John F. or the original JFK, she couldn't tell. Her own face. Lee Harvey Oswald—at last, it came to her. She glanced at her rear-view mirror. LHO. They were trying to upset her. Throw her off-course. Reall Life had put Lee Harvey Oswald's initials on her window, just like they'd put a split in her pajamas way back when. It made her feel sick.

Screens flickered blue like thunder and lightning through white lace curtains. Some houses were dark and quiet. Jackie turned off the navigator. Her skin was goose flesh. Her whole body was vibrating. She had eaten well. Her shoe-laces were tied. Her burqah was on and her speech was ready. Romanzki or Pascillo couldn't do better. She could hear the blood pumping through her head. The pistol was in her pocket.

She stopped the car at Bob Scrutt's. The grass yard at the front was overgrown with weeds. His house was a story and a half. There was a light on inside, but the shades were down. His empty white porch was brightly lit. There were three cement steps up to it.

'This is it,' Jackie said. 'We're going to knock on the door, polite as anything.'

'Trick or treat,' Elwyn said.

'We're going to ask him nicely to let us inside. Then I'm going to ask him to confess to cold-blooded murder in the first degree with malice aforethought. Then we're going to call the police. Then the police will come and arrest him.'

'I'm staying in the car,' Elwyn said.

'No you're not.'

'Oh yes I am,' Elwyn said.

Jackie took the keys out of the ignition and put them into the pocket where her pistol was. She crossed herself and said a silent prayer. She withdrew the weapon and pointed it at Elwyn.

'I saved you. I got you out of Dallas and away from Reall Life. What do you think we've been doing all this driving for?'

'I don't know!' Elwyn cried out. 'It's one of life's fucking mysteries!' He was shivering more now. Poor, frightened, cursing president. He didn't smell too good.

She tried to calm him. 'We made a deal. You don't have to do anything. You're just a witness, that's all.'

'Shoot me then,' he said. 'See where that gets you.'

She couldn't see through his burqah. She couldn't tell if he was play-acting.

212

'Get out of the car or I'll wound you.' She pushed the pistol into his good arm.

He flinched, but he did not move to get out of the car.

'Don't make me do silly things!' She cocked the gun. 'Pretty please!'

Elwyn shuffled out of the car, sluggish and sullen.

Holding onto his bad arm, she followed.

Jack Deer

'Ring the doorbell,' she said.

He obeyed. What else could he do? He was her captive. He was cold and swaying. It was hard enough just to stand. His heart was pounding in his head. She gripped his bad arm. It hurt. She held her other hand in her burqah pocket where the pistol was.

There was no sound from inside.

'Ring again,' Jackie said.

Elwyn obeyed. As he pressed his good hand on the button, he felt a sudden wave of relief: there was nobody home. The flight hormones ebbed away from his muscles. Bobo Scrutt-face was out. The gun-slinging revenge-seeking war-vet was Absent Without Jackie's Leave. She had got it wrong.

Elwyn felt drunk. He wanted to laugh, but he knew he couldn't. His noiseless grin pulled tight under his veil. Not for the first time, he was grateful for the shield that was his burqah.

'Ring again,' Jackie said. 'What time is it?'

'Dinner time,' said Elwyn. 'Maybe he's out chewing the fat with the boys.' It was all he could do to keep the laughter inside. He was shaking with it.

'We're going round the back,' Jackie said, pushing him toward the driveway. 'Nobody uses front doors.'

The back door was unlocked. They walked in, easy as thieves, straight into the kitchen. It was beige, small, fluorescent. The kitchen TV was on.

What's a knoll? Can a knoll be un-grassy? Who says knoll nowadays? In Detroit of course we say berm.

Jackie switched it off.

The house was very quiet. Lights had been left on.

She held onto Elwyn's bad arm, making him move when she did, turn when she did. She opened cupboard doors that revealed nothing special, but he saw mugs arranged in perfectly aligned rows, handles facing the same direction. There were pictures of Mardie fixed with magnets on the fridge door: astride a sand-dune with the man who must be Bob, too small to recognize, featured in a newspaper cutting about her presumed suicide, blowing kisses. Elwyn felt his eyes prickle. He'd ignored her pregnant emails. She was dead. He was looking death in the face. Poor dead Mardie. He didn't care about the jackpot anymore. He'd lost the plot. Everybody had lost the plot. Reall Life had consumed them all. They had all played their part. He felt sick.

'I'll have that,' Jackie said, pocketing an identity badge from Bob Scrutt's place of work.

She led Elwyn to the living room. Nobody was home, he was sure of that now. The place was sad and quiet, all gathered drapes and carpet swirls, beige and pink. The shelves were full of military vehicles, elaborate plastic models glued together and painted with stripes and numbers and camouflage. They were ordered in terms of size. Like the mugs, every one of them pointed the same way. Ready for take-off or launching. A giant silk banner was draped over the main wall. Elwyn read the words: *THE SINBAD CLUB. YOUR HOME AWAY FROM THE TERROR WARS.*

Upstairs in the center hall there was a wall of framed photos. Children small and plump. Teenagers. Bob the husband in his uniform, standing to attention. Bob the soldier smiling, at ease. He was fat-jowled and surprised-looking. There were gaps in his teeth. Bags under his eyes. Red florid cheeks. There was Mardie in full Marilyn regalia, accepting a trophy, leaning forward to show off her cleavage, straddling an air-vent, laughing and holding down her replica dress. Where some photos had gone missing, there were dusty outlines and hooks.

Jackie led Elwyn by his bad arm into the bathroom, then the two bedrooms. With her hand on the pistol in her pocket, she flicked at things, opened drawers and doors, turned things over like a detective with a search warrant. She was playing for time, Elwyn decided. She hadn't accounted for Bob's absence. Or had she?

'Here's the computer,' she said in the main bedroom. 'Good. That's hard evidence. Pick it up.'

Elwyn obeyed. He had no choice. In his daze, he imagined what his lawyers would say. *Hostage. Hijack. Armz. Fever. My client was infected, coerced.* He packed Bob's laptop into his tracksuit waistband like a piece of armor under his burqah. He shivered and swayed, so cold.

Jackie took Bob's identity badge out of her pocket and turned it over.

'We're going to his work,' she said.

They drove downtown, past vacant lots and boarded-up buildings. Massive buildings loomed in the darkness like abandoned citadels. Curved pipes stuck out of the ground, pouring steam downward. Manholes steamed upwards. The sidewalks were bare. Detroit felt like a wounded city, a city that was not healing. New York it was not.

Bob Scrutt's office block was half-lit and empty. Even the lobby was empty. Jackie and Elwyn pressed against the plate glass, peering through their veils.

There were potted plants by the elevator. A couple of monitors at the front desk. One screen was on, flicking automatically from view to view inside the building. The other was dead. A gray plastic object, like a set of odd and cumbersome head-phones, lay on the floor. An empty Drinx bottle had been dropped nearby. The main door was locked.

'Come on.' Jackie grabbed Elwyn by his bad arm and led him back to the SUV.

He felt his wound burst underneath the bandages. It smelled bad. He might have fainted but he was too cold. He fell into the car.

The navigator glowed in the darkness. The voice spoke out, and Elwyn realized it was not maternal at all. Flight attendants were more sincere. Bottled up in the dashboard was the voice of a high-class escort, pricey enough to reflect well on her driver, deflect his lonesomeness, guide his lost and groping hands.

Come this way, Master, she said, oiled and cozy and pat. *Bend over. Turn. Keep going. You're getting close, Master. Prepare to enter here. You're coming. You're coming. You have reached your destination.*

216

Elwyn's wound was wet and malodorous underneath its layers. His head was swimming. Was he delirious? He felt cold all the way through. What was he doing? What was Jackie doing? The SUV had come to a stop.

Jackie turned the engine off.

The street was quiet, full of empty lots. Security fences and warnings, wind-rattled signs of guard-dogs and cameras. Disused warehouses. Skyscrapers against the night sky, impossible to tell how far. Across the street, just thirty feet away, he saw *THE SINBAD CLUB*, a brick bunker with a plastic front as bright as a Foodz outlet.

Music – Good Times – Armz For Life – Thank You Veterans.

There was an empty lot next-door. A life-size model missile lay on the grass. Down the spot-lit side wall someone had painted murals of helicopters and bombers over deserts in the sunset, war-boats bobbing about in fairytale seas.

'We're going in,' Jackie said.

Elwyn knew better than to argue. She had perfected her concealed pistol technique. Perhaps he could give himself up to the war vets, surrender to the enemy. He was dead either way. He stumbled out of the car, caught in the folds of his burqah. He wanted to scream with the pain in his arm, but screaming was a female prerogative, just like screeching or shrieking. He crouched low on the blacktop. He wanted to lie down in the middle of the road and go to sleep with the cold, drift softly into oblivion.

Jackie nudged his back with her foot.

'Get up.'

Harder.

'Get up.'

He had no option but to obey.

John F.'s shoes made him hobble. In slow motion they crossed the street, passed the damaged white car parked out front, and entered the bar.

Jackpot—

Jackie crossed herself and pushed the door open with her foot. The reflectors in her sneakers flashed. She was ready for Bob. She went in.

There were a few veterans slouched at the bar. Flags and ribbons hung off the walls. Photos of servicemen. A kind of shrine in the corner, draped with the banner: *THE SINBAD CLUB. YOUR HOME AWAY FROM THE TERROR WARS.* Guys were sitting at tables that looked too small. Talking to each other. Alone. Watching TV. A big screen hung from the ceiling where a fancy light ought to be. Another hung over the barman. He had on a hat that said *Commodore*.

Jackie couldn't see Bob Scrutt anywhere.

The Commodore turned off the TVs. The place went quiet. There was music coming from somewhere, soft and irritating like insects. One by one the faces turned towards the two burqahs by the door. Conversations halted. Mouths fell open.

Jackie was getting used to this. It was no different from any gas station she had stopped at, or any other place, except Dearborn.

'We don't keep cash here,' the Commodore said. He put his hand under the counter and Jackie knew he had his grip on some kind of weapon. The fat in his forehead bunched into ridges. His nostrils were big and flared. 'We got nothing to steal.'

Jackie wanted to laugh out loud. He had been watching too much news.

'We're looking for Bob Scrutt. Where is he?'

The restroom door opened like an answer to her question, and the hinge made such a noisy squawk that everybody turned to look.

There he was at last. That shiny red pouchy face. Long legs. Out-of-condition hair. He was wearing his field jacket.

Jackie threw her gloves to the floor. She slipped her bare hand into her burqah pocket and clasped the pistol. She wondered whether to draw.

'Some people here to see you, Bob,' the Commodore called out.

218

Bob Scrutt looked bewildered. He picked his way through the tables to the bar where he had a stool. He was drunk.

'What's goin' on around here?' he asked. 'This some kinda joke?'

'Yeah, like a Gulf War joke,' the Commodore said, not moving.

'I got so many jokes about golf it's not funny!' he spluttered.

'Bob Scrutt.' Jackie named him through her veil.

'You gonna sing a song and kiss me? C'mon baby, it's election day and I elected to quit. So you gonna kiss me.' He grinned and showed all the gaps in his teeth. For some reason, he held his foot high in the air, pushed up his army pants and bared his ankle. It was pale and hairless. He tottered and regained his balance. 'Kids get shot for their shoes. I get shot for less. You my tracker?' He reached out to touch Jackie.

'Confess!' She flicked his hand off.

'Tell me how much I drunk, then I'll confess to it. Something musta broke. Don't ask me how it came off. I didn't know if you guys were real or not.' He grasped Elwyn's bad shoulder and gave it a squeeze.

Elwyn whimpered.

Jackie stepped forward. 'You killed my husband.'

Bob Scrutt toed the floor like a kid. 'I killed a lot a men. Killed 'em in the face. That's the Terror Wars for you. It's shoot or be shooten. One man's meat—'

'Shut up,' Jackie said. 'Just shut up.'

He wasn't getting it. She had to unveil, which meant letting go of Elwyn, taking her hand out of her pocket, showing her weapon. But she had prepared for this. Pistol in hand, she bent over, gathered up her skirts and hauled the burqah over her head. The black cloth fell in a heap. Her pale freckled fingers pressed tight on the pistol.

There were clicks and shuffles all around the club. Triggers and ammunition at the ready. Cocked. No words.

'It's a turkey shoot,' Elwyn said out of the blue. In his normal voice.

Bob Scrutt downed the last of his glass and slammed it on the bar. 'So who's the turkey?'

He tried to touch Elwyn's shoulder again, but missed. 'What you got a dress on for?'

Jackie's eyes were still adjusting to the change of light without her veil. Bob was not meant to be drunk. But he was drunk. Why? It was too bad. It was his fault, his choice. He had chosen to be drunk. And Elwyn wasn't meant to be talking. She grabbed his arm and shook the pistol at Bob.

'I want you to confess,' she said as calmly as she could, but she was breathless. She could smell and hear and see everything.

'Which part?' Bob looked down at his ankle, sheepish.

'Admit it!'

'OK, OK, I cut it off.'

Jackie felt her heart in her throat. 'Cut off what?'

Elwyn let out a muffled moan.

The Commodore pulled out his handgun and aimed. 'Listen, lady, we got a club to run here, and you don't look like a member to me, or his tracker, for that matter, so I'm gonna have to ask you to leave. Or else.'

'Or else what?' Jackie shrieked. Some hair caught in her mouth. She pulled it away with her pistol-hand. 'Or else you want to protect the man who killed my husband for all the world to see? The coward who shot him in cold blood, in the back, when he was hired to protect him? Why do you think he's a *Big Dealey* favorite? You want to let him drink liquor and kill people?'

'I didn't do it,' Bob Scrutt said.

She's the hairdresser off the TV! someone called out. *Her pajamas split right down her ass.*

'Liar. Coward. Confess!' Jackie waved the pistol at Bob.

I voted for her husband, someone muttered.

You telling me that's her husband right there? The motel guy?

There's a reward on 'em both. Who saw 'em first?

Bob Scrutt spoke again. 'I didn't do it. I chickened out. I wanted to. He killed my Mardie, but at the last minute—'

'It might be me you want,' another voice said.

Jackie heard a mechanical click. She turned to see a woman in military uniform pointing a revolver at her, its trigger cocked. She was tall and foreign looking. Dark hair streaked with gray.

The Big Dealey—Today's Bets

'THE DARK FILLY' WILD-CARD BET
Suspect: 'Lee' / Billy Lovelady / AJ Hidell / Bobo /
OH Lee / Leona Osborne / Lee Oswald
Firing Line: Texas School Book Depository,
Floor Unknown
No. of bullets: X
Motive: Destiny
Odds at 12:30 p.m. CST: X/X
Total no. of bets placed on all suspects: 54,018,000
No more bets after midnight tonight!
Don't miss out on your last chance
before The Big Dealey *closes—make it a wild card!*

'Lee' is a mystery and she knows it. Ever since her teenage years, she has imagined a kind of veil between her and other people, and she has always liked that feeling. Impersonator or impostor, she is an actor working for Reall Life, or she doesn't quite know who she is working for. She is a maverick, a puppet, a double agent—or a freak of history, born at the very moment Lee Harvey Oswald died on national TV: 11:21 a.m., November 24, 1963. She is an ex-Marine who served in the Terror Wars but there are unexplained gaps in her records, and occasions when her un-American behavior merited disciplinary action—which didn't happen. She is being run by someone.

People say she's 'kind of loco', that she could do anything, go either way. But that's not enough to explain the list of strange appearances, reported by credible witnesses, locating her in different places at the same time. Why was the identity of Officer 1122 concealed by Biological Isolation Garments? Who is the driver of the damaged white sedan with tinted windows? Was someone lurking behind the shelving units in the gas station? Who was the mysterious bakery customer asking burqah questions? And who vandalized the SUV?

But another question must be asked, perhaps the most important of all: why does sharpshooting Lee believe she failed to assassinate John F. Kennedy of Fresno in the Big Day motorcade? Does she really trust news reports more than her own eyes?

Those dark almond eyes famously show no guilt, no shame, no nothing. They are, some might say, inscrutable. She herself has said: 'You will not find anything there.'

—Jackpot

'Why would I want you?' Jackie snapped.

'She's a Marine,' answered the Commodore.

'You should know who I am. I know who you are,' the Marine said. 'We have a meeting with destiny. When you fuck with the lady you fuck with your life.'

The words rang a bell. An alarm bell. Jackie couldn't remember where from. It was like another test. She was in a panic. Nothing was going right, not how she had planned. The emails! *Fuck with the lady*—that's what the emails to John F. said! Jackie wanted a confession. She wanted to send Bob Scrutt to hell. Expiation. She'd had dreams of shooting him, but now she wasn't so sure. She wavered left, right, left, with her pistol. She had two targets.

The Marine didn't seem to like that. She kicked Bob Scrutt in the gut. Then the groin. He fell like a sack of beets, clutching himself and groaning.

'Stay down, you maggot! You're just a cutout! Stay!' the Marine ordered.

Then she spoke like a civilian to Jackie. 'Maybe you forgot who you're dealing with. Like that cheating husband of yours.'

She turned and mock-saluted Elwyn. 'Moving targets, sir! Picked the wrong one, sir! But you didn't pay in full, sir!'

Elwyn swayed. 'I don't know you.'

'Time is money and you're still wasting my time, sir!'

Elwyn fumbled and yanked at his head cover. Jackie let go of him. The burqah came off, revealing his stained tracksuit sleeve, the huge LeizureScape logo, then his stubbly face, sallow against yellow.

Sharp breaths ricocheted around The Sinbad Club.

'See?' Elwyn blinked. He didn't smell good at all, and his hair was a mess, but he did look like John F. Kennedy. 'I don't know you, and you don't know me.'

Somebody laughed. *Hell, we all know you!*

'You don't know Bobo?' the Marine jeered.

'Bobo,' Elwyn said weakly.

'Refer to emails, sir!'

'I thought you said your name was Lee,' the Commodore mumbled.

'Lee. Billy. Bobo. You owe me, Mr John F. Kennedy of Fresno, sir! You've been playing cat and mouse ever since you hired me, sir!'

Jackie suddenly understood John F.'s dying face. The starry look in his eyes as the first bullet found him. He had wanted it all along—he wasn't even surprised. He had hired his own assassin. He had cheated. He had paid to win.

'I never hired anybody,' Elwyn said.

'It was all or nothing for you,' Jackie spoke to the memory of her dead husband. He had no words. No fear. Just soft gratefulness, radiant and shining.

'Well, it's all over now.' The Marine stood forward, took aim and fired at Elwyn. Jackie jumped in fright and squeezed the trigger. The Commodore fired from behind the bar. Bob Scrutt fired from the floor. Bullets fired all around The Sinbad Club.

Within a minute, the place was deadly quiet, except for the moans, and music coming from somewhere, like distant insects.

★ ★ ★ ★ ★ ★ ★ ★ ★ ★ ★ ★ ★ ★ ★ ★ ★

HYPERFRIDAY BLOODBATH

Viewers nationwide watched gripped as HyperFriday tonight drew to a gruesome and dramatic finale. Amazing security footage from a veterans' club in Detroit, Michigan, shows presidential candidate John F. of Fresno and his wife Jackie in a crazy wild-west shoot-out which left at least four people dead and countless others wounded.

The Fresno duo appear to have entered The Sinbad Club wearing outlandish burqah disguises, now familiar to Terror War veterans and home viewers alike. The romantic runaways, who are both said to be in breach of their contracts with Reall Life, dramatically unmasked before exchanging heated words with *Big Dealey* favorite Bob Scrutt.

A mystery female character, claiming to be a Marine and the reincarnation of historic gunman Lee Harvey Oswald, is the seventh and final Suspect to join *The Big Dealey* line-up in a last-minute wild-card twist. Who could have predicted this turn of events? Does history repeat itself?

Unconfirmed rumors suggest that 'Lee' was secretly hired by John F. to perpetrate his own motorcade assassination, thereby confirming him as the candidate 'most like' the original President. Having failed to assassinate him first time around, Lee may have re-appeared for a second take. This unexpected appearance has literally turned the tables.

'In this new and bloody chapter of *The TV President*, anyone and everyone is potentially guilty,' stated *KrimeTime* Detective Oscar Pascillo, chief investigator of the Big Day and its aftermath. 'The first shot at The Sinbad Club was off-camera. After that, it was a turkey shoot. Like a public execution, nobody knows who pulled the lethal switch. And part-way through shooting the principal camera went dead. It was shot out.'

As the clocks approach midnight, election results are STILL too close to call! Voters and gamers are locked in a roller-coaster of thrills and suspense.

Meanwhile, a round-up of other *Big Dealey* suspects has taken place in a synchronized sunset raid across the country.

Santa Cruz, California: Armchair anarchist and reformed alcoholic Patsy Addison was placed under house arrest, confining the Suspect to her home and surf-loving neighborhood. The retired marketeer is believed to be suffering from a terminal illness and is unlikely to be tried. She has been linked to a handgun left unclaimed at the Sixth Floor Museum, formerly the Texas School Book Depository.

Dallas, Texas: Telegenic airside preacher Father Paine, familiar to voters as the priest who heard John F.'s confession just moments before the Big Day motorcade, did not resist arrest nor did he go quietly. He delivered a sermon worthy of Charlton Heston at the peak of his tablet-smashing fury. Catholic supporters from cult organization The Brethren claim that the priest was incapable of clear-sighted vision or rifle handling.

Hot-blooded auto-fanatic Artime Cubela did not resist arrest but announced he would be counter-prosecuting the authorities with charges of anti-competitive business practice and industrial sabotage. Lawyers are lining up to represent him, free of charge. 'One third of the world's lawyers are here in North America,' Cubela's publicity agent said in a press statement. 'Every second person is a lawyer, so it's a tough, competitive market. They love a celebrity case as a way of giving them on-shelf presence, or standout. My client knows he can pick and choose. The customer is king.' The African-Cuban entrepreneur was apprehended in a Dallas suburb.

And Chicagoan wheeler-dealer Jack Mannlicher turned himself in at Dallas Police Headquarters, declaring 'I'm the hero, I did it all by myself, I have been used for a purpose.' The 'Smutman of Stateville' admitted attempting unlawfully to advance the prospects of the presidential candidate who 'put mold on the map'. He expressed a deep desire to return to the security of prison.

Detroit, Michigan: Extremist convert Ali Mohammad Saad was arrested at his home in the heavily Arab suburb of Dearborn. Crowds of bearded men gathered outside in protest. 'Radical Ali' remains the only *Big Dealey* suspect who claims to have been on an official pay-list. He insists that he was obeying orders from above, not committing any crime. Although it is still unclear whether his 'contract' was with

Armz or Reall Life, gamers have not been discouraged from identifying him as the prime Suspect alongside odds-on favorite Bob Scrutt.

Until tonight, the unassuming security guard from Dearborn enjoyed pride of place as the Man Most Likely. Assassinologists refer to him as the Aggrieved Avenger. But fellow veterans claim the former soldier denied using his weapon at any time on the Big Day. Scrutt appears to have been fatally wounded in The Sinbad Club massacre, although his death is yet to be confirmed. His blonde bombshell wife Mardie died earlier this month in suspicious circumstances. War veterans represent at least one person in seven of the general population.

Just in: Paramedics have failed to resuscitate camera-shy hairdresser Fresno Jackie. Premium-rate Reall Life viewers will be the first to see unedited footage of her last moments alive.

★ ★ ★ ★ ★ ★ ★ ★ ★ ★ ★ ★ ★ ★ ★ ★

★ ★ ★ ★ ★ ★ ★ ★ ★ ★ ★ ★ ★ ★ ★ ★

ODD SPOT

In North Little Rock, Arkansas, a hotel manager was admitted to hospital after being sexually assaulted by a coven of traveling nuns. In a critical condition, the victim is a member of The Lot, a bizarre anti-TV sect with few followers.

★ ★ ★ ★ ★ ★ ★ ★ ★ ★ ★ ★ ★ ★ ★ ★

Jack Fell Down

His eyes opened. The lights were bright and made him squint. The ceiling was stamped with brand names. The walls were a blur of logos racing one after the other, edge to edge. His blanket was crawling with them.

He closed his eyes.

There was something breathless and unblinking about the quietness.

He braced himself.

ⒷB *editions*

www.cbeditions.com